D1235078

AT VITORIA

Inspired by actual events

AT VITORIA

A City's Medieval Promise between
Christians and Sephardic Jews

MARCIA RIMAN SELZ

Archway Publishing books may be ordered through booksellers or by contacting:

Archway Publishing
1663 Liberty Drive
Bloomington, IN 47403
www.archwaypublishing.com
1 (888) 242-5904

Because of the dynamic nature of the Internet, any web addresses or links contained in this book may have changed since publication and may no longer be valid. The views expressed in this work are solely those of the author and do not necessarily reflect the views of the publisher, and the publisher hereby disclaims any responsibility for them.

Any people depicted in stock imagery provided by Thinkstock are models, and such images are being used for illustrative purposes only. Certain stock imagery © Thinkstock.

ISBN: 978-1-4808-5297-6 (sc)
ISBN: 978-1-4808-5298-3 (hc)
ISBN: 978-1-4808-5296-9 (e)

Library of Congress Control Number: 2017956017

Print information available on the last page.

Archway Publishing rev. date: 03/23/2018

To my husband, Eduardo Subelman.
Thank you for your loving support and guidance.

And

In loving memory of my niece,
Leslie Fischer, because ironically she made the hours of
concentrated writing possible and regardless of her own personal
circumstances was always interested in my progress.

Foreword

Best efforts have been made to describe the facts to the extent sources were available. The author fictionalized some characters and dramatized some historic events for effect.

This book was inspired by actual events.

Contents

PROLOGUE
When Young Ladies Shave Their Faces

The Saint-Esprit neighborhood of Bayonne, France
November 6, 1951

The sanctuary of Bayonne's oldest synagogue was cold and musty, but the conversation was hot.

The synagogue had flooded years ago, and the dank odor had found a home in the peeling off-white paint and rotting floor moldings. The stone of the building reinforced the chilliness of the large room filled with long brown wooden benches some with family names etched into the brass plates affixed to the back of each seat. These identified priority seating for the High Holy Days.

With the sun having just gone down, whatever warmth had been in the sanctuary had risen to the twenty-foot-high ceiling and escaped through the cracks in the window frames that lined the top portion of the high walls. During the day, sunlight poured in. At night, the windows were large rectangles of blackness.

The building was the synagogue Nefoutsot Juhua. In 1837, when Saint-Esprit was not even part of the city of Bayonne, the great-great-great-grandfathers of some of the men sitting around the long table served on the design committee. In those days, Saint Esprit, the Holy Spirit, was known as the Jewish Quarter on the right bank of the Adour River.

The courtyard of the building was empty. The children who studied their Hebrew lessons after their regular school hours had gone home. The tall iron gates at the synagogue's street entrance were closed.

Only these twelve men, leaders of the congregation, were left after evening prayers. Their families had lived in France since 1492. Their ancestors had come from the medieval city of Vitoria in northern Spain, forced to leave their homes because of the edict of expulsion issued by King Ferdinand and Queen Isabella.

Over the years, as the families prospered, they built large homes in the better parts of Bayonne. However, they still considered Saint Esprit their neighborhood—Their community—even though it was now run-down and populated with war refugees who had survived the Nazi death camps.

Most of these men around the table prayed together every night. Now, as they sat together, two of the men argued. The rest listened to the debate. They were discussing a cemetery in Spain that was over two hundred kilometers away.

"The Spaniards should be released from the oath," Benjamin Crevago said as he sat in the wooden chair in his rumpled dark suit, slightly wrinkled white shirt, and tie that was loosened at the neck. His jostled black hair suggested the need for a haircut. He squinted as he spoke emphatically. "Let Vitoria's Town Council do with the land what they wish. It's time. If the city wants to build apartment buildings on this land, let them do what they want."

Usually Benjamin could not be provoked into a heated discussion. He typically spoke in his dry, controlled lawyer voice—the one he used to explain a boring legal document to a client.

His friends knew the backstory. Their parents and grandparents had told them many times about their history: Leading up to the expulsion, Jews in many parts of Spain were ostracized, robbed, and murdered by Christians during vicious pogroms and riots. However, the ancestors of these men lived in the Basque city of Vitoria (now called Vitoria-Gasteiz) and were not subjected to these types of atrocities. Their Spanish ancestors lived peacefully with their Christian neighbors and that their ancestors had expected to return to their homes within a few years after the expulsion. That's why, just before leaving, they asked the Christian leaders of the town to take care of the Jewish cemetery and keep it as sacred ground. These honorable Christians swore an oath and signed a document agreeing not to desecrate this burial land. The Christians of Vitoria passed this responsibility on to each successive generation.

"I cannot stand by and let staunch defenders of the oath overcome reasonable thinking. Loyalty to an old oath is obsolete. In Bayonne, we celebrate together and grieve together." Benjamin's eyes moved from man to man. "Let's agree that Vitoria can expand the city and use the cemetery land for new buildings." The words poured out of his mouth with force. He wanted to engage these lifelong friends who sat around the table, smoking their cigarettes and exhaling apathy. Their eyelids were heavy after a day's work: Joséph in the bakery, Pierre in the paint store, Boris supervising his landscaping company, and so on. They slouched on their chairs in different directions. Some played with their *tālēt* fringe.

"The oath is outdated," Benjamin said. "Not necessary. Impossible to keep in these times after this second Great War. What is the point of making people abide by an oath that doesn't matter anymore? We will never leave Bayonne and move back to Vitoria."

Benjamin was only thirty, but as he talked, his slender body shook like an old man ill with tremors. His pale white skin turned blush red. He stared directly at the man sitting on the opposite side of the table, who was the only other person in the room who seemed to care about the cemetery's fate. Benjamin lifted his eyebrows and tilted his head as he waited for his older brother to respond.

Michael stared back. Then he stood up, showing his full look as a government official in his navy suit, starched white shirt, and solid blue tie—tied as tightly as if it were still morning. He exuded influence in the same way as when lecturing disadvantaged families on how to improve the sanitation of their homes. That was his job as a public health administrator: to improve the living conditions of others; to be caring but firm, informative but understanding, compassionate and kindhearted.

Michael slowly uttered the words loudly. "No, not ever." He paused to catch his breath.

"We are Sephardim—descendants of Jews from Spain. In 1492, the Spanish forced our ancestors to leave their homes. They had their property, shops, and possessions taken from them. The devils Ferdinand and Isabella cast the Jews out like murderers and thieves. The Nazis learned from them and took it steps further and herded Jews into labor and death camps." Michael spoke with rage in his voice. "They had no control over their lives. Now we have control. We should keep it. Use it. The cemetery is our connection to our ancestors. Let us respect the past and save our ancestors' graves for eternity. We should not let them and their eternal resting place be sacrificed for apartment buildings."

Michael tried to stay calm, but his resentment against those people who tried to obliterate the Jews was overwhelming. Over the past decade, he had nurtured the guise that he could not be unnerved. He was almost thirty-five years old. His joys were his sweet wife, two small sons, and his Jewish community. The synagogue was his refuge from the dirt and squalor he saw as he went from house to house trying to help war refugees—the displaced persons that had been released from postwar relocation centers. He liked attending evening prayers. It gave an orderly structure to his life.

Michael had survived World War II by serving as a physician to partisans. He was a doctor but did not like dressing wounds or doing surgery. Too much blood. Too many compatriots dying. Too much destruction of life. He preferred to help people, not watch people die because he did not have sufficient medicine or bandages. By 1946, he had settled back into his career at Bayonne's public health service. He liked disseminating information and helping families better their lives.

Michael typically hunched his shoulders over paperwork.

However, tonight his shoulders were straight and taut. He moved his chair about slightly and sat back down, waiting for his brother's retort.

Tonight's argument between the brothers was merely a continuation of the same discussion they had picked up and put down during the past several weeks.

Benjamin said, "We will never move back to Vitoria. So what if the Christians promised to preserve the cemetery and even took an oath to not desecrate the land. It's almost five hundred years later. Enough time has passed. It's time. Those buried there centuries ago have become dust. It will not be a desecration to allow the cemetery land to be used for a different purpose. We should be generous and let the people of Vitoria do what they want with the land."

Michael stood up again as he pounded his fist on the table. "Now you are making me mad. They owe us so much. Our ancestors were the physicians of the city who saved many lives during plagues and epidemics. The Christians living today owe us their lives. A promise is a promise."

Michael returned to his chair and made a half-turn in his seat. He took off his jacket and hung it on the back of the chair. Michael was not a good debater. He was more of a listener, a teacher, a negotiator, a compromiser. His friends knew this about him. He never really talked much—unless he had to.

However, tonight Michael's temperament alternated between listening and talking—between ignoring and shouting. He had become like mercury in a thermometer, rising and falling with various levels of heat. He hoped his words would sink in and take hold. A few seconds of silence followed.

Again Michael lifted his tall body off the chair. He walked up the steps to the *Hekhál*, the elaborate ark that housed the synagogue's Torahs. As Michael opened a side door next to the ark, he pointed and said, "This is the Torah our ancestors brought to Saint Esprit after the expulsion. It sits here as a reminder of who we are and where we came from. What our ancestors endured. This is our history."

After a short pause, Michael continued. "I shall be dead and buried before anything changes." He closed the cabinet and walked briskly back to his seat.

"Don't be so controlling," Benjamin said. "Give the land back to the people who live there."

"No," Michael retorted as he again pounded his fist on the table, startling his brother and the others seated in the sanctuary. These men had not seen this side of Michael in a long time—since they were children on the soccer field. Michael was a ferocious guard.

He looked directly at Benjamin. "We just praised God. We said *Kaddish* on the anniversary of our father's death. It is his *nachala*—when we remember his legacy and the lessons we inherited from him." He shifted his gaze back to all the other men. "We pray for the memories of all our parents, our grandparents, and our ancestors. We protect their blessed memories with our prayers, just like we protect and preserve this old building as a place to pray and congregate."

Michael turned to Benjamin. "You rarely come to daily minyans. You have abandoned your Jewish community. So, of course, you don't care about the old town that our families came from centuries ago."

"You are attacking me because I travel for my work. I'm an expert and go where my law firm needs me. I like it that way. Don't chastise me for that."

Benjamin knew why he liked the travel. He was damaged from his time as a partisan, which he spent blowing up railroad tracks, Nazi fuel dumps, and weapon arsenals. He always needed to be active and preoccupied. This kept him from recalling the memories of people being fractionalized by dynamite and seeing limbs blown off.

"I am here tonight," Benjamin defended. "I am a good son and am doing what I should do."

"*La kavesa me se izo un davu.* My head is pounding," piped in Jonah, who had been sitting passively with the other men. This Ladino phrase stopped the conversation. Hearing Jonah speak the family language of Sephardic Jews, the mix of Hebrew, Arabic, and Spanish, caused Michael and Benjamin to pause.

"Let's stop the back-and-forth arguing. You two are like opera singers in a recitative."

Jonah spoke straight to his arguing cousins. He was short, balding, and overweight. His gray V-neck sweater over a white button-down shirt puffed out at his stomach as if he were wearing a pillow under his clothes. Jonah owned a popular restaurant in Bayonne and obviously had eaten too much of his own good food. He had years of experience in dealing with difficult situations: Irate customers who could not get a table, irrational diners who did not like what they ordered, and waiters and cooks with their annoying personal problems that interfered with their jobs.

These experiences made Jonah the most diplomatic person in the group. However, he could also be firm.

He struggled to lift his rotund body off his chair so he could stand up and take jurisdiction of the discussion.

"I am tired of hearing the same arguments repeated," he said.

"We should ask all the families in the community what they think about this," Jonah said. "It should not be solely the decision of the Spanish descendants. It should be a community decision. We should include the Jews whose ancestors came to Saint Esprit after their expulsions from Portugal and Navarre."

"This makes sense," said Saul, the owner of a large fish market.

"Let's move forward on this question," said David, the owner of the Crevago vineyards. He sold Crevago wines in the best restaurants and vintner stores.

Hearing words of compromise, other men started to come alive.

"The Portuguese Jews of Saint Esprit are very important to the community," said Boris.

"They built the chocolate factories," Jonathan added.

"They run the port operations," Nathan said.

"Years ago, all the Jews were classified as Portuguese by the Christians of Bayonne," Eduard, professor at Ecole d'ingénieurs, stated. "We are all Sephardim from the old Iberian Peninsula.

Everyone should have a voice in this decision. It will be good to have a vote."

Jonah added, "And I suggest we include the women. Even the unmarried ones."

"What," said Michael.

"You're kidding," retorted Benjamin. No one had ever thought to include the women in any formal discussion.

However, from sheer exhaustion, the men nodded in agreement. It would be a community decision. With the women.

The Iberian Peninsula (1491)

*Map is not drawn to scale and is an approximate representation of various
locations on the Iberian Peninsula during this time period

Source: Marcia Riman Selz

Crevago Family

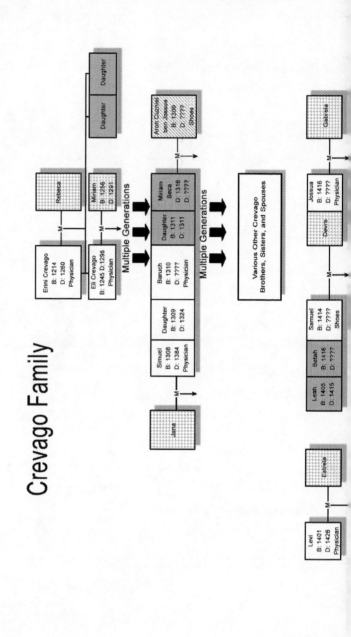

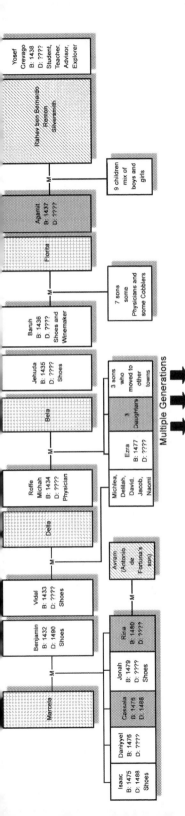

Descendents of Vitoria's Jews and other Jews who escaped the Inquisitions on the Iberian Peninsula

[All dates are approximate]
Source: Marcia Riman Selz

Vitoria Circa 1483*

Jews' Gate

*Reproduced with permission of Agencia Para La Revitalization
Integral de la Ciudad Historica de Vitoria–Gasteiz, Ismael
Garcia Gomez (historian) and Fernando Hierro Diez (artist).

CHAPTER 1

The Sugar Has Not Yet Fallen in the Water

1453

Vidal Crevago was almost home. The road was dry, and when the wind blew, he felt a surge of grit in his nose and eyes. This made it hard to keep admiring the Basque mountains on the horizon.

He had been traveling in Castile and Aragón for several months, visiting artisans who acted as his intermediaries to the Christian nobles, who loved wearing Crevago shoes. Most did not want to consider the possibility that these beautiful shoes were made by Jews.

He had been to Sevilla, Córdoba, Toledo, Segovia, and other cities and towns where the noble-born lived. Upon seeing the new styles, the courtier royals would offer their exclamations:

"Enchanting."

"Wonderful!"

"Most precious gemstones."

"Delicate stitching."

"Sinewy toes."

"The finest fabrics."

However, the servants would snicker when escorting Vidal and his Christian agent out, commenting, "Makes large feet look petite." "Makes big women feel slender."

Vidal wondered how many more successful trips he would have.

Riots against Jews were becoming more commonplace and, certainly, more intense. The Dominican priests were growing bolder, replacing calm homilies with fiery sermons depicting Jews as the children of Satan.

"What can we do to ward off the evils of these religious men?" Vidal said to his horse, Hanna, a strapping brown mare with a swishing tail that moved rhythmically from side to side. With each clop of her hooves, Vidal felt closer to home. She was his traveling companion. The two had been together on many trips. "Should we run away? But where? Britain expelled its Jews. France expelled theirs. Should we go to Jerusalem so the Turks can rule us? The world is small for Jews. Should we stay and see what happens? We are peaceful people. Not since the Maccabees have we successfully resisted our oppressors. In some of Castile and Aragón, Jews are unwelcome. Should we just accept that this is because God made us the Chosen People? In Vitoria, we work and live with the Christians. Leaving is a possibility, but why would we leave when the Christians of Vitoria do us no harm?

Vidal loved Vitoria. He was grateful that, two hundred years before, Erini Crevago *ben Israel Ha Ivri*, son of Israel the Jew, had settled there. Erini came from France as an itinerant physician to the French Army, which he had been drafted into. He tended to the wounds and illnesses of uncouth and foul soldiers. This work kept Erini alive. The French killed Jews as often as they pissed.

Rebeca, Erini's wife, followed with their son, Eli. They lagged behind the army with a band of people who provided services: tinkers who fixed armor, cooks who prepared the meals, animal tenders for horses, and women for entertainment and whoring. Rebeca and Eli, along with others, picked at the dead regardless of whether they were enemies or fallen soldiers. These vagabonds had to get valuables where they could—before anyone else. These could be traded for food and necessities.

When there was no longer an army to serve, Erini, Rebeca, and Eli traveled the Pirineos [Pyrenees], following merchants who went from town to town selling spices and goods brought back from the Indies. The only other Jew in the caravan, a seller of cooking tools, found the Basque people of Vitoria to his liking and invited Erini to settle there with him. Thus, without much thought, the Crevago family stopped its nomadic wanderings and moved into the *Judería*, the Jewish Quarter of Vitoria. Since Roman times, Jews had lived on the eastern side of the city. In the middle of the long *Calle de Judios* (meaning "street of the Jews"), was the synagogue. Erini liked the idea of dwelling with his own kind. He took comfort in knowing men educated in Torah and Talmud who could discuss Hebrew writings as well as history, culture, and commerce, and together observe their religious traditions.

The story of Erini was told within the family like the story of the Exodus. "He found the Basque people agreeable. They were unconcerned with the Jews: the rituals, the holidays, the keeping of Shabbat, the rules of kashruth, the unique clothing." Erini taught healing skills to Eli, who trained his son, Noah, who passed the healing arts onto his younger brother, and so on it would be. In the early 1300s, Aron Cuzniel married Miriam Beca Crevago and introduced the cobbler trade to his nephews. Aron would have preferred to teach his own sons his craft, but to his sadness, they became physicians.

The nephews learned to tan and dye the skins, cut them into shoe shapes, stiffen the hides so they could be covered with fine fabrics, and adorn the fabrics with gemstones. They fashioned exquisite footwear. Shoes and medicine were the livelihoods of the Crevagos. The doctors cured the highborn so they could live to wear Crevago shoes.

L'Dor V'Dor [from generation to generation], thought Vidal. *What a Jewish thought.*

Vidal laughed to himself. He was named after a Portuguese trader who befriended Vidal's father. The trader taught Levi about the cities in Iberia, how to present shoes and boots to Christian agents who could sell to the Christian nobility, and how to increase the extravagance of the shoes to make them more appealing. The trader convinced Levi he should travel through the provinces, even though there were hazards.

When Levi was training Vidal, the father emphasized the dangers for Jews. That is why Vidal was less of a Jew when he traveled. He did not wear the traditional white linen garments with fringes. No skullcap showed his reverence for God. He carried no Bible to study as he navigated his horse and wagon on the potholed roads of rural *Hispania*, the Roman name for the Iberian Peninsula– or Spain as it sometimes was called. It made sense that Vidal hid all signs of his religion. Each year there were more incidents of violence against Jews. Vidal wanted to stay alive.

"We will be home soon, Hanna, to our green forests, where we can smell the freshness of the land, see the tall trees, and find branches that provide firewood to warm us." He silently prayed, "May dangers not approach us."

Vidal knew from family lore that it had not always been so. A hundred years ago, a Crevago was murdered as he tilled his field outside the city walls. From his head covering and dress, renegade soldiers from the Crusades recognized him as a Jew, walked up to him gingerly, and, without fanfare, sliced off his hands with a sword that had killed many Muslim infidels. As this innocent Jew bled to death, these Christians silenced his wife by tearing off a piece of her skirt and stuffing it into her month. They dragged her to a thick clump of trees for their own pleasure. The daughter of this couple had gone to a hillside to pick berries. She found her father lying dead in a pool of blood. She never talked to her mother again. Her mother's ravaged body was found a few days later. The community buried these parents in Vitoria's Jewish cemetery and sat *shiva* for them, one after another.

These thoughts caused Vidal to shiver. Jews must always be fearful.

Vidal had crossed through the forest, and now the land was flat and filled with fields of vegetables that various families farmed. The rows of crops gave a grid pattern to the land. The sun was going down, leaving only a minor amount of light, but seeing Vitoria's city walls in the distance gave him comfort—the same as when he passed by Peio Gartzia tending his sheep in a field. The Christian man was the same age as Vidal, and they had known one another their entire lives. Peio, surrounded by his flock—and with his short stature, distinctive black beret, loose-fitting pants, and red vest—waved at Vidal, who waved back. Vidal smiled as he motioned for Peio to come over. Vidal liked Peio's genial attitude. Vidal dismounted one more time so he could greet his Basque friend. They embraced and kissed one another on each cheek. If they had met in town, they might not have done this, because Christians and Jews typically did not touch each other. However, out in the field, alone, they felt the camaraderie of two men working to earn their livings so they could take care of their families.

"You look well, Vidal," Peio said.

"Same for you. Your family is well?"

"All but my father. He cut himself with a butcher knife, and it is hard for him to work. All these years, my father never had an accident, but with age, he has become unsteady. We will not let him work in the shop anymore. My oldest brother is doing the butchering now."

"So sorry to hear about this. I was away and did not know. Let us meet in the marketplace later this week and tell each other the news of the day."

"Good idea," Peio said. "It will be good to see you again, my friend, and catch up."

As Vidal reboarded the wagon, he said to Hanna, "How can the world outside Vitoria be so violent when I feel so at peace when I come home?"

Vidal was twenty years old. He had started his training as a cobbler when he was seven. By the time he was fourteen, he had advanced from apprentice to cobbler artisan. However, Vidal left the shoemaking and the shop to his older brother, Benjamin. He made beautiful shoes with the best gemstones and materials that the Crevago brothers could find. Vidal preferred to travel, receiving orders from the richest people in the various cities and towns. In the early part of the year, he traveled in the western portion of Castile. In the later part of the year, he traversed the eastern part and on to Aragón, always concluding the trip up the central region of Castile, covering the territory, hearing news, sharing news, and showing shoes.

On this trip, he had done well. He delivered shoes that had been ordered the previous year, took orders for the next year, and showed new possibilities to these customers hungry for elegance and flair. Thoughts of his success were exhilarating. Benjamin made the best shoes. But only Vidal had the finesse to present them to his Christian agents so the aristocracy willingly paid top prices.

The only time Vidal would not travel outside the walls of Vitoria was during the Easter season, which did not always coincide with the dates for *Pesah*. When he was on his first trip through Iberia, he witnessed the *strappado* torture of a Jew accused of desecrating the Eucharist bread. The victim's hands were tied at the wrists behind his back and he was hoisted off his feet by a long rope. On his third trip, he saw a Jewess have two fingers cut off supposedly for touching a Christian boy to extract blood for amulets and religious rites. "At Easter timid Christians become grisly. Jew-hating Christians become truly wicked. All become eager for Jewish deaths. I do not want to be in their path," he told Hanna.

Vidal was anxious to get back to Vitoria so he could give the latest news to Benjamin and the community. As he turned down the last portion of the road to Vitoria, he felt the strong beats of his heart going double time to Hanna's trot.

As Vidal continued up the road, he arrived at a piece of land with burial plots. Tired as he was, he dismounted from his wagon. "Just one moment," he said to Hanna. At the side of the road, Vidal bent down and picked up two stones. He shuffled his feet as he walked to the east side of the cemetery.

"Hello, Papa, my learned father. Hello, Mama, you sweet and

loving woman. I had a good trip and am on my way home." Vidal saw it was getting dark, so he quickly whispered Kaddish, the memorial prayer that praises God. The rabbi had recently introduced this ritual to the men in the congregation. It was supposed to give comfort and hope to mourners. Vidal squatted down, put a stone on each of the two graves, and said good-bye.

Once back on the wagon, Vidal used the reins to command Hanna to go faster. From the road, he could see the main gate. It had elaborate carvings, with heads of animals and ornate designs etched into the stone. The entry extended above the height of the walls to make the city's entrance appear welcoming to travelers and awesome to enemies. As he rode closer, he passed the large monastery that monks had built outside the city's walls. The church, the rectory, and the convent appeared as big, imposing buildings. They had been built with large gray stones to make the walls seem weighty and sufficiently strong to keep the pious in and the uninvited out. The church was its own separate world. It obeyed Rome's rules and regulations—not those of the government. And Rome was not kind to the Jews.

Vidal knew he had to ride by this ominous Christian structure in order to enter Vitoria. "Since I was a child, the church has scared me. The monks in their imposing robes and hoods. The rosary beads clanging from their waists. Always looking serious. Never knowing what they are thinking."

Just before Vidal was about to enter Vitoria's main gate, he directed his horse to take a sharp right turn and commanded the animal to pull the wagon along a well-trodden path that ran parallel to the city's wall. Vidal would enter the city through Portal de Judería (meaning "Jews' Gate"). It was significantly smaller than the main gate and simple in appearance, without any embellishment or ornamentation. But it was nonetheless welcoming to Vidal.

Vidal turned in to the Jewish Quarter. *Home.* The clopping of his horse's hooves on the stone street rhythmically announced his entry into the Judería. He rode up the *Calle.* The shops faced the street, kitchens were in back on the ground floor, and sleeping quarters were on the upper floors and lofts. During the day, wood window coverings were tied open as awnings to protect the workspaces as women threw the contents of *mierda* pots filled with human piss and waste from the upper windows onto the street. The stench would be called horrific by some; however, to Vidal it was the smell of home.

Street frontage was at a premium because land inside the walls of Vitoria was precious. The Crevago shop faced the street and had a slightly larger-than-typical front to entice customers to visit. The wider frontage of twelve feet communicated the prestige of Crevago shoes. Most fronts were only eight to ten feet wide.

The street was almost empty, as most of the men had already shuttered their shops for their evening meal that the women had prepared. Vidal waved to the few men he saw on the street. "See you tomorrow. Cannot linger now," he shouted to each. He had no time for idle conversation. He was anxious to find Benjamin and give him a report on this latest trip. Vidal would see his wife, Della, and the children for dinner, but first he needed to talk to Benjamin.

The Crevago cobbler shop was located about fifty steps past the Jews' gate. The shop was still open because Benjamin worked long days, and even sometimes by candlelight. The smell of hides softened by tanning oils wafted into Vidal's nostrils. He took a deep breath as if to receive a dose that he missed. The shop's disarray was Benjamin's insignia. He was the only one who knew where every tool was, every hide, each gemstone, and fine fabric. This room was Benjamin's domain.

Vidal went through the shop to the courtyard and took the path that led to the rear yard of the Crevago compound. The courtyard had homes built on the sides, and it was in the middle of the yard that the extended family met for meals and gatherings.

Benjamin liked working with his hands. He liked the smell of the tanned hides. He liked designing and creating new looks with unusual gemstones and silken fabrics. He liked working alone, keeping to himself, and not talking to anyone unless he had to—such as when he had to check the work of his apprentices. He did it, but his comments were sparse and terse.

"Benjamin!" Vidal shouted in his typical jovial manner as he approached his older brother, who usually ate dinner after his children had finished theirs. Just seeing this man gave Vidal joy. Benjamin was only fourteen months older, and was Vidal's first friend, and his partner in childhood schemes and pranks. Also, Benjamin had helped Vidal learn the cobbler trade.

The two embraced and kissed. The hug lasted longer than typical because Vidal liked to hug his brother and did not get many chances to do so. The bear hug was out of character for Benjamin. He pulled away—a reminder that he did not like to be touched.

"Glad you are home, Vidal," Benjamin said. These words were as much enthusiasm as Benjamin could muster. The hunch of his back was more pronounced than it had been when Vidal left on his trip. The gray in Benjamin's hair had spread.

Vidal said, "God has been very good to us. We will have prosperous lives for another year. How are my children? How is Della?"

Benjamin watched over Vidal's wife and children when he was traveling.

"How are my boys?" Vidal cared about his daughters, but like most men, he reserved the greater proportion of his emotions for his sons.

"They are good—growing, eating and learning Torah," replied Benjamin. "What news do you have? The caravans brought stories about Christians killing Jews, even women and children. Is this true? I have talked about these rumors with other men in the synagogue, but most think that nothing like this could happen in Vitoria. Most agree that we live calmly with our Christian neighbors. I agree with them. The caravan merchant said these things happened in other parts of the Iberian Peninsula, far away from us. We think that for now, there is no worry in Vitoria. What do you think? Do you think the Christians of Vitoria could be violent? Could killings happen here?"

Vidal shrugged and then straightened up and stood tall as if at attention. "It is not just the future that we should be concerned with. It is the now. In some cities, the present does not look good. Pressure is building from the Church. They want everyone to be Catholic. Our choice is to convert or die. More and more Jews are converting because they fear lost business and lost social position. I heard the Church was also using torture to encourage conversions.

"When I was in Cuenca, I was told that some time earlier Christian Antonio de Suerte, an important magistrate of King Juan II, had been sent there to supervise *conversos* [Jews who had converted to Catholicism] and Jews who collected tax revenue. The Christians rebelled and Juan II had to send soldiers to quell the uprising. The rebels wanted de Suerte, the Jews, and conversos removed from positions of authority over Christians. What made the Christians even madder was that de Suerte urged the king to protect the Jews and conversos of Castile. It was all in self-interest, of course, because they provide significant revenue for the tax coffers. But the Christians did not care." Vidal spoke quickly. "I was told that Jews holding public office were removed with no trial or hearing. A man at the inn told me that the Jews of Cuenca could no longer give testimony in court. In addition, here is what I saw with my own eyes: the body of converso Juan de San Rio, who some years before had been our Christian agent in the city, hanging in the public square with two other men. From their clothes, they looked like important people who had been part of the governance of Cuenca. I did not linger, for fear I might look at someone the wrong way and be accused of wrongdoing.

"Then I went to Madrid. The livery boy said that a few weeks before, Dominican monks took a Jew who was walking alone to synagogue on a Saturday and tortured him until he professed his love for Jesus Christ. They did this in front of the church elders. Monks then took the boy to the outskirts of the city, tied him to a tree, and left him. When he went missing, his friends looked for him and found him dead in the forest.

"I stayed in Avila for Shabbat. I heard from the rabbi that monks hanged some Jews and left them in the plaza for everyone to see. A priest accused them of speaking to Christian women. No one testified to this. The priest accused them, and the city magistrate hanged them.

"In Valencia, Zaragoza, and Sevilla, similar incidents occurred. No city south of Vitoria has been without incident."

Benjamin thought for a moment and said, "These places are far away. We are not affected by these incidents."

Vidal said, "How can we be sure that the harmony between Christians and Jews in Vitoria will last? My inclination is to pack up the family and leave. Go to Holland, where the Dutch are only interested in commerce. They care less about Jews as long as they make money for the government."

Benjamin looked at his younger brother with dismay. He tried to straighten up his body in an effort to stand taller but could not. He was too tired. "You want us to leave Vitoria when nothing has happened to us and our shoes are so well liked by the aristocracy. It would mean starting over. Marcela will not want to move the children away from the only home they have ever known. We live in peace with our Christian neighbors of Vitoria. Why create a panic in our city when none exists?"

"We should have a plan to escape if something does happen."

"Nonsense," Benjamin said. You want to plan in case a house lifts up from the ground and begins to fly like a bird. This will never happen in Vitoria, so why do you need a plan for it? What happens to the Jews in other cities with other Christians is not of concern to us. We can be cautious, but to incite unnecessary fear when our daily lives are peaceful is foolish. We will stay in Vitoria, because this is where our life is and because Vitoria is the place our ancestors chose for us."

"Yes, we have a good life here," said Vidal. "We work with the

Christians; they buy our shoes, value the taxes we pay, and leave us alone to practice our rituals. Our children learn here, have grown here, and our families are happy here. We have built good houses with comfort for our families. But I see what has happened in other parts of the Iberian lands and I ask myself if these things could happen here."

Benjamin said, "Roffe Michah, Juhuda and Baruh will not leave. Our sister, Agamit and her husband, Rahav, will not want to go. He has become the silversmith to the Grandees of Castile. Even though Agamit is younger, she sees herself as the matriarch of the Crevago family. She will want to stay put as long as possible. And what about Yosef?"

Yosef was the youngest of all the brothers. He earned a small wage as a teacher at the synagogue and an even smaller one as an assistant to the rabbi. Because he was the youngest, he stayed in school and studied Torah, languages, classic literature in Greek, Latin, French, and Italian. He learned from everyone—especially travelers who passed through Vitoria. Yosef asked question upon question for hours. He talked with scholars and nonscholars about literature, art, history, and all things within his imagination. "Yosef is set in his positions here. Why would he want to leave?"

The Crevago family had a multigenerational history living in Vitoria. Each member of the family consciously or unconsciously cherished the family's closeness. They gave thanks to God for the serenity provided by living with the Basque people. If one left, they all would leave. But for now, only Vidal was speaking of the danger that existed outside of Vitoria. He could see that Benjamin did not seem much concerned. Or was it that he just did not want to think about it?

CHAPTER 2

Even a Blind Man Can See It

1474

Vidal kept his eyes on the road and the side brush, looking for assailants. Levana, his new mare, seemed to know the way to Segovia without much guidance.

The sights of the city soon came into view. He saw the monstrous Roman aqueduct with its great arches and columns. "I wonder how many Hebrew slaves it took to build this marvelous and huge water system."

Vidal rode farther and entered the city through its San Andrés Gate. As he rode toward the plaza, he saw that it was filled with a large crowd. The people were shouting joyously over the ascension of Isabella *la Catolica* to the crown of Castile. Her brother Enrique IV had died. On this day, Isabella was being proclaimed queen of Castile—a province named for its many fortified castles, the *castillos*, which were also built by the Romans.

Vidal could not get through the square and started to take a side street. But he was blocked by throngs of Spanish subjects who had stopped their day to witness the coronation spectacle. He saw the rich dressed in their finery standing on platforms so they could have the best view. The poorer townsfolk stood in the dirt with royal soldiers holding them back to give the procession space to go through. Travelers with knapsacks had come from the outlying areas to cheer the new queen.

However, Vidal was not excited by the sight of pageantry and excess. He thought to himself, *I do not care about all this festivity. Isabella will become queen, but will this be good for the Jews? This is how I measure things. I have to wait and see.*

Courtiers had whipped the crowd into an emotional throng in advance of Isabella's arrival. The crowd shouted, "Long live Isabella! Long live Ferdinand! Castile! Castile! Aragón! Aragón!" Servants had distributed flags so the subjects could show their loyalty to the crown. Church bells rang. Cannons fired. "Love for Queen Isabella, love for King Ferdinand!"

Isabella had married Ferdinand in 1469. Ferdinand did not attend Isabella's coronation. He was already king of Aragón and did not want to be perceived as power hungry. It would not have mattered. The people loved their royals.

Isabella entered the main plaza on a white horse, in a dress woven with gold and silver, and adorned with spangles and multicolored gemstones. Accompanying her was an entourage of bejeweled riders on horses that collectively formed a singular expression of brilliant sparkle and extravagance. Their dazzle cast a glare as the sun hit the gleaming decorations.

Vidal watched as Isabella rode through the plaza toward the Church of San Miguel de Segovia. He watched the guards dismount and help the about-to-be-crowned queen off her large Arabian steed. She walked majestically into the church. Vidal had never been inside a Catholic house of worship but imagined it had many crucifixes of Jesus like those worn around the necks of priests, and maybe statues of saints and famous religious people. Nuns dressed in black habits with white cloth framing their faces, stood outside the church. They sang solemn hymns, which were lovely in their melodies but not understandable, as the songs were being sung in Latin.

Vidal wanted to move on. He feared evil spirits might be lurking around some corner of the plaza and planning to put him in danger.

He did not believe in superstitions as his wife did. She wore blue beads and constantly uttered prohibitions against the evil eye. However nonetheless, he knew he should be cautious.

"Best to not take any chances with this horde in its uproar of joy over the new queen. These peasants could turn ugly and want to torture this Jew."

As Vidal sat on the wagon seat smelling the sweat of the excited crowd, it reminded him of the crowd he had seen and putrid smells he had experienced several years before. It was in Toledo. As he entered the city's central square, people were shouting as they stood around a platform in the middle of the plaza. The square was too small for the mob, and some people were spilling onto the side streets. Other people were hanging out of windows and standing on the balconies that surrounded the square. They were shouting just as they were doing today for Isabella's coronation. Except instead of cheers for the monarch, the outcry was, "Death to the false Christians! Kill the conversos!"

Vidal had caught sight of a platform with two naked men hanging from the gallows, their private parts exposed, their heads cocked to the side from the nooses around their necks. Nearby an unwashed peasant dressed in tattered clothes stood in the back of the crowd and said, "I cannot see if they have a *prepucio.*" The knotted hair of this lowlife was attracting gnats.

His companion, an equally dirty ne'er-do-well, had started to push people aside, all in an effort to get a better view. "None," he said, laughing to his friend. "These *Marranos* cannot fool us—not even with their fine clothes that make these pretend Christians look like important Spanish gentlemen. The Archbishop Alfonso Carrillo de Acuña and the priests will seek their kind out and have them sleep with pigs. Then hang them. It is the right thing to do."

The gawkers shoved each other in an effort to get a better look at the hanging men. Vidal watched a beggar climb onto the platform and swing one of the dead bodies from its rope. He made gestures as if he were pushing a side of mutton hanging in the slaughterhouse.

Vidal remembered how the food left in his stomach had risen into his throat. He swallowed numerous times as he silently struggled to keep it from entering his mouth and being coughed up onto the street. He felt his body get hot from anger at the notion that living people could be so cruel and hateful. He thought, *The priests want us to convert, but even that is not a good choice.*

"Death to the Jews! Death to the heretics! Death to the Marrano liars!" the beggar shouted to the audience. And in response, the audience shouted back, "Death! Death! Death!"

On that day in Toledo, not only did the Jewish community suffer, Vidal lost a friend. He had driven his horse to the casita of Sancho—his Christian contact in Toledo who bought goods for local royals of moderate and high importance. He and Sancho had worked together for some years. The shop was on *Zapatos* Street, where all the shoemakers in Toledo resided. The smell from the tanning oils reminded Vidal of home. But on this day, there was no humming in the background of customers bickering over prices. Most of the shopkeepers, their apprentices, and buyers were in the square. Vidal stopped his horse and wagon in front of Sancho's shop. It was a small structure with brown wooden slats. The awning was down, and the door was closed. Vidal decided to go in just the same. He saw Sancho, a man large in girth, at his workbench. His long hair tied tightly at the back of his neck. His brown leather work apron showed stains of use over the linen gown that he wore for daily work in the shop.

"Sancho, my friend," Vidal said as he approached the cobbler's bench. They always greeted each other with big hugs and many kisses on each cheek. Sancho would honor Vidal with food and wine at a lavish dinner. Vidal looked forward to it. Sancho's wife, children, and extended family would join in the frivolity and laughter and enjoy receiving word from other cities. Afterward, Vidal and Sancho would talk leather, hides, fabrics, gemstones, and new styles for the next batch of aristocratic shoes.

However, this time was different. Sancho did not look up from his cobbler's bench. He kept working and merely said, "Leave what you have for me. I will pay you. Then leave my workplace and do not return to Toledo. The danger is immense—for you and for me. I can no longer do business with a Jew. I did not go to the square because I did not want to participate in this contemptible activity of hanging men who committed no crime and were not fairly tried. But that does not mean that I can continue to be a correspondent of yours."

Vidal's first thought was one of resentment. However, he very quickly realized that this decision by Sancho was a sign of the times.

Vidal said, "I understand. I do not like it, but I understand. I do not want to endanger you or your family by my presence."

Vidal hastily unloaded the sacks of shoes from his wagon.

He never saw Sancho again. Vidal never went to Toledo again.

As Vidal let this recollection linger in his mind, he thought of how Toledo had slipped away from its Jewish community. However, sitting on his wagon in Segovia watching this crowd fete the new queen, he would not allow his sadness or fear to become evident to onlookers or to disrupt his purpose in Segovia. Vidal knew it was on with business, regardless of Castilian jubilation or memories of Christian cruelty.

CHAPTER 3
Whoever Wants the Rose Also Gets the Thorns

1479

Vidal hurried to Antonio's. Levana's hoofs clopped on the stones of the road leading to the city. Segovia was always one of Vidal's favorite stops. He urged Levana on toward the Judería. On his way, he rode past the large Church of the Corpus Christi, which had once been the city's main synagogue. Sometime in the early years of the century, around 1420, the Catholic Church expropriated the building, declaring it a house of blasphemous speech. Then the bishops turned it into a church.

Vidal looked over toward the jutting heights of the *Alcázar*—a favorite palace of the royals. Vidal thought, *They are probably inside somewhere, reclining on a chaise covered in satin, enjoying themselves; or maybe they are dining on feasts of roasted lamb, black sausage, botillo, or roasted suckling pig, all the while trying to develop new schemes to make life harder for the Jews.*

Vidal passed through the streets of Christian merchants. Unlike streets in the Judería, where all different types of shops existed on one street, in the Christian quarters, each trade was confined to a specific street. As Vidal rode down Calle de Zapateros for the shoemakers, shop after shop gave off the familiar smell of tanning oils, which went up his nostrils. *Smells like home*, Vidal thought.

Next he came upon Calle de Panadería for the bakers. The aroma of fresh bread reminded Vidal that he had not eaten since the afternoon meal and was hungry.

Vidal turned onto Calle de la Judería, he saw the various shops on the street: the tinker, the silversmith, the butcher, and so on. He noted in his mind the mix of smells and sounds that made this street different from the Christian quarter. The street teemed with people shopping before sundown on Friday, talking to friends and neighbors. Children were playing in the street. Women were leaning out the second-story windows, shaking rags being used to clean their homes and shouting greetings to people they saw on the street.

The block was long, but within minutes, Vidal was in front of his destination. Antonio de Fortuna sold fine silks, woolens, and linens. Vidal would buy some for the next generation of Crevago shoes.

Vidal could see inside through a small opening in the wall of the shop. Antonio, wearing a typical leather apron with pockets for scissors and threads, saw Vidal dismount from his wagon. As the traveler stepped through the doorway and into the shop, Antonio said, with the warmth of a man greeting a brother, "Welcome. I have missed your company."

The workshop was filled with tatters and cuttings from rich fabrics that Antonio bought from nomadic traders. Bolts of fabric lined the walls. In the center was a large table that Antonio used as his cutting board. It had shiny red brocaded fabric lying across it. Several pairs of variously sized scissors sat on the edge of the board. Spools of thread were scattered around. In the back of the shop, a boy sat at a loom where Antonio created his own designs. Nobles wanted uniqueness, and Antonio knew how to deliver on this desire.

"Same for me. How are you, my friend? I hope your world is happy," said Vidal.

Antonio's face became serious. His brow furrowed as the corners of his mouth took decided downturns. "I am not happy or sad," he said. "I live in the world as it is. I face the world as it is. I change only what I can change, like the buttons on a vest or the lace on a bodice. What I cannot change I do not think about."

Antonio's family had lived in Segovia for more than a century. For this entire time, they were *draperos*—cloth merchants who customized fabrics, which became magnificent clothes for the nobility of Segovia. The family enjoyed high social standing as established members of the city's expanding urban commercial community.

Nonetheless, Antonio, his wife, and children had converted to Christianity four years before. Since the ascension of Isabella la Catolica, passions had risen against Jews. Priests were deemed unfit if they supported tolerance of the Jews. Some nobles wanted more action to restrain these infidels. Accusations of excessive tolerance by the previous kings of Castile, Enrique IV and his father Juan II, grew.

Nobles had pressured Antonio to convert. They wanted to keep buying the luxurious clothes that Antonio tailored from his unique fabrics. However, with the new laws and regulations, the nobles could not buy from a Jew. "Nobles have split into camps," Antonio said to Vidal. "They have settled into pro- versus anti-Jewish campaigns. Those against the Jews want to confiscate our properties. Nobles tolerating the Jews do so because Jews manage tax collections and give financial advice. Such is the world for the Jew."

With conversion, Antonio continued to create fine clothes for the richest people of Segovia. However, because Segovia was thus far a city of peace between Christians and Jews, he had not moved to the Christian quarter.

Antonio's face flushed as he said, "Change happens. I have accepted Christianity. Change is what I did to preserve my family and my life in Segovia. Whether it is a good change I do not know. I cannot think about that very much. Tonight I want to celebrate that you are with us. Supper will be ready soon."

A young boy approached Antonio to show his work to the master craftsman. Not speaking, Roaldo put the newly woven cloth in front of the master weaver. Roaldo was small for being sixteen. He did not have any of the vestiges of manhood: no hair on his face, a weak jaw with only a slight chin, no show of muscles in his arms, and childish long hair.

"Not right," Antonio bellowed. "I have shown you how to weave this cloth and its pattern three times. Go back and do it over again. You waste too much yarn with your mistakes."

Then, with a mellowing of his voice, Antonio looked at the boy, whose eyes had started to well up with tears. "I am sorry to be so abrupt with you, Roaldo. My compassion is not where it should be."

Roaldo had been an apprentice with Antonio for less than a year. His family lived in the poorest section of Segovia. His brothers and sisters numbered more than ten, and as each son came of age, he was put out as an apprentice to a craftsman. The daughters were married off. Roaldo had been put to Antonio. None of the Christian craftsmen would take him in. They called him *estupido*. Roaldo's behaviors were erratic, but he was not stupid. He had trouble staying focused on his work. Antonio had understanding for this boy, so the master weaver had accepted him as an apprentice.

Nonetheless, Roaldo resented Antonio's criticism even as Antonio put his arm around the boy and walked him to the large loom in the back of the shop. Roaldo returned to his seat at the loom and took a new ball of wool from the pile in the basket. He removed his shoes and placed his feet on the wooden pedals that were used to pull the strands of wool through the elements of the loom. His face glowered with anger. He sat up rigidly as if to show his resentment at being in this room. The humming of the loom could have softened Roaldo's hardened expression, but Roaldo refused to be softened. He was required to do his work but would not do it happily.

Antonio turned his attention back to Vidal, and Vidal was happy for the unpleasant episode that he had witnessed to be over. He was relieved to be in this home of safety. He did not feel threatened here, even though Antonio had converted to Christianity.

Vidal proceeded to look at Antonio's newest cloth creations. The men did their exchange of selling and purchasing, packing, and storing of the goods so Vidal would be ready to leave when the time came.

Antonio looked over at the irritated boy sitting at the loom. "Roaldo, let us close up the shop. Go to your room. The señora will bring you your supper after we have had ours."

For some, weaving produced a rhythm that resounded in a tune that most lovers of the loom found melodic. However, for Roaldo, the sounds were closer to slavery chains whose links were clanging against one another. Roaldo said, "Thank you, Master Antonio, for letting me leave this drudgery." He felt humiliated by having to work for a converso. It made him feel small and less esteemed than his brothers, who were working at Christian shops they could be proud of—not in a converso's shop.

Roaldo exited the shop, but instead of going to his room in the rear of the courtyard, he lingered out of view on the side of the back house, where the family's dining area was. He peeped through a crack in the wood of Antonio's house. Roaldo was bitter that he could not sit with the family for dinner; nor could he go home to be with his parents. He secretly watched as Maria set the table.

Antonio shuttered the shop, locking out the activities on the street. "Follow me," he said to Vidal. "Maria is finishing supper preparations. It is almost sundown." The two men walked to the washbasin sitting on a table by the kitchen door. They splashed water on themselves and used the soaps that Maria had made from ash and plants to clean their faces, necks, and hands. Then, in an odd movement, they checked their fingernails for cleanliness, turning their hands inward and outward in various positions.

Maria appeared in the doorway dressed in finer clothes than she would normally wear for housework. Her lustrous dark brown hair was pinned back, and her face looked fresh and clean.

"Come in, Vidal. Hello, my darling Antonio. We will all celebrate tonight with food and wine. The children are waiting for us."

Antonio greeted his children, all of whom had been studying by the fireplace. Everyone except Maria sat down at the table.

Maria went over to a cabinet and took out a big black cloth. She unfurled it and hung it across the top of the door from hooks. She then went over to a bowl of salt and put salt in each of the oil lamps so these pots of oil would burn longer and she would not have to relight the lamps before the next day's sundown.

Once the lamps were primed, Maria knelt down on her hands and knees and removed a floorboard. In the floor's compartment were two silver candlesticks and two candles made from mutton fat and beeswax. Vidal, Antonio, and the children watched Maria in silence. Vidal looked at the faces of this family, which glowed as Maria lit the Shabbat candles. She moved her hands three times gracefully and slowly above the flames as a gesture to welcome Shabbat. She then brought her hands to her face, covered her eyes, and recited in an almost inaudible voice the Hebrew blessing over the candles: "Baruh attah Adonay, eloheinu melech haolam, asher Kiddush shan nu bimitzvoh tav vetzivanu, lehadnick nel shel Shabbat. Shabbat Shalom."

Maria then bent over and unceremoniously blew the candles out, saying under her breath, "Forgive me, Adonay, for not letting the Shabbat candles burn to their end." Everyone at the table waited and watched as Maria quickly put the candlesticks away in their hiding place.

As soon as Maria returned to the table, Antonio lifted his cup of wine and, in a whisper even lower than the level of sound Maria had used for the prayer over the Shabbat candles, said the prayer he had repeated throughout his life for as long as he could remember. "Baruh attah Adonay eloheinu melech haolam borah pri hagafen."

As each person at the table took a sip from the silver chalice, Antonio added a personal statement. "Thank you, Adonay, that our friend Vidal Crevago is with us tonight." Antonio knew that Vidal could be depended on to keep the secret of their clandestine Shabbat ritual.

When Antonio had reseated himself, Maria stood up. In a calm and hushed voice, she said, "Dear Lord, King of the universe, we ask you to bless this bread that we pray over. We have baked it for tonight's Shabbat meal, and we thank you for all the manna you provide. We say this blessing to show our unity with you and as our way of praising you and giving glory to your name."

Maria uncovered the two loaves of bread and said the traditional Hebrew prayer: "Baruh attah Adonay eloheinu, melech hoalam, ha motzi lechem min haaretz."

In tranquility and stillness, the group, almost in a pantomime, said, "Amen."

Antonio then rose out of his seat and explained to his children, "For fear of being heard, I cannot raise my voice in joy and take each of you into my arms, put my hands on your head, and bless you in the manner I would like to. I can only say to all of you a prayer in the tradition of Aaron, brother of Moises:

May the Lord bless you and keep you;

May the Lord make his face to shine upon you and be gracious to you;

May the Lord lift up his countenance upon you and give you peace.

Ye'varech'echa Adonay ve'yish'merecha.

Ya'ir Adonay panav eilecha viy-chuneka.

Yisa Adonay panav eilecha, ve'yasim lecha shalom.

Antonio paused after he finished the prayer over his children. He stepped back three paces and lifted his arms toward the heavens, and with quiet dedication he said, "Lord, I am Yuda ben Lousada, and this is my wife, Benita bat Nahon, and these are my children."

With that utterance, Pedro, Antonio's oldest son, although only six years old, stood and said, "I am Avram ben Yuda Ha Ivri."

Next, Antonio's little daughter, Gaila, spoke. "I am Sarah bat Yuda Ha Ivri."

"I am not Esteban, I am Esau ben Yuda Ha Ivri," Antonio's second son said.

Then Maria spoke, as if offering an apology to God for their conversion. "I hold my arms around my son—not Nuño, but Jeremiyo ben Yuda Ha Ivri."

Their words offered a virtual pledge that in their hearts they had remained Jewish. Antonio concluded with "Children, we keep this secret and tell no one what we have just said."

Then the group ate their Shabbat meal. On the table were fresh greens and a small stew pot of lamb and cooked vegetables—foods appropriate for a Shabbat dinner. Also on the table was a platter of fish; in the event that an untrustworthy outsider stopped by, the lamb would be removed from the table and hidden. No meat was to be eaten by Christians on Fridays.

Vidal enjoyed the restful Shabbat evening with Antonio. In the privacy of this converso's home, they talked quietly about the weekly Torah portion, the Talmud, and the politics of the day.

"Segovia is becoming a place of danger for conversos. Maria and I have been talking about leaving and going to Portugal. But my commercial interests are doing so well. It would be difficult to become established somewhere else. And Maria does not want to leave her family and friends. If I were younger and without children, I would go."

"You still could leave," Vidal responded. "I have tried to convince my brother Benjamin to go to Holland, but he says the same as you, that business is good and he does not want to uproot the family."

"I feel fear in celebrating Shabbat but do not feel an aversion to doing so. I still feel Jewish. My conversion was forced for economic and social reasons, to protect my family. An oath that is given by force and taken because of force is not valid. I will not become a new Christian who detaches from the beliefs and traditions of my ancestors. I will have my children learn about our forefathers and know their teachings. More than fear of Christian betrayal, I fear for the loss of our heritage."

"I am not accustomed to these fears in Vitoria," Vidal said. "There, the Christians and Jews work together and have friendships, although we all know our places."

Vidal and Antonio talked until their strength was gone.

On Saturday morning, the men continued their conversation while they ate a light breakfast of bread and jam made from berries found in the groves near Antonio's home.

Maria served a cold lunch from the food that had been prepared before the Shabbat began. On Saturday evening, Maria and her neighbors stood in their doorways, munching on cold green vegetables. As the stars came out, more neighbors congregated in front of their homes and chattered about how beautiful the evening was.

On Sunday, Antonio and Vidal talked more about business and the politics of the day. Vidal could not leave because it would arouse suspicion to see a merchant traveling with goods on the Christian Sabbath. On the Monday morning, Vidal embraced each of Antonio's children until all had received his words and gestures of farewell. He kissed Maria and Antonio and offered wishes for their health and prosperity.

Vidal said, "It was a blessing to have these few days with your loving family." But what he thought to himself was *I wonder what type of future these children will have in Segovia. Living in secret breeds a danger that cannot be good.*

CHAPTER 4

A Good Son-in-Law Is One Who Sees His Mother-in-Law Burning and Saves Her

1484

The morning rain had not yet evaporated, and the smell from the wet brush around the graves was sweet. The cemetery in Vitoria dated back five hundred years. Creating a Jewish cemetery was always one of the first things Jews did when moving to a new area. The Talmud teaches that Jews have to be ready for death because it never arrives at an opportune moment.

Vidal walked on the worn path as he navigated the row of graves. After his latest travels, the visit with his parents and grandparents would be a first step in settling back into his family life. His dirty clothes and his exhaustion did not seem important. He considered these visits replacements for missing the nachala of each parent, the annual Hebrew remembrance, when Vidal should have memorialized their deaths.

When Vidal reached his parents, Levi and Estrela Crevago, he paused to study the pile of stones on each grave. Each stone represented a visit by their children, grandchildren, family, and friends. There were no names marking the graves. He just knew where they were. In the Jewish tradition, Vidal said the Mourner's Kaddish, and then he put a stone on each grave.

Vidal also visited the graves of his dead children. Three had been born dead. Two had died just weeks after their births. One had died of disease when he was three years old. Vidal did not feel attached to these children, which gave him pangs of guilt, but he was sad enough just knowing these young ones had joined the dead too soon. Vidal took strength from the knowledge that the souls of these babies had risen to be with the Almighty, the one who gives and who takes away. They would never feel grief from their parents dying or from losing their own children. Vidal put a stone on each grave as he said Kaddish.

He walked a few feet more to the graves of his grandparents. He walked on until he reached the graves of Erini and Rebecca, Eli and Miriam, and other ancestors. At each site, Vidal repeated the prayer and stone ritual.

Vidal walked back to the wagon, careful to stay on the paths and not walk on the graves. Respect for the dead, those who had lived long lives and those who had died young, was a lesson he learned as a child when he accompanied his father to the cemetery.

Because Vidal's trip had been routine, he decided to see Della before Benjamin. Vidal accessed his home through the back alley that ran along the rear of the houses on Calle de Judios. The back door of his townhouse was open and he could see into the kitchen. Winding stairs went to the second and third floors, where the family slept on rectangular wooden frames topped with mattresses filled with wool. The second floor also had a built-in window seat niche for the mierda pot. The window was open in all types of weather so the odors could be released into the air. However, sometimes the wind blew the smells deeper into the house, which made sleeping almost unbearable.

Vidal found his wife laboring by the fire. She was leaning over the stew pot and stirring the food. She looked tired. Della was a short woman who had become rather stout after bearing twelve children and losing so many to early deaths. Regardless of these tragedies, Vidal thought she had a kindly face.

Vidal tapped on the table, and Della turned around.

"Welcome home," she said. Della was always happy to see her husband. Even with all the children, in-laws, and multitudes of people enmeshed in her family, home was less joyous when Vidal was gone. She missed his good humor. And she missed him in bed. When he held her, she felt safe. When he stroked her hair, she felt young again. When he caressed her cheek, her body became hot. When he touched her private places, she invited him in.

The younger children scampered about, hugging the father they had not seen for months. Vidal picked up each one as the two older girls, Michlea and Delilah, looked on. Vidal shook hands with his seven-year-old son, David, and the six-year-old Gabriel. He loved all his children, but he favored the boys because they would be able to work with him and learn his route of stops throughout Iberia. Of the girls, Naomi, the five-year-old, had stolen his heart. She had Della's face and an always happy disposition.

"Naomi, come to me so I can hug you more," he said after all the children had welcomed him home.

Naomi threw her head back and glanced at her sisters as she ran back to her father for additional affection. "You are brighter than the gems on Crevago shoes," Vidal said as he patted her head and wrapped his arms around her. Vidal kissed the girl again and looked up at Della, who was watching the welcome-home celebration.

"I missed you, my husband," Della said as she hugged Vidal after the children had had their fill and gone back to the learning of their Hebrew and reading a Bible story about how Joshua sent spies into Jericho. "Tonight will be special."

"I would have been here sooner, but I stopped at the cemetery. It is just a gesture, but it is odd how this act connects me to the heritage of our people. Now it will be time for us. Just being with you is special for me." Vidal stroked Della's hair. "It is good to be home for the Pesah Seder. I am looking forward to being with the family."

Della whispered, "I have not been to the *mikveh* yet but I want you tonight. Would it be bad if we slept together even though it is not on the prescribed days? I have missed you so much." Della and Vidal knew that a Jewish woman only could have sex with her husband if seven days had elapsed since the end of her menstrual bleeding and she had taken a ritual bath in the mikveh.

Vidal said, "Tonight will be beautiful for us. Serve fish for dinner and give the children berry juice. Let them eat as many nuts and as much bread as they want. This will fill their bodies. Even give them some eggs to help them sleep soundly through the night. We will have quiet in the house. I will pray to God for his forgiveness after we show our love for each other on the wrong day."

After Vidal had rested, he went to see Benjamin to detail the results of his trip. "Mostly good. Could be worse. Macario de Alba in Peñafiel will not buy from us anymore. Nor will Don Inocencio of Mélida. But we have many orders. As we expected, by lowering the prices, more shoes were purchased. We will have another good year."

Benjamin said, "I am not surprised at this loss of customers. This trend in the South of Christians and conversos not wanting to work with us is only going to get worse. We should congratulate ourselves on planning for it. I have been buying cheaper lambskins from the Basque shepherds in the hills. Juhuda has negotiated better pricing for gemstones and has done well in keeping a tally of costs, orders, and distribution of payments to each family. Baruh is now spending only half his time in the vineyards so he can spend more time in the shop. We also have the nephews and cousins working smartly. But the most important thing is that you have returned safely."

Once the assessment of business with Benjamin was completed, Vidal felt free to spend time with his family and friends, especially Roffe Michah who was the only physician among the brothers and with his youngest brother, Yosef, the most studious of Levi and Estrela's sons. Yosef was not required to make shoes or become a physician. Levi hoped that since Benjamin did not become a rabbi, perhaps with Hebrew scholarship Yosef would. However, by the time he was old enough to start learning a profession, the family was economically comfortable, so Levi allowed Yosef to continue his studies.

Even as a child, Yosef wanted to discuss philosophy and worldly subjects. Vidal teased him mercilessly, saying that he had a *kavesa de a granada* (the head of a pomegranate), but in truth, the older brothers were proud of Yosef for his intelligence and dedication to his studies. He could speak Spanish, Hebrew, Portuguese, French, Latin, Aramaic, and Arabic. He had spent years learning Torah and Talmud, but he mostly loved the more worldly subjects of history and the Greek classics. However, he wanted more.

After Levi died, Benjamin allowed Yosef to continue his studies and live in the family housing complex with their sister, Agamit, her husband, Rahav the silversmith, and their children. Agamit was a feisty woman—the only girl among her brothers. When Estrela died, Agamit took on the role of managing the females in the Crevago family, deciding who should cook what for holiday dinners, whose children would be watched by what wife when the others went to the market, how family birthdays should be celebrated, and such. "She is big and bossy," Vidal would say in fun, but also with a tinge of seriousness in an effort to protect Della from his sister. Agamit's figure matched her outsized personality. She was bigger in girth than the other women, had graying hair that made her look older, and a wrinkled face that gave harsh expression to her commands. Being the only Crevago sister gave Agamit prestige among the women who had married into the family. They respected her leadership, but feared her sharp words of derision if they did not precisely obey her orders. Agamit never hesitated to call a sister-in-law lazy if she was not moving fast enough, shout an insult to another sister-in-law in front of everyone else, or describe someone's cooking as sickly.

Yosef knew Agamit would not be happy with his plan. However, before informing Agamit, he needed to speak with Benjamin—a conversation he did not relish.

On an evening after Shabbat, Yosef summoned his courage and

crossed the courtyard to Benjamin's house. Benjamin was sitting by the fire drawing a new design for a Crevago shoe.

"Brother, Verino, a merchant from the caravan, told of the university in Murcia. It has many manuscripts and books that have been printed on a press. In fact, the university has acquired more books than exist in all of Vitoria. Murcia is a nice place to live."

Benjamin did not look up.

"Brother, did you hear me?"

Benjamin still did not look up.

After several long, uncomfortable pauses, Yosef asked, "Brother, may I go to Murcia to study?"

With this direct question, Benjamin lifted his head and replied, "Yes. It is with great pleasure that I grant you leave from Vitoria to study in Murcia. I think this is what Papa would have said. However, there is a condition. You must come back and spend the most holy of holy days, Rosh Hashana and Yom Kippur, praying in synagogue with your brothers, and that you return to Vitoria for the Pesah Seder so you can hear the story of our exodus from Egypt with your family."

With joy, Yosef agreed to these terms. He was not sure if he would be able to keep this promise, but he would try.

"Now go tell Agamit."

As he crossed back to Agamit's house, Yosef had an epiphany. "With my leaving, Agamit will feel a diminishment of her power in the family. She brags to the other women about how she takes care of her little brother. With me gone, she will have only her children to preen over. How shall I tell her so she does not go into a rage?"

Yosef opened the door and saw Agamit sitting on a stool, alone by the fire and sewing. The shirt she was mending lay across her lap, with her basket of threads positioned next to her. She looked up at her charge and asked, "Where did you go?"

"To speak with Benjamin. He is quiet but is wise with his words."

"About what?" Agamit asked in a meddling tone.

"I know you will not like it, but Benjamin consented to my going to Murcia to study."

Once Agamit heard that Benjamin had blessed Yosef's venture, there was no way the decision could be overturned. But that did not keep her from trying in a tone of authority. "You will be alone. You are too young. Who will take care of you?"

Yosef, almost in a whisper, said, "All good questions, my sister. You have been kind to me. But it is time that I forge my future." He decided to not engage Agamit in a shouting match.

"To do what? Read books all day? Write manuscripts? Talk, talk, talk. I value scholarship, but you, my little brother, will not be able to fend for yourself. You have never and will never survive without the comfort of my home."

"Maybe so, but you are foolish with this chatter," Yosef said. "What you are saying is selfish. You do not want me to go so you can keep me under your roof and treat me like a child." Yosef's fingers became rigid as he pointed them at Agamit with determination. "You do not want me to go so you can say that you take care of me and that I depend on you. This does not matter to me. If I cannot sustain myself, I will come home to live. I need to venture out on my own. I have no wife and no children, so now is the time."

"I do not agree. Now is the time to find a wife in Vitoria. You could still live with me, and Rahav could build a separate room so you would not sleep with my children anymore."

"Agamit, it is not a wife that I want. My decision is made, and Benjamin has consented. Accept this and keep me as your loving brother. If you do not, you will lose me."

Agamit had lost the argument. With this ultimatum, Agamit knew the conversation was over. As her eyes filled with tears, Yosef was not sure if Agamit's sadness was the result of her failure to impose her will or his decision to leave. However, as her grim look of fortitude turned into a face of softness, he wanted to believe that it was her genuine love for him that caused the tears. Agamit looked into Yosef's eyes and said softly, "May God watch over you and keep you safe."

Yosef left for Murcia with the next full moon. Upon his arrival in the new city, he headed toward the Jewish quarter, taking refuge at the inn near the entry gate. The innkeeper welcomed him and asked, "Can I provide you with a drink? You have the look of a traveler who has come a far distance."

Yosef sat on a bench near the fire and, for the first time in days, started to relax. He welcomed the drink. "I am worn," Yosef replied. "Very worn, but very excited about my future in this city of learning. Tomorrow I will go to the university and see if they will hire a Jew."

"I have a bed that I can give you for the night," offered the innkeeper, wiping his hands on his grimy apron.

Yosef opened the bag hanging from his waistband. "With pleasure, I will take it," Yosef replied. With that, he paid with some coins Benjamin had given him and followed the innkeeper up a narrow stairway.

"Is this it?" asked Yosef as he looked at the large room with many beds of straw stuffed into sacks and covered with linens. The noise from the snoring of the dozen or so men in the attic was deafening.

No answer followed. The innkeeper had already gone downstairs to greet other travelers.

Yosef was so tired that once he lay down, the deafening noise disappeared. He fell into a deep sleep.

As the morning light came through the cracks in the roof, the men began to stir. Slowly, one by one, they filed out to go downstairs to use the forest as a latrine and eat a mix of grains and nuts for breakfast.

Yosef was the last to get up. He felt exhausted but excited. He had never been away from Vitoria. His body felt liberated. He was on the cusp of an adventure.

Yosef grabbed up his travel bag and went downstairs. He was anxious to see what awaited him.

The Universitas Studiorum Murciana, established in the

thirteenth century, presented Yosef with the inspiration and challenge he had yearned for. The school had become one of the most well respected educational institutions in Castile.

After a few weeks, Yosef wrote Benjamin and sent the letter with a traveling merchant going to Vitoria. He wrote about his lengthy discussions with the North Africa–based *Almohades*. "These Moors are brilliant. Their scholarship is excellent. They are great teachers."

Soon the clerics recognized Yosef for his breadth of knowledge. They granted him a teaching position, and a few months later, the governor of Murcia appointed Yosef to be provincial cultural adviser.

The Crevagos were proud of Yosef, as was the entire Jewish community of Vitoria. A revered nobleman on the Iberian Peninsula had elevated one of their own, a Jew.

CHAPTER 5

Every Rooster Sings in Its Coop

1487

Vidal dismounted from his wagon and stood in front of the doors of Segovia's Corpus Christi Church. Since the street was empty, he wanted to take a moment to see the remnants of Stars of David and Jewish carvings on the large wooden panels. Vidal contemplated the evolution of the building when a priest in fancy vestments pushed the church doors open. As the priest exited the church, he almost knocked Vidal over. An entourage of obviously lesser priests, who were dressed in simple black robes and hoods, followed.

The priest offered no apology. "Get out of my way," he said. The lesser priests did not even look at Vidal. They just plowed on after their leader.

Vidal did not respond. He was awestruck. He had never been this close to a priest.

Vidal had thought the priest would ask him if he was entering the church for confession or counseling. Vidal had never spoken with a priest, and although he had had many dealings with Christians, he feared priests because of the evil they spread with their desires to convert all Jews to Christianity. Vidal knew that Don Moises, a jeweler in Segovia, had been tortured by the Dominicans until he converted. Then they forced Moises to testify against his brother

Abraham, who was accused of being a false Christian. After Abraham was hanged, the Church confiscated his property.

So, after due consideration, Vidal felt relieved that he had not had to respond to the man in the long red velvet robe with a huge silver crucifix hanging around his neck. The priest, with all his finery, seemed concerned only with himself and where he was hurrying to, with no concern for anyone else.

Best to get on with my annual visit with Antonio, Vidal thought. He climbed onto the wagon and urged his horse to hurry.

As Vidal entered Antonio's shop, he saw that it was empty. He called out, "Antonio, where are you?" No one returned any echo of greeting.

He walked through the shop as he had done many times before. It was ominously quiet, with no sounds of the loom going and no one hustling around the cutting table. Threads lay on the table, ready for use but with no one there to use them.

Vidal slowly walked where Maria would typically be cooking. Food was on the table. Soup was in the pot sitting on the hearth, but the emptiness of the room made the stone walls very gloomy. Looking around, Vidal noticed that the yard seemed awkwardly cold and silent.

"Antonio! Maria!" Vidal called out.

After a few pregnant moments, Vidal heard some noise from behind a row of barrels. Cautiously Pedro stepped out of the shadows that were hiding him from view. Vidal gasped as he raised his eyebrows. Pedro appeared gaunt, with his eyes hollowed out from lack of sleep.

"Don Vidal? What are you doing here? Why have you come? It is dangerous for you," the boy fearfully whispered. His body shook as he talked in uneven tones. The boy's left eye had a slight uncontrollable tic that Vidal had never seen before.

"Pedro, sit here on the steps," Vidal said taking the boy's hand in his. Pedro had grown since Vidal had last seen him. He looked older than his fourteen years. His eyes had a knowing look as he listened to Vidal's questions. Vidal did not have much experience in helping people overcome sadness. He ran his fingers through Pedro's hair and rubbed the back of his neck.

"Where is your father? Your mother?" Vidal asked.

Trying to hold back tears, Pedro said, "A few days ago priests and soldiers took them to the court of Inquisition. My brothers and sisters are hiding in the cellar. I was coming back from the groves when I heard the commotion in the courtyard. I sneaked into the house and watched through a crack in the door. The men tied my parents' hands, put white garments on them, and put large white cone-shaped hats on their heads. I followed them and saw the men took my parents to the cathedral."

Vidal was so stunned that he almost fell off the step he was sitting on. He felt ill equipped for this news.

"I don't understand," Vidal said. "The Jews and Christians of Segovia have lived in peace for decades, doing business together and privately socializing as much as acquaintances might. For decades, there was no Judería in Segovia. The streets were open. Laws against the Jews were not enforced. No Jewish curfew existed. It is only in the last few years that the seven gates closed off the Judería at night."

"The Dominicans have been preaching more hate and more conversos have been tried," Pedro said. My father told me this, but he assured me that he never would be taken,

Vidal asked, "Why would churchmen come after your father? He probably pays a lot of money for renting a house owned by the Church." After a pause Vidal said, "I guess it does not matter. The Church hates Jews and will do whatever it wants."

Vidal knew of violence against Jews since the 1400s, when Father Vincent Ferrer preached in Sevilla, Córdoba, Cuenca, Toledo, Madrid, Burgos, and Logroño,. He used his charismatic charm and torture to convert Jews to Catholicism. About the same time, the laws of Ayllón were enacted in Castile. These pronouncements restricted the authority of *aljamas* (the self-governing committee of the Jewish community), barred Jews from living in integrated communities with Christians, and from congregating with Christians in any social situations. The laws also limited the professions that Jews could have, thus relegating many to financial jobs, such as tax collectors. Most of the Jews who were truly affected by these laws, like Antonio, converted to Christianity so they could keep their professions and social standing.

"My father told me that a court of Inquisition had been set up in Segovia. He said the Dominicans from Santa Cruz Church were running the whole thing."

Vidal knew this was where Father Tomás de Torquemada lived. A rabid and fanatic Jew-hater, he had encouraged his most important worshippers Ferdinand and Isabella to introduce the first royal Inquisition. The priest did not trust the Church to be sufficiently strict. He wanted total control over the process and the victims, without interference from Rome. When the monarchs named Father Torquemada grand inquisitor, he created courts of Inquisition throughout Castile and Aragón, and rewrote Inquisition procedures. Torquemada believed that no converso could ever be a true Christian. Things changed for the worse when he came to Segovia. Arrests began to occur.

Pedro told Vidal, "I know that once the court of Inquisition was established, fewer weaving orders came from the royals and nobles. There was less for me to do in the shop, and my father let our apprentice go. Our business dwindled to mostly Jews and conversos, and even the conversos started going to Christian weavers as a show of loyalty to the Church.

"I know that last year bakers could not bake *matzo* for Pesah, candle makers were forbidden to sell candles for Shabbat, weavers could not sell cloth for religious garments, and the butcher on Avenida La Almuzara could not slaughter according to Jewish law. There was a day some months ago when soldiers forced Jews and conversos to stand in the square and listen to speeches by Francisco de la Peña of the Knights Templar. My father and I felt humiliated as this priest urged the townspeople to kill us, with statements like 'sy non ponen fuego al monte, que non podría echar los lobos fuera [If you do not set the forest on fire, you cannot throw the wolves out].' We stood in disbelief. It was degrading to hear this language from a supposed man of God."

Pedro continued. "A few weeks ago, my father went to see Don Juan Bravo. They had worked together to solve a problem with some traveling vandals, and my father had secretly lent money to Don Juan when his son was kidnapped for ransom. On this last visit, my father asked Don Juan for help in earning business back from the nobles. Don Juan did nothing to help my father. Then the soldiers and priests took my parents. I have been hiding and caring for my brothers and sisters since that time." Pedro covered his face with his hands. He leaned into Vidal's arm and rested his body against Vidal's.

Pedro said, "Two of my father's customers became inquisitors, Dr. de Mora and the *Licenciado* De Cañas. My father has a good relationship with these men, but I am worried that this might not matter. Priests compel Jews and Christians to testify out of fear and greed. Priests use whatever means necessary to achieve the verdicts they want."

"Things have changed," Vidal said as he looked into Pedro's face. Vidal kissed him on both cheeks and then stood up. But he quickly sat back down. "I need to be quiet for a few minutes so my heart will stop pounding." Vidal needed to pull himself together, because he knew what he had to do next. "I am going to the court," Vidal said. He was calm and determined to see what was going on.

Pedro lifted his head from its resting place on his knees and wiped his tears. "It is too dangerous. If they recognize you as a Jew, you might be taken."

"I am a traveler selling goods and looking for sights to see. I will stand in the back of the room, which is sure to be large enough to accommodate all the Christian spectators. I know the danger. The rumor is that Ferdinand has Jewish blood from his ancestors, so he needs to show that he is truly devoted to Christ. He likes that the

Jews pay and are helpful to him, but he needs to demonstrate how Christian he is. And the Inquisition is how he has chosen to do it.

"Gather the younger children. Take them into the groves. I will come back for you."

Vidal could see that Pedro looked somewhat relieved. "Thank you, Don Vidal."

Vidal wanted Pedro to feel hopeful that his parents could be helped. Vidal saw the corners of Pedro's lips curl upward as he gave Vidal a small smile.

As Pedro went to find the other children Vidal left the courtyard.

He walked through the narrow streets, blending in with some Christians who were heading in the same direction. His thoughts focused on memories of Antonio. How could this happen? How could the Iberian Peninsula become so inhospitable to good people who willingly or under duress had forsaken Judaism for Christianity? Being born Jewish had once more put people in jeopardy.

What hypocrisy. Vidal thought. *The priests want you to convert, but your conversion will never be good enough.*

As he instinctively moved along with the crowd, Vidal got lost in his thoughts. He had heard something about how the popes invented the scheme of Inquisition to wipe out errant thinking. Vidal remembered Yosef talking about the Cathars who in the thirteenth century wanted to separate from the Church of Rome and abolish the need to talk with or pay a priest before absolution for a sin. Pope Honorius III created the Dominican Order and instructed the founding priest, Father Dominic de Guzman, to eliminate Cathar heresy. The priest went to the largest Cathar community and urged them to return to the fold of true Christianity. However, the Cathars rejected Father Dominic's plea. After some experimentation, Father Dominic concluded that torture, not talk, was the only persuasive method to induce the Cathars to return to Catholicism. A popular technique consisted of Dominican friars tying men to large wooden posts with nooses around their necks. Priests then inserted sharp knives into the prisoner's genitals. This kept the heretics alive so that at their public trials, they could atone for the sin of oppositional beliefs. After confession, the priests burned the heretics at the stake. Father Dominic presided over many *autos-da-fés* [acts of faith]. It took more than one hundred years to eradicate the Cathar movement. The Church had learned an important lesson: an Inquisition must move swiftly and harshly if it is to be successful.

Vidal entered the cathedral with the horde of observers and moved to the back of the sanctuary as inconspicuously as possible.

Although the Inquisition was a government-endorsed mandate, no rules of due process were enforced. Defendants could not present evidence opposing the accusations. Nor could legal advocates speak on behalf of the accused. Religious people managed the proceedings.

The church sanctuary loomed large with its vaulted ceiling, arches for support, and its huge crucifix of Jesus standing on the altar. Priests and nuns stood on one side of the sanctuary. Their black garb created a core of dark with white faces peering out of habits and hoods. Wooden crosses hung from their necks. The Christian laity of the city stood on the opposite side of the sanctuary. Vidal could see the rich standing closer to the front of the hall, with a rope barrier separating them from the poor. The men and women talked to each other excitedly in anticipation of what was to come.

After the inquisitors had stepped up onto the judges' platform, the chief inquisitor of this tribunal, Father Benito de Diego, walked in. Vidal recognized him as the priest who had come out of the Church of the Corpus Christi.

The judges sat down and the trial started. Father Benito said, "By the order of the Tribunal of the Holy Office of the Inquisition, as ordered by our royal monarchs, we begin these proceedings against the accused."

Six people walked through the prisoner's entrance with an unearthly cadence, staring straight ahead but seemingly not looking anywhere. Each wore a long yellow *sambenito*, the shroud of shame with its large red crosses on the chest and on back, and a tall conical hat. The accused walked barefoot. One woman had bald spots where her hair had been pulled out.

Antonio and Maria were the last two to enter. Vidal assumed that the yellow garments hid whatever wounds they might have from torture. Antonio could not lift his head. It was as though his neck no longer worked. Maria's hair had turned completely gray.

Vidal stood too far in the back of the sanctuary to catch their attention. Wanting to remain inconspicuous, he could do nothing to comfort them. He saw their faces. The fear was evident. Maria frowned as she looked with disgust at her judges. She turned to look at her fellow prisoners, and her face softened with sadness.

The bailiff read out their names: "Converso Antonio de Fortuna, also known as Yuda ben Lousada and his wife, conversa Maria de Antonio de Fortuna, also known as Benita de Yuda Lousada."

The chief inquisitor read the indictments: "You are accused of one or more of the following: you have celebrated the Jewish Sabbath by washing your body before sundown, by wearing a clean shirt or better garments, by spreading a clean tablecloth, by refraining from lighting a fire on Saturday, by eating food that was taken from a sealed pot that was kept warm but not cooked on Saturday, by not performing work on that day, and by visiting with neighbors on Saturday afternoon and chewing green vegetables. Who has seen the accused do any of these things?"

Hidden voices rang out from the audience.

"I have."

"I saw them secretly being Jews."

"They would not eat pig meat."

"They did not cook on Saturday."

Vidal recognized only one voice. It was a young voice. It came from the side of the sanctuary where witnesses sat.

"It is true. I saw Don Antonio bless wine. I saw *la señora* light candles on the eve of the Jewish Sabbath." The voice belonged to Roaldo, the apprentice. Feeling the protection of the court, he spoke strongly, with assurance and arrogance, happy to be participating in the trial of the Jew who had made him work long hours at the loom. Roaldo gladly showed off his loyalty to the Church.

"Who saw the accused decline to eat or drink on the Day of Atonement? Did the accused go barefoot or ask forgiveness of another on that day?"

Voices chimed in like bells calling Catholics to mass. "I saw Antonio go barefoot on the Day of Atonement. I heard him ask for forgiveness."

The inquisitor continued. "Converso Antonio de Fortuna and your wife. You are accused of celebrating Passover with unleavened bread, eating bitter herbs, telling the story of the Exodus, celebrating the Feast of Tabernacles, circumcising your sons, washing your hands before praying, blessing a cup of wine, performing rituals of cleanliness over food, giving Old Testament names to your children, blessing your children by putting your hands on their heads, washing a corpse with warm water, and praying without saying 'Glory be to the Father, the Son, and the Holy Ghost.' These are the sins you have committed by not being genuine in your conversion to Christ."

More voices rang out in a din of noise, each certifying the sins asserted.

The process was repeated for the other husbands and wives.

Then the chief inquisitor prayed for the redemption of all and celebrated Mass.

Dr. Mora, an esteemed citizen of Segovia chosen by the Dominicans to give the tribunal greater communal significance, rose to his feet. The priest rose with him. They had not gone out of the room to discuss the evidence against these individuals; they simply stood up. Dr. Mora spoke the name of each of the accused, followed by the verdict. "Guilty." Then he gave the sentence for all: "In an auto-da-fé, an act of faith, they will be burned at the stake."

The crowd in the sanctuary hummed with excitement. These people were the presumed faithful, and the auto-da-fé helped them confirm their own faith. The crowd showed its passion as the inquisitors shouted some real and some made-up biblical axioms to the crowd.

"An eye for an eye."

"Love thy neighbor, but not a Jew."

"Be humble, but stand against the Jew."

Vidal's heart ached as he faked his actions and words to conform with the crowd. "Cristianos Nuevos, Falso Cristianos!" he shouted. "Marranos!" He tried to hide the tears that were about to run down his puffy cheeks.

The three men and their wives looked stunned. Vidal thought, *Why should they be so shocked? When arrested, they must have surmised that their lives were over. There have been other autos-da-fés in Segovia. Each ended with a guilty verdict. Did these conversos feel so invulnerable? How could they be so ignorant of the times? Antonio considers himself too much a Castilian and too little a Jew. How could he so badly underestimate the Church's reach into his life?"* Vidal thought about how Antonio and Maria were participants in the society of Segovia. If this travesty could happen to them, it could happen to anyone. Vidal did not want to think these thoughts. He had no power to change what was happening. He did not want to think that trials could happen in Vitoria. He gave thanks that he and his brothers had not converted to Christianity. "It is dangerous to be a Jew in Iberia, but it is more dangerous to be a converso."

A procession formed with the Dominicans in the lead. Their robes dragged on the ground with each new step. Their cowls bobbed up and down, suggesting that the men inside this garb were bouncing with some joy. Some of the priests had their hands folded inside their large sleeves. Others held the banner of the Inquisition, showing off its green cross of knotted wood, flanked by an olive branch signifying forgiveness and reconciliation, and with a sword that stood for justice. On the banner around the cross was the phrase "Exsurge, Domine, et Judica causam tuam" (Rise up, Master, and pursue your Judaic cause).

Vidal watched as the priests headed out of the church. These hooded men of God followed, with their crucifixes dangling from their necks. The priests sang specially composed Inquisition chants urging the condemned to do acts of repentance and deliverance.

The city leaders of Segovia—magistrates of big and little importance, followed. Vidal noticed that the administrators portrayed themselves as men of good even as they participated in a horrific spectacle in the name of God.

Next were soldiers of Ferdinand and Isabella, wearing yellow and red belted tunics and round metal helmets that made each man look like an ominous combatant.

Vidal was sickened as each member of these supervising groups passed by him, walking slowly as if to show off the goods that followed—the goods they had captured.

Antonio and Maria followed with their group of accused heretics. Vidal watched as they passed by him, trying even more desperately to withhold the tears in his eyes and heart. "This loving couple. These good people. Parents who love their children." However, Vidal realized that even though Antonio had not planned for this capture, he had not done anything to prevent it."

People gawked at Antonio, Maria, their fellow heretics, and at the spectacle. Vidal wondered if some of the spectators maybe were once Antonio's friends and customers—fellow citizens of Segovia.

Antonio tried to get close to Maria so he could whisper his love to her, but he could not get the words out. Nor could he move his head. His body was decimated, as was his spirit. He kept stepping forward toward his fate.

Vidal wanted to say some words of comfort to Antonio, but could not. This action would reveal Vidal's identity. He knew all was lost for Antonio and Maria. He did not see any purpose or benefit in putting his own life in jeopardy. However, as Antonio walked by, Vidal caught the prisoner's eye and gave him a grimace to show the pain he felt for his friend.

No acknowledgement came from Antonio.

The group of prisoners walked slowly with their hands bound

in front by rope, and each held a devotional candle. The flames flickered, and the warmth of the candle reached Antonio's face. Nonetheless, he felt cold.

Halberdiers, the guards of the Church, provided a border around the condemned. Each guard held his five-foot-long metal-shafted pole high, to show the crowd that the weapon was crowned with an oversize curved axe blade and pointed spike for spearing combatants. These armed soldiers symbolically served to protect the crowd from the heretics. As one prisoner tried to escape from the group, a guard prevented it by using the pole to hit the accused on the shoulder and push him back into the procession. The sound of pain blended with the shouts of the crowd.

"Scum!"

"Kill the fakes!"

The drummers brought up the rear of the processional. They beat out the sounds of impending death with their kettledrums, slowly pounding out a mournful rhythmic sound. Maria walked to the pace of the drums. She attempted to look over at Antonio but could not. She stared straight ahead and said to the crowd in the loudest voice she could muster, "You are not creatures of God. You are monsters." In embarrassment for humanity, her eyes looked to the ground.

Vidal watched tears roll down Antonio's cheeks as he heard his wife's voice. Vidal knew the tears came from Antonio's grief for himself, his wife, and fear for his children. Antonio had no way of knowing that his children would escape to a place of safety, that Vidal would take them in.

Antonio tried to touch Maria with his arm. She did not feel this gesture. As Antonio looked at his wife, he whispered, "I love you, my precious." In that moment, Maria looked up and saw Antonio's loving look. She pursed her lips in a silent gesture of kissing him.

Just then, a guard used a long, thick baton to give Antonio a swift hit to the back of his neck. Antonio gave a slight howl and hung his head forward, putting his chin on his chest.

Vidal melted into the seemingly obsessed crowd of Segovians who wanted to witness the result of the trial. As the procession marched around the plaza and through the narrow streets surrounding the square, the crowd yelled epithets at the condemned:

"Jew dogs!"

"Marranos!"

"Liars!"

With each turn and twist of a street, the onlookers renewed their vigorous attention to the yellow-robed six. As the procession started down a new street, other people leaned out the windows of their homes, ridiculed the accused, and cheered the accusers. Some people stopped their daily work to join the frenzied crowd. A baker in his flour-covered clothes with his hands on his hips joined in the chanting as he stretched his neck for a better view. A woman gawking at the accused carried a basket of vegetables.

The procession arrived at the *quemadero,* the burning place, and the accused climbed the stone steps of the scaffold. Executioners tied the condemned to the slender stone pillars that masons had built for this purpose.

As the mob closed in on the quemadero, Father Benito, stepped forward and spoke to the heretics and the crowd. He was short in stature, with a pocked face. His odor traveled on the breeze and was strong enough for Vidal, who was standing in the back of the crowd, to smell it. The priest had the rancid odor of rotten eggs—clearly the label of an unclean, infected man. Vidal wondered why he had not noticed the smell earlier in the day, outside the Corpus Christi Church.

Father Benito bellowed, "We are here today to bring hellfire to heretics who have defiled the Catholic Church by pretending. We cannot have people who pretend to be Catholic still be loyal to their Judaism. We must purify, purify, purify." The crowd met each statement with cheers. They roared a return restatement of "Purify, purify, purify."

"These Marranos belong in hell's fire. They are evildoers. They pollute our Catholic world. We must send them to hell and be saved from their presence." The cadence of his words seemed melodic.

The priest delivered his message replete with passages from the New Testament. These seemingly gave authority to the tribunal that delivered the guilty verdict.

After the priest finished his sermon, the proceedings moved to the next phase. The notary again detailed the crimes of the condemned persons. The list had expanded from the list of crimes that had been read in the church.

"Ate meat that had been salted and had veins removed, talked about Judaism with a Jew, did not believe in the trinity, did not believe in Jesus as the messiah, did not believe in a Christian Paradise, did not believe that the Host was the body and blood of Christ, did not observe the sacred rites of true Christians, did not eat on the Fast of Esther..."

So on and so on ran the list of sins and misdeeds of the accused.

The repetition made the charges seem true.

In the front of the crowd, Vidal spied Roaldo. He was relishing the attention he received as a witness to Antonio and Maria's crimes. A smirk-like smile graced his face.

Vidal felt only hatred for this boy.

Vidal was never tongue-tied. He usually could muster words even in the most awkward situations. He could tell humorous stories at inappropriate moments in conversation. But at this moment, he could not move a muscle in his face and could not move his tongue to utter a word. His thoughts rang in his head. *I can say nothing. I can do nothing. Their fate is their own. I do not understand this cruelty and this disregard for human life. Where is God? Who can believe in God if these atrocities happen? I will never put my trust in God again.*

The priest on the platform interrupted Vidal's thoughts with orders for execution. "Death by fire!" the priest yelled out triumphantly, as though he had just won a prize from the pope. "But not before each has one last chance to repent so they can meet God with their remorse in full display. Who will truly convert to

Catholicism now, at the moment of condemnation, so you can receive the gift of being strangled before you are burned?"

No one in a yellow robe spoke. Their shock at this choice was evident. Death by strangling or death by burning—was this a fair choice?

However, with no other option, the less painful death seemed to be by strangling, and soon four of the six conversos were released from their posts. They crouched on their knees in front of Father Benito, reciting conversion prayers and giving statements of loyalty to the Roman church. "I repent," they shouted. "I proclaim my loyalty to Jesus Christ."

Immediately following their repentance, the executioner retied each of the four in a standing position and then strangled them, one by one. With each death, a wave of supportive cheers of elation was heard from the crowd. The townspeople were mesmerized by the death ritual. Then, as instructed, the executioner took the dead conversos, who were limply standing tied to their pillars, and chopped off their hair so that when their bodies burned strands of hair would not flitter about the courtyard.

Only Antonio and Maria refused to repent. "I am who I am and should not be burned at the stake for it," Antonio said. "My family became Christians to have a safer life. Christianity did not do this. Better to be an authentic Jew. The God of Abraham, Isaac, and Jacob will wrap me in the fire's heat and take me to our forefathers."

The inquisitor looked at Antonio with disgust and anger. Vidal watched as the official stood directly in front of Antonio, their faces not more than six inches apart. The inquisitor wrinkled his forehead and began poking Antonio. "This man has not repented as he should." The inquisitor turned toward the crowd, madly waving his hands in the air, and said, "He has robbed us of a victory. I shall see that your fire is hot and burns slowly, to give you as much time for repentance as possible."

The executioner cut Antonio's hair, careful that the razor did not scrape the scalp.

"Spill no blood!" yelled Father Benito.

The inquisitor stepped in front of Maria. He looked at her and said, "I give you this opportunity to repent, to save yourself from a tragic death, to ease your pain and suffering."

Maria glanced at her husband and then to the inquisitor. She looked out at the whipped-up crowd and back to the inquisitor. In her head, she heard Hebrew melodies of her childhood singing.

Calmly, but firmly, Maria said, "I am Benita bat Nahon ha Ivri. I am a daughter of Israel—of Sarah, Rebecca, Leah, and Rachel. I lift up my eyes to heaven and say, "Sh'ma Yis'ra'eil Adonay Eloheinu Adonay echad. Hear, Israel; the Lord is our God. The Lord is One."

With these words, the inquisitor spoke in a loud and hysterical voice, with his arms flying about. "Executioner, cut this heretic's hair close to her scalp. Let us get on with it."

As the man with the black mask over his face started to clip Maria's hair, the inquisitor turned to the crowd and shouted in a crazed tone, "Who will light the fire of these heretics, these blasphemers? Who will bring these heretics to an end?"

Within seconds, fervent residents of Segovia who believed they would be rewarded in heaven for the deed they were about to do jumped onto the stone stage. They responded to the urgings of the inquisitors to pile the straw high about each body of the four that had repented and the two who had not. The do-gooders acted quickly. They surrounded each stone post and accused heretic with straw and wood.

On the signal from the chief inquisitor, in all piety, several Christians of Segovia took the torches from the Dominican priests and lit each pyre.

Spectators in the crowd shrieked. The gruesome, ghastly nature of this shocking exhibition appealed to the ardent Christians. The townspeople reveled in the moment and in the belief that they were getting closer to God with the burning of these humans. The exhilaration was evident. Some in the audience knelt and prayed to Jesus for their own salvation. Others prayed to the Virgin Mary for divine intervention for heavenly deliverance. They thought their participation in this demonstration of faith would give them a passage to heaven. Few in the audience thought their participation in the spectacle doomed them to the fires of hell.

Antonio cried out, "You cannot force me to believe what I do not believe!" Looking at the nobles he used to serve, Antonio said, "You Christianized me. I converted because you forced me to do so. Now you condemn me for your evil act. You are evil. Evil. You are the workers of evil."

As the flames started to burn Antonio's legs, he spotted Vidal. The two men looked at each other for just a passing moment. Even at his last instant of life, Antonio would not betray his friend to the crowd. Not even to save his own life or make his own death more palatable.

Vidal wished he could shower Antonio with words of respect. Antonio was showing courage and honesty at the stake. Vidal wanted to tell Antonio that he had seen Pedro and that all the children were safe. But Vidal could do nothing but offer silent prayers for Antonio and Maria.

As the heat rose about him, Antonio shouted out in Hebrew, "Ye'varech'echa Adonay ve'yish'merecha. Ya'ir Adonay panav eilecha viy-chuneka. Yisa Adonay panav eilecha, ve'yasim lecha shalom. [May the Lord bless you and keep you; May the Lord make his face to shine upon you and be gracious to you; May the Lord lift up his countenance upon you and give you peace.]"

Antonio slipped into unconsciousness, and his body, engulfed in flames, burned.

With the roar of Antonio's flames in the background and the crowd praying and shouting, Vidal heard Maria say the twenty-third psalm. "The Lord is my shepherd, I shall not want…" But the heat of the flames caused her to drop into nothingness before she finished the prayer.

In time, the ashes from their bodies mixed with the residue of straw and wood. Collectively they spiraled into the air. The wind carried ashes to places outside the plaza. Some even landed on the house in the Judería, where Antonio had been born, where his children had been born, and where his life had been content up to a short time ago.

Vidal walked slowly from the crowd. Once around the corner, out of the eyes of those still reveling in the grotesqueness of the afternoon, he bent over and puked a gush of what seemed to be his guts. He wiped off his mouth and clothes, which had been tainted by his bile, and he walked back to Antonio's shop as nonchalantly as he could.

Vidal found Pedro and the other children hiding in the groves of berry bushes. With as comforting a voice as he could muster, Vidal said, "Let me join you for a moment." As he spoke, the tears that he had been holding back poured from his eyes. "You cannot go back to your home. Your parents are dead."

"The worst has happened," said Pedro. His face turned white. He put his arms around as many of his brothers and sisters as he could and asked Vidal, "What will happen to us? Where shall we go?"

The younger children looked at Pedro as he asked these questions. Adela, who was only four years old, asked, "When will Mama and Papa be coming home?" She knew that information had been delivered, but she could not grasp the gravity of what she had been told.

"They are not returning," Gaila, the oldest girl, said. She was one year younger than Pedro. She moved over to be closer to Adela. Gaila stroked Adela's hair and attempted to envelop her as best as possible. "I am the new *Mamita* of this family." Her voice broke as she said these words. She had not yet come into her own womanhood, but she knew that she had to step in to comfort the young ones. "I would like to burn the priests and every Christian in this city, but we cannot."

Nuño, the seven-year-old, said nothing. He was as confused and unknowing as Adela but was too scared to talk. Esteban, who was twelve, sputtered, "What is going on?" His face showed his confusion and dismay.

Vidal said, "Sweet children, I grieve with you for the lives of your parents. You will come with me to Vitoria. I will tell my family what happened here, and we will all leave the Iberian Peninsula together. You will live with the Crevagos, and where we go, you will go. Let us be on our way now."

Vidal pushed the few bags of shoes left in the wagon to one side. He loaded the younger children into the remaining space. Pedro climbed in front with Vidal.

"Move forward," Vidal commanded the horse pulling the heavy load.

With that pronouncement, Adela began to cry. "Where are we going?" she asked.

Pedro turned toward her and said, "Wherever we go, it will be better than here."

⊱━◆━○━◆━⊰

Vidal arrived in Vitoria with Antonio's children and believed Della would nurture and love them like a mother who had found a litter of lost kittens. Vidal deviated from his usual arrival routine of stopping at the cemetery. Instead, he went directly to his own home.

"Stay in the wagon. I will be right back."

Vidal found Della alone in the kitchen, making bread for Shabbat. The oldest girls, Michlea and Delilah were married and living in the homes of their husbands' families. David was working as an apprentice to Benjamin, and Jacob was learning medicine from Roffe Michah. The youngest girl—Naomi, had gone to the market to buy meats for Shabbat meals.

After embracing Della, Vidal quickly described the events in Segovia and stated that he had brought Antonio and Maria's children to live with him and Della.

"These children need to stay with us until we can convince my brothers' and sister's families that we must leave Iberia and make arrangements to go to Holland, where there is tolerance and it is safe for Jews."

Della said, "I know these children have suffered the loss of their parents. Life has displaced them, but they cannot stay with us forever. There is no room. Often Michlea and Delilah's children sleep here. These are our grandchildren, and they have to come first. We cannot afford to feed five more mouths. You leave for months, and the raising of these orphans will fall to me. How can I care for five more children? I spend my days helping Michlea and Deliah take care of their children and cooking for them. I still have our own unmarried children to care for. As for leaving Vitoria, I will not do it. No harm has ever come to us. We get along well with the Christians. You have Christians that you have known your whole life, and you speak in a friendly way to them. The churches in Vitoria do not posture against the Jews. Do not ask me to leave, because I will not. I do not see the need to do so; nor will I keep these displaced children for more than a short time."

Vidal looked at Della's face, which had become hardened over time. Her expression did not convey the recognition that she would be doing a *mitzva* by taking care of these orphans.

"You are being unkind. This is not what I expected. Why should we not keep them until they are grown," Vidal said. "Antonio and Maria sheltered me when I was in Segovia. They did not tell me how long I could stay."

"They knew you would not stay for months. There was no reason to ask you to leave. They knew you would."

"The children have endured a terrible grief. They should be with someone they know who will care for them. To give them off to people they do not know will be another blow. I cannot do that. We must keep them. It would be heartless to do otherwise."

Della was firm. "They can stay with us for a few days. Then permanent homes must be found. For tonight, the boys can sleep with our sons. The girls will sleep on the floor near the piss pot. Tomorrow you will go to the rabbi."

Like most synagogues on the Iberian Peninsula, Vitoria's had a help and welfare committee that fed the Jewish poor and aided families in times of illness and need. The men of this committee would understand that it was the community's obligation of benevolence to find permanent homes for these orphans.

When Vidal told the children to come into the house, they stood in a huddle with fear of the unknown in their eyes. Adela started to cry and repeated, "I want my mama." Gaila tried to comfort her, but without success. Della went over to the young child and gave her an embrace, as any mother might do. Della looked at the group of orphans and said, "Go sit by the fire and have some sweet cakes. I made them for Shabbat, but you can have them now." Her tone let the children know they should feel guilty that they were eating food intended for others.

As Della walked to the cupboard, she scowled at Vidal and moved her head from side to side, visibly saying no to this situation. It was at this moment that Vidal fell out of love with Della. He had never before noticed that she had become so selfish and protective of her own family and possessions, to the point that she had no love left over for these homeless souls.

Vidal said, "You are the woman in this household. I will make the decision as to what is best for this family."

The two did not talk about the subject again.

Within a few days, Pedro and his oldest brother, Esteban, went to live with a drapero.

Gaila, Nuño, and Adela went to live with a childless couple— Joshua and Ester Levi. Joshua was the apothecary for the Judería. He and his wife welcomed the instant family. For months Adela had nightmares, until she learned that Ester would comfort her.

All the children settled into their new homes with memories of their parents and gratitude for these people in Vitoria. Pedro and Gaila were relieved that they could be openly Jewish in their new homes. The younger children just accepted that they would now be called by their Hebrew names.

Vidal wanted to describe to his brothers what he had witnessed in Segovia. He felt certain that, given the events that had befallen Antonio and Maria and people in other parts of the Iberian Peninsula, all would agree that it was time to leave and begin making plans for the move to Holland. Vidal called a meeting of his brothers.

>─┤─◆>─•─O─•─<◆─┤─◁

Vidal breathed in the aroma of the cakes Della had put on the kitchen table. The pastries filled the small room with the scents of spice. Six cups sat on the table with a jug of Baruh's sweet wine. Della had wiped the benches, swept the floor, and put the big pots and pans on their hangers to give the room a tidy appearance. She did not know why Vidal had called the family meeting but could sense from his demeanor that it was to be an important conversation. As usual, she was not invited to participate. However, since Vidal had brought Antonio's children, he had not engaged her in much of anything— just conversation that was essential to daily living.

One by one, the brothers filed in. Only Yosef was missing, since he was in Murcia. Once Benjamin, Roffe Michah, Juhuda, Baruh, and Agamit's husband, Rahav, were seated around the kitchen table Vidal retold in greater detail what he had witnessed in Segovia.

"We must be fearful of what Christians can do when stirred up by a priest. We should leave Castile and go to Holland, where people are more tolerant of Jews."

Benjamin's voice became deeper than his usual solemn speech. "I know you think the risks to us are great, brother, but how do we know if what happened in Segovia will happen here? We live with the Basque, who have never harmed us. We have been in Vitoria for many years with no incidents of violence by our neighbors. They think of us as Jews but also consider us as Spanish as they are. What the priests did in Segovia does not mean it will happen in the Basque country."

"No," said Vidal forcefully. "I have told you about various towns in Castile and Aragón where riots of Christians killed Jews. If the violence moves north into the Basque country, I do not think we can count on the Christians in Vitoria to shield us. We separate ourselves from our Christian neighbors because we are different from them. Our rites and rituals. Shabbat. Feast days. Our Day of Atonement. We do not mix with them, go to their homes, attend their celebrations, or eat meals with them. It might not take much for them to turn on us."

Roffe Michah said, "As a physician, I am more concerned about the illness that is striking Christians than I am about Christians hurting us."

Benjamin agreed. "Merchants told me they first saw the disease in Italy. It traveled through France with caravans. And they saw it in Iberia. They saw the dead piled up in Burgos. No one wanted to go near them. No one wanted to tend to the sick … the soon-to-be dead."

"The country is good for growing crops but also for fostering the spread of disease," said Roffe Michah. "But I have not heard anyone say that the Jews caused the sickness like they did a hundred years ago when the plague struck. I am confident that no one will harm us. Why would they? We have not harmed them." Roffe Michah was two years younger than Vidal but believed himself wiser. "I know these people. They respect us. They would not do harm."

Baruh said, "We have built our business and contacts here. Christians buy most of my wine regardless of the law prohibiting Christians from drinking wine that was made by Jews. Christians buy Crevago shoes. They buy Rahav's silver plates and goblets. Our life is here. Our prosperity is here."

"Brother, you are making too much of what you have seen elsewhere," Benjamin said with somberness. "The Inquisition searches for conversos. This is why Antonio and Maria were condemned. They had forsaken their Judaism. We do not need to be as afraid as you make it seem. We were born Jews and have stayed Jewish. We have not succumbed to the pressure to convert and never will."

Baruh's hands were trembling. The tremors were normal for him. He had always been the sickly brother. He had a compassionate soul. "Vidal," Baruh said, "we know you want the best for us, but you need to soften your thinking that a move to Holland is needed. We have lived in Vitoria since Erini Crevago ben Israel ha Ivri arrived here more than two hundred years ago. Jews were already living on our Calle. Our ancestor wanted this as our home. I do not see that our families are at risk here. If anything, we are safer here than anywhere else on the Iberian Peninsula. Holland is far away. Old Erini made a good decision to settle in Vitoria."

"Erini found the Basque country agreeable," Roffe Michah said by rote. "Its scenery of green hills and woods were beautiful. The berry groves and nut trees provided delicious treats."

Juhuda, who was fifteen months younger than Roffe Michah and the second-most-skilled cobbler in the Crevago shop after Benjamin, agreed. "Vidal, you overstate the concerns. The Basques do not care about us except for the taxes we pay. Kashruth. Our different clothing. The Basques are strange in their own way. They have their own foods... their mix of Christianity and unusual pagan rituals. They are not typical Christians and will not harm us. We are safe with the Basques. I do not want to think of having to leave Vitoria."

Benjamin asked, "Vidal, do you think Della would move away from your married daughters and their children—her grandchildren? Have you asked her? This will never happen."

Vidal could not answer his brother. Just like Benjamin's wife, Marcela, Della was devoted to her children and grandchildren. She would rather die than leave them.

Rahav sat with his brothers-in-law. As was typical, he would not enter a conversation until everyone else had spoken. He accepted his outsider status. However, he was also self-conscious about his scarred, pockmarked face, which would not allow him to grow a beard that fully covered his cheeks. As a child, he had been sick with itchy sores all over his face. His scratching scarred his skin. Rahav sat with his shoulders rounded and his head resting in his palms with his fingers extended, almost in an effort to hide his cheeks. "Agamit will not want to leave Vitoria. This is where her friends on the Calle live." Agamit dominated Rahav just as she did her sisters-in-law. "She is happy living in Vitoria. The children are in school or learning trades. Our oldest studies with the rabbi."

"You are all wrong in how you are looking at this," Vidal said, "not wanting to see what could be ahead of us. The fact is that it does not matter how prosperous we are or how well we live with the Christians. They will turn on us in a moment if the priests of Vitoria urge them to. What if Dominicans come here from other parts of Iberia? I remind you of what happened when Father Ferrer came to Vitoria. He used torture to convert Jews to Christianity. How many of us could withstand torture and remain Jewish? We need to protect our families and leave."

The discussion among the brothers went on, but in the end, most agreed that no events in Vitoria warranted an upheaval of the family. Vidal had lost the argument.

CHAPTER 6

Give Thanks for Living Whatever Is Your Life

1488 Early Summer Afternoon

The Crevagos took advantage of the warm months and ate Shabbat lunch together in the long courtyard surrounded by the townhouses where the families lived. Long tables with benches filled the space on this balmy afternoon. There was a table for men and those boys who had completed their *Bar Mitzvas*, all of whom wrapped tefillin for prayer. There was also a table for boys who were approaching their Bar Mitzvas. The unmarried girls and the very young children sat at a table with the women.

Agamit, Crevago wives, and the older daughters brought out jugs of thick, syrupy wine that Baruh had made and poured it into cups. The family said Kiddush and drank the thick liquid and chewed the grape skins and stems that were included with the juice.

As soon as the *HaMotzi* prayer over the bread was said, the women started to serve the men. Chimes of "May I serve you?" filled the courtyard as women heaped food on the plates. The smell of roasted lamb that had taken days to cook swirled in the courtyard space. The women filled bowls with a thick soup of beans and leafy greens.

After the men and younger boys were served, the women, girls, and younger children ate. The mothers talked about various foods, cooking, children, and the new gossip they had heard at the well and the marketplace. All while nursing babies and helping the smaller children with their food.

The men talked of their workdays and any new events that had occurred since the day before. No one mentioned the evils that had brought Antonio and Maria's children to Vitoria. No one mentioned anything about the courts of Inquisition that were taking place elsewhere on the Iberian Peninsula. Instead the conversation went to a different topic.

Benjamin asked Roffe Michah, "Did you tell everyone who you saw yesterday and what you saw?"

Roffe Michah, without looking up from his plate, said, "I was called to the shop of Muni, the soap maker." He spoke in hushed tones so his talk would not alarm the women and children. The men leaned in so each could hear what seemed to be important news.

"He is the first one in the Judería that I have seen fall ill to the disease that has been plaguing the Christians. Muni had a great deal of heat in his body. When I touched his neck, he whimpered with pain. He could hardly move because of the weakness in his arms and legs. He said his head was pounding like the banging of church bells. His eyes were red, and he had a cough that came from deep down in his belly. Then his nose started bleeding. His wife said Muni could not keep any food down. And he was shitting a river of mierda. He is sure to die within days."

Benjamin said, "What did we expect? We have known for weeks that an epidemic of sickness has been among the Christians."

"Maybe this is punishment from God for what the Christians have done to the Jews," Vidal said sarcastically. He had evolved into a nonbeliever after seeing Antonio and Maria burned at the stake. The memory was still as fresh as the day he witnessed this horrific event.

Roffe Michah, who, unlike Vidal, was completely observant of Jewish traditions and rituals, said, "Our God is not one that seeks revenge upon people who harm us."

"Not true," argued Benjamin. "He made sure Pharaoh's men

drowned in the Red Sea after Moses led the Hebrews through to safety."

Roffe Michah argued back. "I cannot believe that our almighty God would curse the Christians of Vitoria, whom we have lived with in calm and peace for centuries. Our physician ancestors saved the Christians of Vitoria when the black death came to them. Many of Vitoria's Christians would not be alive today if our ancestors had not saved theirs. Why would God strike these people when they have not done us any harm? And do we want to say that our God is vengeful? Do we want Christians to think that the God of the Hebrew people is responsible for this tragedy of illness where women and children are dying? I do not think so."

"We cannot trust that God will help us in our time of need. God did not help Antonio and Maria, or the Jews of Toledo when the Christians rioted there," Vidal said. "It is foolish to put our faith in God when God lets people burn at the stake. We must always think of ourselves first."

Vidal did not give Benjamin a chance to respond. Instead he looked directly at Roffe Michah and said, "If the Christians ask you, will you help them? Will you tend to their sick and dying? Will you put yourself in danger of illness for the Christians?"

Roffe Michah did not hesitate. "I am already treating Vitoria's Christian sick. Yes. If I am asked to do more, I will. I took an oath to help those in need." Roffe Michah started to recite portions of his physician's oath. "'I will take care that they suffer no hurt or damage ... I will comport myself and use my knowledge in a godly manner.' So I really have no choice."

"Let us stop this talk of sickness," Benjamin requested. "One ill soap maker does not mean disease for the Jews of Vitoria.

Benjamin called to his children, "Isaac, Daniyyel, Cassela, Jonah, and Rina! Come here!" They immediately got up from their seats and surrounded their father. "What are the three obligations Jews have?"

In unison, the children repeated what their father had taught them. "Give service to God. Study Torah. Repair the world. And if we cannot repair the whole world, we must do what we can in whatever way we can." Isaac spoke the loudest. He wanted to show that he was the smartest, and he wanted to curry favor with his father. The children rarely received favorable comments about their learning, although Benjamin was very interested in scholarship. "I am ready for my Bar Mitzva," Isaac said with his chest puffed up.

Vidal listened to Benjamin's children spout off Jewish teachings and said, "I am hardened to the difficulties of Christians. The sickness that has penetrated their homes seems minor compared to the riots, torture, and burnings that Jews have endured at the hands of the priests."

As the family talked and ate, two men poked their heads into the courtyard at the rear entrance that backed up to Calle Abrevadero. Crevagos who did not live on Calle de Judios used this Calle Abrevadero entrance.

The pair took a few hesitant steps toward the men's table.

"Physician Crevago Roffe Michah? It is Argi Bakar, a shoemaker from Calle Zapatería. I am with my cousin, Kaver Borcero, the tinker. May we enter?"

As Roffe Michah nodded, Argi and Kaver walked over to him.

The seated men stopped their discussions. The women stopped talking their gossip. They glared at these odd-looking men in their Christian clothes with their flat, wide berets, heavy red shirts, and black woolen pants. The children moved closer to their mothers and to each other. Most had never been off the Calle, so they had not seen very many Christians. A hushing quiet came over the courtyard.

"You know me," Kaver said. "I made some metal instruments for you."

Kaver was a large man with wide shoulders. His dark skin was ruddy from growing up in the cold hills around Vitoria.

"Hello, Don Benjamin," Argi, the shorter and squatter Christian, said. The Jew was his competitor, but Argi respected Benjamin's skill and artistry.

Kaver turned to the other men sitting at the table and said, "I know this Crevago family, and you know me. Many times you have seen me at the market and in the square with my children."

Argi and Kaver were oblivious to how odd they looked to the family. Vidal thought that to these men, the Jews sitting at the table must look strange, with their skullcaps and white garments with fringes.

The Christians had never before been in the courtyard of a Jew. And the Jews had never had a Christian in their courtyard.

Roffe Michah was the exception. He visited wealthy sick Christians in their homes. He was the least horrified at the sight of these Basque men.

Benjamin gestured to Argi and Kaver. "Join us in some food and drink." He beckoned to the men with a welcoming motion of his hand, behaving with the normal politeness one might expect.

However, the two men did not respond.

Vidal said, "You look upset. What is it you want?"

Argi's head reared back at Vidal's bluntness. Argi kept his hands in front of him in case any of these Jews tried to attack him. Argi had learned to be fearful of Jews. The priests had voiced the dangers of cavorting with Jews, because according to Christian lore, they had killed Jesus Christ.

Kaver saw Argi's reaction and put his hand on his shoulder. "We need to be here," Argi nodded in agreement and whispered, "No more can we have barbers act as physicians. We need better."

Argi told Roffe Michah, "I do not know much. I am not a learned man. I can read and write only a little. Still, I have come to plead for your help."

Kaver added, "We do not mean to disrupt your afternoon meal," as he realized that all eyes in the courtyard were staring at his brown face.

"What do you want?" Vidal said with lifted eyebrows and a sideward glance to his older brother, who was seated at the head of the table. Vidal's skepticism of Christians had grown significantly since he had witnessed their capabilities for terror.

Argi seemed to know that he had to defend his countrymen before he could ask his favor. "As we walked through the city, my cousin and I talked of how Vitoria has not experienced any of the terrible brutal events that have gone on in other parts of Castile, Aragón, in the kingdom of Navarre, or in the southern cities of Sevilla, Granada, and Valencia. We want to keep the harmony of our city and keep the generations of peacefulness that we have been told about by our fathers and grandfathers."

Kaver said, "I represent the tinker craftsmen on the city magistrate. The town council has always looked to the Jews of Vitoria for helping us with taxes demanded by the crown and nobles. We know Jews pay more in taxes than Christians do. You take care of your poor and downtrodden in ways that we Christians do not. I say this freely because it is true. Now we need more from you."

"What is it you want?" asked Vidal a third time.

"Physician Crevago, I was asked to speak with you because I work with Jews who need metal tools and fittings. The leaders on the city council, house of officers, and the lesser open council beg that the physicians of the Judería come to the Calle Nuestra Señora del Cabello and help the sick who have been quarantined in the Pilgrim's Hospital. More than forty have died—men, women, and children. Triple that are sick and likely will die if nothing is done to help them. They are already lifeless. You know the baker Arbone Amalure. His wife and all his children are sick. You helped his wife when she could not birth her youngest child. And Motea Tolar, the shepherd—he died yesterday. We ask that you also visit the families who have not put their sick in the hospital but whose servants are taking care of them. We see the illness spreading from home to home, and we fear for the lives of the old and young in Vitoria."

Vidal said abruptly, "Why can the Christian physicians not tend to your people?"

Kaver waited to answer. He looked at his wrinkled hands rather than into the faces of those seated before him and said, "I am in shame to tell you. The Christian physicians cannot help, and the dead are piling up."

"Why can the Christian physicians not help?" Vidal asked, pressing Kaver.

"The Christian doctors and their families have fled the city. These physicians saw patients with symptoms, tried to cure some, but could not. They treated the cough unsuccessfully, and then chills and body heat occurred. These barbers left us. I am not proud of these Christians. We understand that they feared for the lives of their families, but we do not understand how they could abandon their friends and their responsibilities at this time of need. When we learned that the physicians had left, the council met to see what could be done. Only half of the men showed for the meeting because the other half was sick."

Argi added, "We come to you because you and the other Jewish physicians are held in high esteem. You already treat some Christians, and they have told us of your skills. Through the stories of our fathers and grandfathers, we know that the Crevago family helped us when the black death came to Vitoria a hundred years ago. We need you again."

Benjamin looked at Roffe Michah. "Can you? Do you want to?"

Roffe Michah, without hesitation, responded, "I will go myself and see what the situation is. I will take my son Ezra with me. This will be good training for him. Once I know what needs to be done, I will ask my fellow Jewish physicians to help with the healing. The esteemed physician Antonio de Tornay. And others."

Vidal leaned over to his brother and whispered, "Is it safe for Ezra? He could become sick."

Roffe Michah said loudly in reply, "Ezra needs to know the dangers of being a physician. Going with me will provide good lessons for him."

Argi heard this and said, "We know the size of what we ask you to do. We do not have enough money to pay you and your fellows for your service."

Benjamin said to Roffe Michah, "Go with this man. See what you can do for his people."

Isaac walked over to his father and said, "I want to go too."

Turning toward his nephew, Benjamin said, "Ezra, take your cousin Isaac with you, and the two of you should be a comfort to the sick children." Benjamin had no choice but to let Isaac go with Roffe Michah after the boy had spouted off about the Jewish obligation to repair the world.

Vidal leaned over to Benjamin so Argi could not hear. "Brother, you are sending our dear boys to be with Christian children. What if our boys get sick? Do not forget Muni and his family. What if there are other Jews who may already be sick? You are leaving our fellow Hebrews without care and their children without comfort."

"The Christians have asked for our help," said Benjamin. "We have needs in our own community, but the younger Jewish physicians, including your son Jacob, can take charge of them for now. Roffe Michah should help this man, who loves his children as much as you love yours. He has shown courage by coming here to ask for help. Our sons must learn to give help even when it is dangerous."

The other brothers—Juhuda, Baruh, and Rahav—kept their heads down and said nothing. Benjamin had decided, and as the oldest brother and the main cobbler for Crevago shoes, no one wanted to disagree after his public pronouncement to the Christians.

Benjamin said to Argi and Kaver, "We will not take anything in payment for this. It is to fulfill God's charge to us that we will help you."

With his unfinished meal in front of him, Roffe Michah stood up and climbed over his bench seat. Ezra, who had been sitting next to his father, immediately got up. He felt honored to have been chosen to accompany his father on this mission. Ezra's eyes widened with excitement. The mission seemed scary, since he had never ventured onto Christian streets.

Benjamin's wife, Marcela, who had been listening intently, also stood up and walked over to her husband.

"Is it necessary that you send our son into this den of sickness? Roffe Michah is used to it, and he can do what he thinks best for Ezra. But why must you offer Isaac, who has never been with Christians? I do not want him to go. He might get sick. I beg you. Isaac is to be a shoemaker, not a physician. He does not need to learn the ways of medicine."

Marcela loved her husband, but since their wedding day, she had not understood him—his turn to coldness and lack of affection. He took care in monetary ways but never doting on the children or fooling with them. Benjamin touched Marcela only when it was permissible according to Jewish marriage laws and when his body demanded it. "I dislike that you care more for Christian children than your own."

Benjamin looked at Marcela. Her youthfulness was apparent under the tired lines that ran through her face. After pausing for a moment, as was his custom, Benjamin ignored Marcela. He always avoided arguing with her. Marcela watched him go sit at the other end of the men's table.

Roffe Michah's wife, Bela, followed him into the house. As he began to check the tools and potions in his medical satchel, Bela beseeched her husband, "I never said anything when Ezra started to go with you on your house visits in the Judería. I understood this is what you wanted for him so he would learn his trade. It has been good for you to have his help. But rooms of sick Christians could be dangerous. These people could become wild from their illness. Please do not take Ezra."

"Woman, go tend to the other children. Ezra belongs to me now," Roffe Michah said.

Each woman knew her man very well and knew that each had an oath he needed to fulfill—Roffe Michah as a physician and Benjamin as a Jew. Without wishing harm on either child, each woman said her own secret prayer that her child would not be sickened.

CHAPTER 7

Things Are Good as Long as We Are Alive

1488 Later that Summer Afternoon and Weeks Afterward

Benjamin escorted the Christians and the medical troupe into the shop so they could exit onto Calle de Judios. This would shorten the walk to Pilgrim's Hospital. Benjamin said good-bye and wished them success in saving lives.

As they walked on the Calle, the Jewish physician and the boys lagged behind the Christians. This gave Argi the opportunity to speak privately with Kaver. "In the saints' name, this street is clean. No garbage. No bodies piled up. The cobblestones are washed. The houses are made of stone. They look sturdier than our wooden huts. Ours are made of wood strips woven together and covered with a mud plaster of hair and clay. These stone houses look cleaner than ours."

"It is probably part of their strange Hebrew rituals," Kaver said. "Hand washing before eating and after pissing. Wiping their asses with plant leaves. Burying their dead fast, not even letting relatives visit with the dead for several days to ward off evil spirits. All very strange."

As they walked toward Pilgrim's Hospital, Kaver said to Argi, "This physician is about to enter a den of sickness. Besides the sickness, we should be honest with him about what else he might find." Argi gave a nod in agreement. The Christians looked back and waited for the Jews to catch up with them.

As they all walked together, Kaver said, "Physician Crevago, after meeting with my fellow town councilmen, Argi and I were told to go to the priest of the Cathedral of Santa Maria and ask for permission to seek your help."

Kaver's comment distracted Roffe Michah from watching out for uneven cobblestones and potholes. At the mention of needing permission from a priest, Roffe thought about what Vidal had seen in Segovia. Goose bumps popped up on Roffe's arms.

"We met with Father Joaquin. He came to Vitoria from Lisbon. I think he must have committed some enormous sin to be sent to our small city. He is not as tall as me, but in his black robes, he looks like a strong man of authority."

Kaver did not say how truly insignificant he felt in the cathedral, which was so much larger and more ornate than the small church where he normally took communion and gave confession.

"Father Joaquin was aware that Christians had died from the illness. He had said funeral masses and buried the dead. I asked the Father to grant permission for the Hebrews for help. I told him they seem less affected by the disease. I asked for his prayers and blessing. And do you know what he answered me?" Kaver paused before he told Roffe Michah. "He said, 'no'. Argi and I were stunned."

Roffe Michah tripped and almost fell when he heard Kaver's story. "I cannot believe that a priest would say this. People dying and the priest resists going to Jews for help. It does not make sense."

Kaver continued. "Father Joaquin told us to not have contact with the Jews. He said you would kill our children and take the blood, boil it, and then drink it to preserve your own lives. Then Father made the sign of the cross."

Kaver looked back and forth from Roffe Michah to Argi.

"But Argi was brave."

"I did not do much," Argi said. "I merely did something that I have never done before. I questioned a priest. I asked him, 'how do you know this?' I said, 'no child is missing; nor have we found any dismembered or mutilated bodies.' I asked, 'They do not mingle with us. They do not come to our streets or care about our children or their blood. Moreover, on the rare occasions when I have seen Jews at the market or in town, I have seen how loving they are to their own children. I think they value life and would not kill any children—even Christian children.' Father Joaquin could not say anything, because he was shocked that I had even spoken to him this way. All he said was 'The Church does not approve of you seeking medicine from Jews.'"

Roffe Michah said nothing and kept his face from revealing his dismay.

Argi continued. "For whatever reason, I felt fearless after rebutting the priest's outrageous comments. Kaver and I left the cathedral, and instead of reporting to the other men on the town council, we went straight to speak with you. I hope I will not end up in hell."

Roffe Michah hesitated speaking, in fear of saying the wrong thing. "I am confused by what you tell me. I thought priests were all-powerful among Christians. Will this priest seek retribution against you for talking to me? Might he forbid you or your family from worship or do worse to you?"

"Maybe, but too many people are sick to be fearful about this now but some people at Pilgrim's may not want a Jew to touch them."

Roffe Michah said, "You probably saved Christian lives by asking a Jew for help."

"Christians have covered up their relationships with Jews for years." Argi said. "Let us walk on, and I will tell you a story. A long time ago, my great-great-great-grandfather was a cobbler apprentice to his uncle. This grandfather, Zuzen, was sent on an errand into the Judería. It seems the uncle had received a request for two pairs of shoes from a *vizconde* (viscount) who was known for his elegance and grandiosity. One pair was for his wife, and the other was for himself. He was also known for his unprovoked fits and swings to violence and bravado. And he was anti-Jew. It was even rumored that he had killed some Jews for sport. His moods came on quickly and generated intense anger. His servants would sometimes receive punishment for no reason. They never ventured a word unless spoken to, and even then, conversation with the vizconde was limited to what was necessary.

"The shoemaker uncle did not want to be the object of the vizconde's anger. At the same time, he had to be sure that the shoes would be well received as the most beautiful ever seen and the most comfortable. He had heard about the Jew Aron Cuzniel. This Jew made shoes woven with gold and decorated with elegant trimmings. Of course, the uncle did not want to walk on Calle de Judios, so he sent Zuzen to see what the shoes of the Jew looked like. Grandfather returned to the uncle's shop with visual images of the handsomest shoes he had ever seen.

"The next day, around sunset, the shoemaker and his apprentice dressed as Italian traders in coveralls and wide-brimmed hats. They slipped into the Judería to engage Cuzniel. The uncle requested that the Jew make two pairs of beautiful shoes but did not say that they were for the vizconde and his wife. The Jew said he only made fancy shoes for brides who lived on the calle, but after persuasion, Cuzniel agreed to make the requested fancy shoes. Within a fortnight, the shoes were ready, and Grandfather Zuzen was sent to secretly pick up the goods. When the vizconde saw them, he showered praise on the Christian shoemaker. After that, each time the vizconde requested shoes of unnatural beauty, the Christian cobbler went to Aron Cuzniel and somehow persuaded him to make more shoes for the vizconde. However, the Christian shoemaker, who valued his own life and the vizconde's high praise, never told the noble that a Jew had made the shoes. That would have put lives in jeopardy. Moreover, the Jew never told anyone either."

Roffe Michah laughed. "Aron Cuzniel ben Jossua is my ancestor. He married into our family, and he is the one who taught the Crevagos how to make shoes."

The men walked down the streets of the Christian quarter toward Pilgrim's Hospital as if they were old friends.

Ezra and Isaac lagged behind. They were dumbfounded to see that Christian streets were still dirt roads. The boys had never been on this side of Vitoria. Their mothers would not let them venture this far from home.

The group walked the narrow streets, avoiding the ruts left by wagon wheels and horses after the rains. They passed in front of the Christian stores, where baby Jesuses, crucifixes, copies of holy relics, and garlic hung for protection. They passed by the inn, where some traveling peddlers and local shopkeepers sat on benches at tables. Clay jugs and cups contained rich, dark wine, and metal plates with half-eaten mutton rested in front of the diners. The roof overhangs shielded the diners from the light rain that was falling.

Ezra and Isaac also saw people sitting on the ground and leaning against buildings, moaning and calling for help. They ignored the Jews who walked down the dirt street. The dead bodies were piled up and surrounded by bugs feasting off the flesh. Flies infiltrated the dead to lay eggs. Nearby, babies and small children dressed in tattered garments cried. They had been abandoned by their parents who had died or were close to death.

Isaac wanted to close his eyes and turn back toward home. He felt his lunch meal returning to his mouth. "I am barely able to keep myself together," he said to his cousin. However, Ezra was busy looking all around. As a physician in training, he wanted to remember this scene with as much detail as possible. He would need to report the details when his father asked questions. "I have been around sick people before with my father, but nothing like this. What a sad, horrible sight. I think Christians smell when they are alive because they are dirty people, but this must be the smell of death. I can barely breathe. It is putrid but is somehow mixed with a very sickly sweet odor. This must come from the mierda seeping out of the dead bodies."

"Cover your nose and mouth," Roffe Michah said. "Stay close to me."

The Crevagos turned a corner with Argi and Kaver. They had just a few more steps to go on Calle Nuestra Señora del Cabello. City officials were waiting at an arched doorway to usher the men inside.

An official in a gray coat offered a "Hello, Physician Crevago. Thank you for coming to the hospital." The man uncharacteristically bowed to Roffe Michah in deference.

Roffe Michah nodded. He felt off-balance at this high level of respect. Roffe Michah knew these men, but none had ever shown such regard before.

Ezra's eyes widened as he walked into the hospital's vestibule and saw the many crucifixes on the walls. He brushed against the long, flowing black garb of the women carrying food and water. Stiff white linen caps with ties under their chins framed their faces. Some of these women looked wrinkled with age, and others had the smoothness of youth. Each wore a plain black gown covered with a full-length white apron that had a slit cut across the neck for easy donning. Each apron had ties at the waist. Long sleeves covered their arms, with the cloth narrowing tightly around their wrists.

The stones that made up the walls of the building were pockmarked and roughly hewn. The plaster used to seal the spaces between the rocks was crumbling, and small bits lay on the floor. As Ezra looked around and up, he saw the arches that bolstered the building. They formed an ominous protective shield against the heavens.

Roffe Michah introduced the men to Ezra and Isaac. Although Ezra listened carefully, he could remember only one name—that of the man in gray. He was Don Alvarez, head of Vitoria's city council. His clothes revealed his stature in the community. His coat of soft, colorful yellow and red material was loosely draped over his body so the robe of the same material peeked out from underneath. The sleeves were short and wide for ease of motion. Hose covered his legs.

Knee-high black trousers covered his loins and privates. His equally colorful felt cap was edged with curly black lamb's wool.

Ezra looked at the impressively dressed man but did not say a word. Isaac was trying to acclimate himself to the stench of sweating people in the room.

"Physician Crevago, I am grateful that you are willing to look at the ones who have fallen sick. Come this way."

The group walked through the arched hallway and entered a large room with many bundles of straw stuffed into sacks that lay on the floor. Many dozens of people lay moaning. Lying on top of the bundles were men, women, and children. Most wore clothes that denoted these were people of lesser class. The men wore long tunics tied loosely at the waist with a linen belt. The weather was hot, so most did not wear any trousers. The women lay with longer dresses of plain linen. Ezra could see how uncomfortable these people were. They looked ragged, weak, and in pain. Squalid smells of vomit and moaning created a foul reality. Soft rhythmic prayers of "Our father who art in heaven" and rattling rosary beads created a musical background of sounds.

Roffe Michah saw Vidal's friend Peio lying with his eyes closed. Roffe walked over to him, bent down, and said, "I am Vidal's younger brother, Physician Roffe." The man did not answer. He was already dead. Sadness came over Roffe Michah. He would have to tell his brother about Peio—and the many others that were dead or dying.

Roffe Michah put his satchel of medical supplies on a table. He took his long medical gown out of the bag. He removed his *kippa* and slipped his head through the hole at the neck. He tied the strings on each side that would hold the overall in place so his street clothes and religious garment with fringes hanging out were covered. He put his kippa back on and turned to Don Alvarez. "Please, may I please have a clean apron?"

Don Alvarez turned to Sister Angelina and nodded. The young woman in her black nursing garb stood in stark contrast to Don Alvarez's fancy dress. She looked somewhat disoriented at Don

Alvarez's quick fulfillment of the Jew's request. The older Sister Constanza looked around for a priest to consult, but since she did not see any, she said, "Comply with the request."

The physician walked over to an old man of about fifty years who lay on the bundle of straw closest to the entrance. Roffe bent down and felt the man's forehead. As Roffe knelt down to gain a better look at the patient, he knew from the redness of his patient's skin that the man was burning up with fever. The physician laid his hand about two inches over the man's stomach to estimate the amount of heat that was radiating from his body. Roffe picked up the man's arm, examining its movements, shape, size, and mobility. He looked into the man's mouth and eyes and felt his neck and throat.

"What hurts inside you?" Roffe asked.

"My head hurts, and my eyes are feeling so painful," the man said.

Roffe put his ear to the patient's chest. The learned physician said, "Breathe in and out slowly." The man obeyed.

"Put some *orina* in here," Roffe said giving the man a urine bottle.

The man quickly pissed into the container. Roffe looked at the liquid. He pulled out a paper from his satchel and compared the orina's dark orange, almost amber hue to a rough chart showing various diagnoses based on urine color. Roffe lifted the urine bottle to under his nose and smelled the bitter odor.

In this same manner, Roffe examined four more patients of varying ages and genders.

"No need to taste the urine this time," Roffe said to Ezra. "Color and smell are enough for a diagnosis. The dark urine, its pungent smell, the coughing, muffled breath sounds, the aches, and pains tell me that these people need to drink hearty liquids."

Roffe Michah turned to Don Alvarez. "They are suffering from a pestilence of the throat and lungs. I have never seen so many people ill at the same time. Many more people will die. We can try to treat them and see if we can stop the illness from spreading to others."

The physician offered up a series of orders to the nuns standing nearby. "Go to the berry groves and find enough blackberries to fill four large baskets. Cook them in hot, hot water until the fruit juices bubble. Cook them some more for a short time. Let the mixture cool. Each sick person should drink several cups full. Then they should drink more. Give them many cups of berry juice so they can piss out the bad elements from their bodies. Have each patient eat walnuts and hazelnuts. This will bring about more shitting. Bring blankets to keep people warm until their bodies sweat out the illness. Put cloths soaked in cold water on their foreheads to relieve the headaches and eye pain. Give them food to build their strength. Also, heat water in a big pot until the water is very hot. Empty out that water and put new water in the pot. Heat it again until it is bubbling. Then bring a fresh pot of bubbled water with clean cloths to me and I will show you how to wash the patients to treat the heat in their bodies. Remove all the straw from this room and burn it at once. Put the sick on piles of freshly washed blankets over new sacks filled with clean wool from fields and homes where no one is sick. Wash the floor and walls with hot water. Keep washing the floors and walls until the foul smell is gone."

The nuns looked quizzically at Don Alvarez. They had never seen a Jew take such assertive command over Christians. Then the sisters looked at Father Carmelo, who had been giving last rites to a young girl. He looked up for a moment to catch the eyes of the confused nuns. His sad expression over the loss of another child became a nod of approval. The priest did not know what else to do. The nuns set to work following Roffe Michah's instructions.

Don Alvarez said, "Please come over here and look at this boy."

Roffe Michah moved slowly through the rows of people lying on the ground. He knelt down next to the boy that Don Alvarez pointed out.

"This is my son Alvaro. We moved him here from our home so he would not be near our other children. He is my oldest and most precious. My other children are girls. They are important to me, but this is my son. Can you help him?"

The boy was purplish and red in color. The fever consumed him. As Roffe examined him, he thought, *He is almost the same age as Ezra.*

Roffe Michah removed the boy's shirting and checked his neck, joints, chest, and arms. The physician continued until he had made a complete examination.

"My neck hurts," the boy whimpered as he pointed to his throat. His sentence was followed by coughing that exhausted him. I am so tired, but I cannot sleep because my whole body aches."

"Use bubbled water that has cooled and a clean cloth to wash him down," Roffe Michah said to Sister Constanza. "Bring him hot soup made from the meat of a chicken. Add vegetables that are green in color, and chop them very fine. Make him drink it. Then bring him some more. And more. And more. Fill him with soup, nuts, and berry juice. Make sure he pisses often. Let him sleep for one hour. Then he must have more to drink and eat."

Roffe Michah turned to Don Alvarez and said, "I do not know if I can save your son, but I will try. There is more to do here and in the homes where there is sickness. Have your servants remove all dead bodies and garbage near your house. Take these to a field outside the walls of the city. Dig a deep pit. Pile up the bodies and trash in the pit, cover it with lye and then cover the pit with dirt.

"Here are other things you must do if you want to save your Christian families: If someone dies, wash the body with lye. Bury that person immediately, alone—not with anyone else in the grave. Make a solution of animal fat and ash, and wash in hot water the tables, chairs, plates, utensils, clothes, walls, and floors. Wash your hands often—your bodies at least one time a week. In your house, burn incense of camphor, rosemary and sulfur to keep your house cleansed. Before you drink water put it in cleaned pots and heat it until it bubbles, let it cool, and then drink it. Do not drink water that has not bubbled. Do not allow any food scraps to be on the floor. Do not allow any animals in this hospital or in any houses. Tell everyone in Vitoria to do the same."

Don Alvarez was awed that Roffe Michah could enumerate these instructions without any book or written aid in front of him.

"Physician Crevago," Don Alvarez said, using Roffe Michah's official title in a sign of additional respect, "can you please repeat these instructions for Sister Angelina and Sister Constanza to hear. I will write down exactly what the physician said, and Argi, you will take the instructions to the Town Council. This information must be spoken in all Mass and Church services. Post these necessities around the city, and appoint inspectors to make sure Physician Crevago's instructions are enforced. This will save lives."

Roffe Michah repeated his instructions and then turned his attention to other patients in the room. At the same time, he spoke to his nephew, who had been watching intently.

"Isaac, go to the Judería and fetch the physician Antonio de Tornay. Ask him to bring other men learned in healing ways and medical cures. Ezra, you will stay here and assist me." Ezra was glad Roffe Michah had not asked him to be the messenger. He wanted to learn how to be a physician.

Isaac was grateful for the order that allowed him to exit this room of illness. He wanted to breathe deeply and feel the fresh air of the evening. Isaac stepped outside and proceeded on the return route toward the Judería.

Isaac ran through the streets of Vitoria, past the dead and moaning, past the flies and maggots, past the children crying in the street. Once he had left the streets of death, he slowed to a reasonable pace.

Isaac turned left onto the Calle instead of right, which he would have done if he had been going home. Antonio de Tornay lived on the Calle de Judios, which was a long street, but at the opposite end from where the Crevagos lived.

How wonderful to be in the Judería, Isaac thought as he walked through the street. *Away from the death. I will double my efforts to learn cobbling.*

Isaac panted as he knocked on the door of Physician de Tornay's home. A small woman with dark hair opened the top half of the door. Isaac did not wait for her to ask any questions. In breathy tones, he said, "My uncle Roffe Michah has sent me to fetch Physician Tornay to Pilgrim's Hospital. Is he here?"

The woman turned away from the door. "Antonio, you are needed."

A slender man stepped to the door. Isaac had seen him on the Calle but had never talked to him. "My uncle is Roffe Michah Crevago. He instructed me to request that you go to Pilgrim's Hospital immediately."

"Why?" the physician asked.

"Christians are sick, and he needs help in tending to them."

"Ah, yes. I thought this might happen." Physician Tornay grabbed his medical satchel, unlatched the bottom half of the door, and exited his home with his two sons, who were a few years older than Isaac. "Let us go now. On the way, we will find Physicians Benleon and Sarnory, who can also help."

The physician and the boys walked a short distance down the Calle and stopped in the middle of the long block. Tornay shouted into an open door, "Benleon, grab your cousin and meet us at Pilgrim's Hospital. A load of illness waits for us."

When Isaac and Physician de Tornay entered the hospital, some of the nuns were busy bathing patients, while others were busy washing the walls, floors and furniture.

Within a few minutes, Physicians Benleon and Sarnory arrived with their sons, who were also in training to be physicians.

Roffe Michah greeted his fellow physicians but did not waste time with the traditional handshakes and kisses. Instead he briefed them quickly and divided the workload.

"We need to tend to the ill here, but we have to find all those in the city who are sick. They must be tended to properly so the disease will not spread to others. Benleon and Sarnory, you stay at the hospital and work over the remaining patients. Tornay, you know the wealthy Christians, so you and your sons go to their homes where the sick need attention. I will continue here with my son and nephew."

Physicians Benleon and Sarnory immediately started to examine the remaining patients and apply treatments using the techniques that Roffe Michah prescribed.

>-+-+>-+-O-+-+>-+-<

Roffe Michah, Ezra, Isaac, and the other Jewish physicians worked diligently for weeks until no new cases developed.

"Keep on with the cleaning regimen of hot water and soap from tree ash," Roffe Michah told Sister Angelina as he was about to leave the hospital and return to his regular routines in the Judería. "Treat the ill as you have been, and the number of sick will continue to decline. All will recover as Don Alvarez's son Alvaro did and as the others did."

"Thank you for all you have done," said Sister Angelina as she kissed Roffe Michah's hand in reverence as she might a bishop's or cardinal's. Roffe Michah stayed steady as the woman held his hand in hers.

She said, "I watched as the sick, one by one, grew stronger. I witnessed people getting up from bed and walking out the door to go home. I heard the words of gratitude to you and the other physicians flow out of their mouths and the mouths of their families. They cried tears of joy as their children survived."

She gave a curtsy to Roffe Michah—something she had never done to a Jew. She then turned to Ezra and kissed him gently on both cheeks. "You boys have been a great help to the people in this hospital. They will remember how attentive and kind you have been." She took a step to the right and, in the same manner, kissed Isaac. Sister Angelina said to him, "Holy Father! You are hot." Suddenly,

Isaac fainted. He had not grown accustomed to seeing mounds of dead or rows of sick people, but that was not why he fell to the floor.

Sister Angelina knelt over the boy and felt his body. "Don Crevago, feel his skin; look at this arms. Your nephew is limp."

Roffe Michah saw Sister Angelica's face. She was naturally pale from a lack of sunlight, but her skin was snow white as she looked up at the physician. "He is burning up."

"Let me bring him to this fresh bed of straw, Sister."

Roffe Michah and Ezra put their arms around Isaac and felt the heat of the boy's body through his clothes. "Bring me cool water and rags to wash him," Roffe said as he started to undress his nephew.

Isaac opened his eyes and looked at his uncle. "I am sorry to be sick. I have not felt well for more than a week, but I did not tell anyone. I did not want to disappoint my father, you, or Ezra. I hid it very well until now, did I not?"

"Do not worry about that now. You have never given your father or the family shame of any kind. It is time for you to rest. We have been working long hours for many weeks. We did not even stop for Shabbat so we could save lives. You did everything you could to be helpful."

"My throat and chest have hurt for many days. I am so tired now. I wanted to make my father proud of me. If someone had to get sick, I am glad it was not Ezra. He will be a physician like you. I would have been only a shoemaker."

Isaac's head fell to the side and his hands loosened their grip on his uncle. He drifted to the other side of God's world and never spoke a word again. As his body filled with death, it began to lose its heat. Eventually Roffe Michah took a blanket and covered Isaac with it. The uncle lifted the boy and put him in a wagon that Father Joaquin had sent over to pick up recovering Christian patients and return them to their homes. A man offered to pull the wagon for Roffe. "No, I need to do this myself as I mourn for my nephew."

Ezra walked alongside the wagon as his father pulled it through the Christian quarter, into the Judería, and onto Calle Abrevadero.

Ezra was stunned by how fast Isaac had died. He had not had a chance to speak with him and tell him how much he valued his cousin as a friend. Ezra and Isaac had shared their Hebrew learning, their ambitions, and secrets about how they were changing from boys to men. The sense of loss from the death of his cousin began to set in.

Once on the back street, Roffe Michah went through the alleyway and entered the Crevago courtyard. He set the wagon in front of the entrance to Benjamin's house.

"Stay here with Isaac. I will tell Tio Benjamin."

Roffe Michah entered Benjamin's house. Roffe was so intent on his purpose he did not see Marcela sitting on a stool in the dark corner of the room sewing. The smell from the lamb stew nauseated Roffe Michah.

Marcela looked up without much expression, even though it was unusual for her brother-in-law to be in her kitchen. She went back to her sewing, and he went straight through to the cobbler shop. Vidal's son David was working in a corner, cutting hides that he would make into soft-sided shoes. Scraps of skin lay on the floor at his feet. Another apprentice sat at a grinding mill, polishing stones that were destined for royal shoes. The smell of lambskin and ground stones permeated the space.

Roffe Michah saw Benjamin leaning over his bench. He was verifying that shoes made by an apprentice were fashioned exactly according to the design.

"Brother, stop what you are doing. I need to speak with you."

Benjamin stiffened at Roffe's deep tone of voice. He looked up and saw the grim look on Roffe's face and knew that whatever Roffe Michah was about to say would not be good news.

"Isaac took sick. He was so good with the children in the hospital, but he took sick himself."

Benjamin rose to his feet. "Where is he? I will go to him."

"He is in the courtyard in a wagon. You can go to him, but he will not be able to talk to you. He is there, but his soul awaits its call to be with God. Isaac died not an hour ago."

Benjamin fell back to his seat. After a brief pause of silence, he said, "How could you let this happen to my boy?" Benjamin's forehead furrowed to the center. His eyes focused on his brother. "Why my son? You should have protected him. I let him help you because we are people who do good deeds, but the price is too high. You are my brother, but you took my son from me. You could have sent him home after one or two days. Why did you keep him with the sick for so long?" Benjamin's face was wet with tears. "I have to tell Marcela. She already hates me because I wanted Isaac to go with you and feel the righteousness of caring for the sick. Now she will hate me forever."

Benjamin stood up and walked to the kitchen in a daze. Marcela, still in the corner with her sewing, looked at her husband and then over to his brother. "Why are you ..." her voice trailed off once she saw the sadness in Benjamin's face. "What is it?"

"Look out the back door into the courtyard," Roffe Michah said.

Marcela looked to the yard and saw Ezra standing by the wagon.

"Tell me what you need to tell me," Marcela said. She dropped her sewing as she got off her stool. The kitchen was empty of children. No laughter existed.

"Isaac is gone."

"Gone where?"

"To the heavens."

"No. This cannot be."

"It is. He had been carrying the sickness without letting on. I was too busy to notice. I am sorry."

Marcela sat back down on the stool and started to sob. The other children, who had been upstairs, came down to see their mother in an immediate state of grief.

Through her wailing Marcela cried, "You did this, husband. You sent my first born to his death by giving him to God to work with the sick." She got up from the stool and walked slowly over to her husband and slapped him across the face—a gesture no wife would ever think to do, especially in front of others. Roffe said nothing but was shocked by his sister-in-law's behavior. Benjamin just stood like stone.

"You will never be near me again. You can never make up for sending Isaac to the hospital for no good reason. I am done with your speeches about repairing the world. We may be Jews, but we do not have to give our children so others can live. That is what you have done. You have traded our son for Christian sons."

With these pronouncements, Marcela started to sob as Benjamin had never seen. It was as though all the sadness she carried in this marriage came out at this moment. She never understood why her husband had changed so drastically after their wedding. She had loved him regardless, but no more. "I will not speak with you again." Marcela went upstairs, and her remaining children followed her, perhaps as a gesture of agreement with her.

"Ezra, go fetch the rabbi from the synagogue. Then tell your uncles to come," Roffe Michah said from inside the doorway.

Roffe walked to the wagon and gently carried his dead nephew into the house and put him on the table where the family ate their meals.

"Benjamin, you did for Isaac what you thought was right and good. Marcela will soften with time. I have seen this before when there is a death in a family. There are rarely answers—only the question of why do bad things happen to good people. Do not be in despair. We will mourn as we should mourn at this sad time."

The brothers stood over Isaac. Benjamin took Isaac's now-cold hand and kissed it. "I am sorry, my son." He continued to repeat this phrase. He prayed over Isaac's body until the rabbi arrived.

Ezra found Rahav at his silversmith shop and Baruh in his vineyards. He asked each to go to Benjamin's house. Once there Roffe explained what had happened, and the brothers began the ritual of *tahara*, washing the dead boy's body to purify it and prepare it for burial. Filling the room were the sounds of crying mixed with the rabbi's prayers.

Vidal and Juhuda, who had been on Calle de Zapatos, walked into this scene of mourning.

"Isaac caught the illness and died. I did not see that he was sick during the weeks that he sat with Christian children in the hospital. I blame myself for his death," said Roffe Michah.

"This is a loss," Vidal said. "How is Marcela? How are the other children? I thought he would be taking over for you, Benjamin, and now that plan is lost."

"You have a crass and uncaring soul. Do not talk to me of business. I have lost my son, and I have lost my wife."

Vidal and Juhuda joined the rabbi in prayer. Roffe Michah, Baruh, and Rahav continued with the washing. They recited verses from the Psalms.

Benjamin stood next to his son in silence, holding his hand. Marcela did not come down to the kitchen. Ezra went to tell his mother and spread the word in the Judería that his cousin died. Ezra cried as he spoke, but it did not deter him from his task. *It could have been me*, he thought. He tried to suppress this thought as an evil spirit that had entered his body.

Residents of the Judería visited and joined in the praying over Isaac's body.

Benjamin wrapped Isaac in a clean white cloth. In the late afternoon, the uncles and cousins carried the young man to the cemetery.

Marcela would not walk with Benjamin. The other children enveloped her, not their father. Cassela took her mother's arm on the left. Daniyyel escorted his mother on the right. Jonah and Rina walked in back of her in case she stumbled. Marcela had not stopped crying since she had received the news of Isaac's death. Benjamin walked with the rabbi.

The cemetery was about a fifteen-minute walk from the Judería.

The procession moved slowly. There was no haste to bury this young man.

The air seemed colder. The land seemed gloomier. The moisture on the trees seemed to weigh the leaves down. The sky was not its usual blue but more gray on this day.

Isaac was buried in a plot not too far from Erini, Rebeca, Eli, and all the family's dead. This was where his soul would ascend to heaven with the rituals and prayers of his ancestors.

It was right that Isaac's living relatives surrounded him, gently putting him into the ground, and covering him with dirt.

Isaac needed to be buried quickly as proscribed by Jewish law. The family would mourn and then move forward with their lives. Benjamin and Marcela would not forget this child. However, their sadness needed to start dissipating so they could again feel happiness.

The seven-day mourning period of shiva started as soon as the prayer for Isaac's soul to ascend to heaven was said. For the following seven days, just as their ancestor Jacob had mourned the loss of his son Joseph, Isaac's family mourned. The community visited Benjamin and Marcela. They brought food and simple cakes so the family would not need to cook for themselves. Each mourner recited a blessing in Isaac's name over each type of food eaten, since each blessing helped elevate his *neshama* (soul) to reach heaven. During the seven days, soft conversation echoed through the home. Friends listened to Roffe Michah talk about Isaac. "He was young, but with promise. He had not committed any sins." Condolences were given with the prayer "May heaven comfort you."

The family wore no shoes. They sat on the cold floor in grief. They used no combs and did not bathe. Men came to the house at sundown and said Kaddish.

Marcela watched as their many neighbors crowded into the small house. She did not speak to the people who came to comfort her. She sat silently with her children around her, exactly where Isaac would sit when studying the Torah. Her eyes were glassy. Her mind seemed locked.

"Marcela is not eating," Bela told Roffe Michah. "She is not talking to anyone. She is just so still."

"She has buried her oldest son," Roffe Michah said. "What do you expect? Have no expectation for how a mother will be when she loses a child."

Benjamin had been an isolate for many years. This tragedy had not changed him. The family and neighbors spoke with each other, but Benjamin would not mingle with them.

Compared to when Isaac was born, these days were so different. For the covenant event of his *Berit Milá*, very few people came to the house. Marcela was sick from the birth. Isaac received his name and the blessing for a long and productive life with only a few family members present.

Bela said to Agamit, "If more people had come for Isaac's circumcision, maybe this would not have happened. Instead, they came for this sadness."

Argi and Kaver came too. As they walked to Benjamin's house, Argi said, "What can we do for this family?"

"We can say prayers for this boy," Kaver responded.

"We are responsible for his death," Argi said.

"No, God is responsible. God took us to the Jewish physicians, and the Jews saved us. This was God's plan. At Sunday Mass, we will give thanks to the Virgin Mary for the Jewish physicians. The boy was good and kind. Jesus must need him in Heaven."

CHAPTER 8

A Woman Is Not a Shirt That You Can Change at Will

Early spring 1491

The room was cold. The morning sun had just started lifting itself up over the hills and onto the streets of Vitoria's Judería. The heat from the sun had not yet reached the house. The chill winds of the Vascos Mountains blew with domination over the land.

Cassela Crevago was glad she lived in the Judería. She felt safe here. This was her nest. She was like a baby bird sitting amid the twigs and leaves that its mama had placed in a grand tree.

Cassela sat on the hard floor of the upstairs room she shared with Rina, who was still sleeping. Cassela put her very petite feet into her suede shoes with their soft soles. *The floor is so cold*, she thought. *Papa and Daniyyel make glorious shoes, but I am only given the lowest shoes to wear. Just leather and ties to keep them closed. The winter season will remain for a time. My feet need to stay warm just so I can do my chores.*

Cassela walked down the winding stairs and saw Marcela was already cooking. Cassela could hear the snipping of scissors and beating of hides, as her father, Daniyyel, Jonah, Ezra, and the apprentices were already working in the shop. Ezra had switched from medicine to cobbling. After Isaac's death, he refused to tend to any more sick with Roffe Michah. The conversation between the two was coarse. Roffe demanded that Ezra become a physician, and Ezra completely rejected the idea.

Ezra said, "I will not do it. People will die if I tend them. I will take Isaac's place in the shop."

"It is my profession and I want to pass it along to you," Roffe countered. "You will do as I say and work with me."

"I will never be part of a profession surrounded by death. I want to apprentice with Tio Benjamin. I have seen enough death to last me until I am an old man. No one ever died from wearing shoes."

The father had lost the argument.

Vidal's son David had left the cobbler shop to learn wine making. He worked with Tio Baruh. David thought he could improve the vines. He had planted new vineyards and experimented with different types of soil mixtures.

Marcela cooked a breakfast of oats and berries that would become a sweet gruel. The aroma floated through the house. A pitcher of fresh milk sat on the kitchen table next to a platter of bread that Cassela had baked the day prior. On the bench lay the blanket that Marcela used to keep herself warm until the fire heated the kitchen.

"Good morning, Mama." No response came from Marcela. She hardly talked anymore. Since Isaac's death, she was no longer her previous joyful self. She had become more like Benjamin: reclusive, speaking only when necessary. There was none of the old chatter she used to make when doing chores with her daughters.

"I will fetch Papa and the boys for breakfast," Cassela said, "and bring the others their food." The apprentices ate sitting on their stools in the shop.

Benjamin was in his usual position at his worktable, leaning hunchbacked over pieces of tanned leather. Daniyyel and Ezra were at the cutting table, where piles of forms for future shoes lay. They were sorting sizes and checking the quality of the leather tanning. Jonah was sorting and cleaning beads that would be affixed to shoes for highborn women. Once finished, the shoes would be stacked and stored until Vidal could deliver them. The other apprentices were beating and culling the hides.

Cassela walked over to Benjamin. "Mama asks that you come for breakfast." Cassela would never tell her father what to do. She would only ask reverently. There was no hugging, no good-morning kisses, and no smiles—just the terse announcement of breakfast.

Daniyyel looked at his sister. She had just turned thirteen years old, and he saw that she was becoming a beauty with her long brown hair, big brown eyes, and pink skin that looked as soft as the petals of a newly bloomed flower. "Come here, little girl," he said with the voice of authority. "Is there breakfast for me? I am working as hard as Papa. I hope your long hair did not dangle in the oats."

Cassela loved when Daniyyel paid attention to her. "You can eat after the dog has his breakfast," she said, teasing him back.

Ezra looked up with derision at this frivolous conversation between Daniyyel and Cassela. "Tio Vidal will need shoes for his next trip. Before breakfast, let us see how much we can accomplish with our work."

Daniyyel said, "Ezra, you are more like my father than my father is. Be still. The shoes will be made. You can work if you want, but I am eating when Papa goes for breakfast."

Ezra nodded with acceptance. He did not want to eat at the same table with Benjamin and be subjected to more of his uncle's criticism. The shift in Benjamin's attitude toward Ezra since Isaac's death had been jarring.

"Someday I will leave Vitoria," Ezra said. However, he had no plan. He thought about going to Murcia to live with his Tio Yosef, but without money for the journey and no trade for earning a living, he did not have any choice but to stay in Vitoria.

Jonah said nothing. He did not want to be part of this chatter. He just did what he was told, and that was enough of a life for him.

Benjamin, Daniyyel, Jonah, and Ezra entered the kitchen from the shop. The benches screeched on the floor as they moved them to sit at the long table where Isaac had lain. They immediately began slurping their oats without talking, just listening to the blowing wind outside and to the sounds of eating.

Cassela started to help Marcela with cleaning and chopping the greens for lunch. She was pounding them when Marcela caught Benjamin's look at the noise Cassela was making with her vegetable hammer.

"You can do that later," Marcela said. "Go to the butcher now. I will keep your breakfast warm. Get lamb for our midday meal. You can finish the vegetables and wash the dishes when you come back."

Cassela nodded. She put on her shawl and skipped out the back door to the courtyard. She needed to go on Calle Abrevadero, walk two streets, and then go around the corner to Solomon the butcher. He blessed and slaughtered animals in accordance with the rules of kashruth. Marcela had told her, "The knife has to be freshly sharpened and cannot have any nicks or breaks. The blade must be twice the width of the animal's neck. The animal cannot be hurt or injured in any way. The animal must be humanely held so the slaughter is fast and painless. The cut of throat and blood veins must be done in one quick motion so the animal dies immediately without suffering. The animal's blood must be drained completely, because it is forbidden to eat blood since it contains the soul of the animal. The dead animal's insides must be examined to ensure there is no disease. The internal fat and blood sources must be removed." This was the knowledge that mothers passed to their daughters while boys learned Torah,

Solomon's family had been the Judería's butchers since early times when Jews first came to Vitoria with the Romans.

Cassela did not mind going to the butcher, but she did not like seeing all the dead animals hanging with their blood dripping. She did not like hearing the lambs and knowing that they might be someone's dinner within the next few days. She liked when her mother made lamb stew, but did not want to think about how the lambs arrived in her mother's stew pot.

As Cassela walked out of the Crevago courtyard, she was thinking about what it would feel like to be married. She would teach her own daughters kitchen work, and how to be a Jewish woman. Her thoughts took her to when she would have her own home and children. She did not know whom she would marry, but she knew she would marry someone.

Immersed in these thoughts, Cassela walked down two-thirds of the small Calle de Morano before she realized she had made a wrong turn onto a street that bordered the Jewish and Christian quarters. On both sides of the street, the houses were in various states of disrepair. The calle had cobblestones like Calle de Judios, but these stones were chipped and cracked, and some were coming loose. *It is really dingy and deserted*, Cassela thought. She turned around to go back to the main street when she saw an older boy lingering nearby. His clothes were clean and looked well made. As she walked down this narrow street, the teenager sidled up to her and started talking.

"Do I know you from the market?" he asked. "Or is it from the bakery? Is your father a baker?"

Cassela said politely, "No, I have not seen you in the market. No, my father is not a baker." A small smile graced her face.

The young man, looking about eighteen, offered to buy her some sweets. "I know a place through this walkway."

"How nice you are," Cassela said.

"It is right this way." He led her into a back room of an empty shop that a Jewish family had recently vacated after their conversion to Christianity. Very little sun reached this dwelling, making it dark and leaving it with a dank smell. The walls were tinted greenish with moss growing between the stones.

"This does not look like the way to anything," Cassela said.

As Cassela turned to go out of the house, the boy tripped her. Once she was on all fours, he flipped her over so she was lying flat with her back on the ground. With one hand and his legs, he held her down. With his other hand, he took his neck scarf and stuffed it in Cassela's mouth so she could not scream for help.

"Stay still and it will not hurt," he said with a smirk on his face, pleased with his conquest. "Do not talk, or I will punch your face and give you a scar that you will never forget. I need some release."

As Cassela tried to fight the boy, he slapped her hard. Her cheek immediately turned red and started to bruise. As she struggled, her dark eyes looked in all directions, hoping to see someone who could help her. She struggled and tried to free her arms, but the young man held her arms down and was too strong for her. She tried to move her legs so she could kick him or wriggle out from under him, but with the weight of his body, and with his knees digging into her thighs, this was impossible. She knew she was powerless to overcome this assailant. Her thoughts raced to anger that she had even talked to this stranger. Why was she so stupid as to believe that he was going to be kind to her? She did not think of herself as particularly pretty. Not many boys had ever talked to her. She felt scared as she struggled to free herself.

Cassela continued to fight off her attacker.

"Take this again," he said as he slapped her one more time. "This is just for good measure."

Then he used his legs to spread hers, pulled himself out of his pants, and took advantage of the child. Her fear was not diminished, but her strength was spent. She kept her eyes on him as he showed his pleasure in completing the act.

"I am going to hit you one more time to let you know that I am a man," he said. Cassela closed her eyes as she felt the pain of his hand cross her face. Her mind went blank. He pulled his scarf from her mouth and quickly left the house, leaving Cassela in the dim, damp room of rape.

It was an hour or so later when Moises, an old beggar who had been searching back alleys for food, found Cassela. He was horrified to see the young girl, her face bruised and her skirt pulled above her waist.

"Girl, girl," Moises said as he gently picked up her hand.

Cassela did not answer. Her eyes were puffing up and closing tightly shut. She was limp.

Moises was too weak to lift the child. After he pulled her dress down over her private parts, as quickly as he could, he shuffled to the front door of the dwelling and out to the street. "Come here right now. Come here. Follow me." He called and motioned to the first man he saw. It was a street vendor pushing a cart filled with bolts of cloth.

The street vendor followed Moises into the empty house and to the back room.

"Do you know this girl?"

"Oh my heavenly God. Who did this? Yes, I know her. She is Benjamin the cobbler's daughter," said Pedro, Antonio's son, one of the children that Vidal had brought back from Segovia." He approached her. "Cassela. Cassela. Talk to me. It is Avram," he said, using his Hebrew name. "Cassela. Cassela." Avram lifted her hand, but it was lifeless. He lifted her head, but she did not open her eyes. He put his long finger under her nose to see if she was breathing. He could feel some slight air coming out.

Avram lifted Cassela and carried her to the street. A group of people had gathered in the small walkway at the timorous voice of the beggar when he had called for help. They saw Cassela as she lay lifeless in Avram's arms.

The crowd murmured Cassela's name as they made an aisle for Avram to walk through.

He continued to talk quietly to Cassela as he carried her up Calle Abrevadero to the Crevago courtyard. He saw Daniyyel outside by a dye vat.

"Your sister has been harmed."

"What happened?" Daniyyel asked as he saw her lying in Avram's arms. Daniyyel walked over to Avram with large steps to shorten the distance.

"Aach," he shouted. His mouth opened in disbelief. He took the girl from Avram and carried her to the house.

"Papa, Cassela has been hurt!" Daniyyel yelled as he carried her into the house.

"Rina!" he shouted to his younger sister, who was in the garden. "Get some water so you can wash Cassela. Help me."

Rina, although horrified by her sister's condition, brought the water. Avram took the heavy pail from her. "I will do this. Get a cloth." Avram paused. "Are you all right?" he asked the young girl.

Rina was stunned by the question. She did not answer. No one had ever asked how she was. The young girl caught a look into Avram's eyes. She was only eleven years old but saw that this man was kind and caring. *So different from my father,* she thought.

Benjamin went into the kitchen and saw Cassela in Daniyyel's arms with her bruised face. "I do not know what happened to her, but she is not awake," Daniyyel said.

Benjamin did not answer. The sadness in his face was sufficient for Daniyyel to know his father was horror-struck by Cassela's appearance.

Marcela watched as Daniyyel started to carry Cassela upstairs to her sleeping room. As Daniyyel put his foot on the first step, he paused and looked at his mother.

"Cassela has been hurt. I do not know what happened, but I know she is not good." Daniyyel thought this news would cause his mother to snap out of her malaise. Instead Marcela walked to the bed that had been moved into the kitchen so she could rest during the day. She lay down, and covered herself. She said nothing to her son or her husband.

Benjamin looked at Marcela lying in her bed by the fire and said to Daniyyel, "It is good that your mother is not interested. She is not strong enough to see Cassela like this. Take Cassela upstairs."

"I will send Ezra to get Roffe Michah. And I will get Tia Agamit to tend to Cassela," Daniyyel said.

"No," Benjamin said with a snap of his head so he did not have to look directly at Cassela or Daniyyel. "Not Agamit. Rina will take care of her."

Daniyyel did not understand why Benjamin did not want Tia

Agamit to be called, but he did not question his father and with a grimace, took Cassela upstairs.

Benjamin did not want his pushy sister disrupting his household. He feared she would come in and start ordering his children around—and him too. He thought to himself, *Agamit asks too many questions. Once she gets involved, she puts her nose in my soup.*

>—+◆>—◯—◆+—<

Cassela lay in her bed for days, not moving or eating.

"Sister," Rina would say as she washed Cassela's face with a cool cloth, "can you hear me? Do not die and leave me alone with Father, Daniyyel, and Jonah. Mother sleeps most of the day, as you do. Do not leave me to this world without you. I need you to teach me how to be a woman, since mother does not care about these things anymore."

Cassela did not stir at these comments. She did not open her eyes or speak in any way.

Benjamin walked over to her, placed his hand on her forehead, and walked away. He did not know what happened to her, but he feared the worst. It was as if he could not bear to be near to her. He could not tolerate his pain of believing someone had violated Cassela, but it was also difficult to bear the pain of not knowing what had actually happened.

"Your father is so cold," Ezra would say to Daniyyel as they worked at the cutting board. "I cannot do what my father does, but at least he talks to us. And helps people when they are ill. Your father makes me feel invisible."

Daniyyel had no rebuttal to these comments. He could say only, "He is my father, and he is who he is." But Daniyyel resented the coldness that Benjamin showed to Cassela and their mother.

Except in the evening as he passed by Cassela's room to go to his own, Benjamin stayed away from Cassela. He would pause in the doorway but not go into the room.

Cassela stayed in an unconscious state until she died. The family buried Cassela near Isaac and not too far from her grandparents, great-grandparents, and other ancestors who were buried in Vitoria's Jewish cemetery. Benjamin, Daniyyel, Jonah, and Rina sat shiva for seven days, but few people came to their house. Minyan was held at Roffe Michah's so Marcela would not know that Cassela had died.

Marcela did nothing. She just lay in bed with a glassy stare in her eyes.

On the last night of shiva, when prayers were finished, Daniyyel, Jonah, and Ezra went back to work in the shop, but would do little else during the thirty-day *sheloshim* mourning period. They would not join in any celebrations, cut their hair or listen to people playing musical instruments. Benjamin would mourn for his daughter for a longer time, saying Kaddish for her each evening.

A few days after shiva, Rina said to her father, "I'm going to talk to Tia Della for a few moments. She wants to show me how to make a sweet fish stew."

Benjamin did not answer his daughter so she walked out the door with quiet pervading the room. As Benjamin was alone in the kitchen with Marcela, he sat down next to her on the bed.

"You will not see Cassela anymore," he said to Marcela. "She has married and left Vitoria." Benjamin preferred to live with this lie rather than tell Marcela the horrendous truth.

Marcela opened her eyes. She lifted her hand and put it gently on Benjamin's cheek before her hand fell back to her side and her eyes closed again. Benjamin pulled back. But then he took Marcela's hand and put it back on his cheek. The softness of this motion brought tears to Benjamin's eyes.

"I have something to tell you, Marcela. I cannot hide it from you any longer."

Marcela opened her eyes with great effort. She wanted to be as alert as possible for whatever Benjamin had to say.

"When we were young and I walked home from Torah study, I would walk very slowly by your house to try to get another look at you, maybe in the garden picking vegetables or drying herbs. Your long brown hair with its ringlet curls became almost copper-colored when you stood in the sunlight with its shine on you. Your skin looked so soft and delicate. Your round eyes looked as big as two side-by-side full moons. You had a glow of brightness and strength. You looked so sweet. My body would get excited whenever I saw you—even when I just thought about you."

Benjamin had never talked like this to Marcela. As weak as she was, Marcela managed a small smile as she thought about the happiness of her childhood. The entire time since Isaac's death, Benjamin and Marcela had not talked. Marcela had wanted to speak with her husband, but in her grief, she refused to. Now she could barely talk, but she managed.

"I tried to be in the garden when you walked home from the rabbi's. I wanted to see you so I could call to you with my eyes and a sashay of my hips. I just hoped that no one else saw me do this. I could not speak to you without Mama or one of my sisters present. In synagogue, I would look at you from the women's side and watch you pray. When you came to see my brother and I heard you laughing with him, it was thrilling for me. You were so joyful and pleasant with people."

"That is how I was as a boy. As I grew up, I always thought you were pretty. I liked when I would see you laughing with your sisters in the street. I was happy when the match was made and I knew we would marry."

"I was happy too," Marcela said.

Benjamin said, "Just a few days before we married—it was the Shabbat before our wedding—I was walking home from the other side of Vitoria where I had been delivering some shoes to a Christian. I remember the daylight was going and I did not want to be late for the Shabbat celebration with our families. I decided to cut through some streets that were not familiar to me but that I thought would get me home sooner. One street was narrow and dark. I remember the big walls of stone, with the dirty paste between the rocks. The steps were wide, making it easy to walk up the gloomy street. There were not too many people out walking around. Shops were closed, and dinner was being served in most homes.

"I passed three men in the shadows but did not think much about them lurking there. I was just thinking about being late for Shabbat and that the next day would be restful and holy. But the three came up on me quickly and without warning. They pulled me into a small alleyway. I stumbled as I heard them say, 'Jew, we have you now.' I tried to struggle free, but a big heavy man pulled a knife from his waistband and put it to my throat. Marcela, I remember this as if it were yesterday. He said, 'If you scream or say one word, you will be a dead Jew.'"

Marcela looked at her husband with pity and sadness in her eyes. "I am so sorry, my husband, that you could not tell me before this."

Benjamin ignored Marcela's words. He was intent on telling the whole story.

"The attackers laughed as they pulled off my jacket and saw my white shirt and fringes. 'What is this, Jew? We have never seen Jews dress like this in Pamplona,' one said. These men smelled of wine as they breathed heavily on me. Then another said, 'Take his pants down. Let us see his *pene*. Maybe we will do his cutting again.'"

Marcela, as weak as she was, understood the humiliation Benjamin was feeling as he told her this. She did not say anything but just listened.

"I could not defend myself. I kept thinking, *How can this be happening to me?* Two of the men held my arms to the street while the third pulled my pants down to my ankles and held my legs. The skinny one with a large scar on his cheek held me down by kneeling on my arms. He made disgusting guttural comments about Jews and about my parts. Another attacker took one hand and roughly pulled on my part and laughed. He used his other hand to reach under me to my rear. The third man, who was husky and well built, took out his own *el pene,* pulled back the foreskin, and put the stiff organ close to my face. He said, 'Open your *boca.* Do some work on me, Jew. If you make a sound or hurt me, my friend will take his knife and slit your throat.' Within a minute or so, I was wet with the brute's slime."

"Oh, my darling," Marcela said. "I cannot imagine the horror of this moment for you."

"It is worse than this. The skinny one whispered to his friends, 'Turn him over. Let me at him.' I was close to losing all thought when I was flipped over and put in a kneeling position with my forehead touching the ground. With a knife to my neck, I felt each man go inside me. I said the Shema in my head. This kept me from fully feeling the pain of entry and the revulsion of what was happening to me. I felt the wetness that they left on me, and I saw my blood dripping onto the street. When the attackers finished, they walked away laughing."

Marcela was crying softly.

"I dressed myself and sat for a few minutes thinking about what I would tell my family. Why was I late for Shabbat? Why did I look wrecked? I decided to tell no one what had happened. The shame was too much. So was the pain in my body. I would think of something to say, but not the truth. It would be my secret forever. When I arrived home, my mother was concerned about my lateness and my father was concerned that I had missed candle-lighting and kiddush, but no one asked any questions.

"Benjamin, how you have suffered—from the attack and all these years of hiding this secret from me. I always thought you did not love me anymore. Why are you telling me this now?"

Benjamin thought for a moment. He knew that the death of Cassela and the details of his attack were two horrendous secrets. The pain from having to keep both was too much. He preferred Marcela know the gruesome details of his attack rather than the truth of what had happened to their daughter. However, instead of revealing his true rationale, Benjamin said, "I am sorry I did not tell you. I thought you would look at me differently because of the attack. I was more scared of that than of the attackers."

Marcela's strength was waning. "Do not worry about me. I forgive you for not telling me. And I forgive you for Isaac's death. God wanted it this way."

With those words, Marcela closed her eyes and drifted off to sleep. Benjamin's tears fell on Marcela's blanket. He felt relief from revealing his secret and blessed because of Marcela's forgiveness. Benjamin kissed her forehead and cheeks. He had never before kissed his wife with such enormous love and emotion in his heart. Benjamin took Marcela's hand in his and sat by her side for a long time.

CHAPTER 9

From the Rose Comes a Thorn and from the Thorn Comes a Rose

Summer 1491

Rina wanted happiness in her life. Rays from the midday sun streamed through the windows. They warmed the kitchen and made the room feel cheerful. Rina was grateful for this. She wanted the house to have a happy feeling.

Rina turned to the small fire and said, "I am doing my best for Daniyyel and Jonah." She felt the heat of the fire on her face.

No one answered back. Rina moved closer to the wood logs in the fire. Looking directly into the hearth, she said, "I will visit with you later." Rina almost expected to hear someone say "Thank you" or to see a message of "Talk to you soon" in the ashes. But nothing happened.

"Benjamin," she whispered, using the given name of her father. "Papa, I watched you work hard for us. You were so dedicated." But no one responded.

"Marcela," she whispered. "Mama, stay my rock. Speak to me." But no reply came forth.

Rina was looking for a message from her dead parents. Marcela had died a few weeks after Cassela. Benjamin died a month after

Marcela. He stopped eating and died. They were buried in the cemetery near Isaac.

Rina believed that some of her thoughts came to her from her dead parents.

"You each loved me in your own way, as best you could." Rina always spoke to the souls of her parents when the kitchen was quiet. It gave her the solace she needed to grieve for her parents, her sister, and her brother. She could not go to the cemetery as often as she wanted, because of her daily chores. The rabbi had told her that Jewish tradition required her to mourn but also to focus on renewing her life without her parents, Cassela and Isaac. She reminded herself: *Jews do not stay stuck in their grief.* In the past few months, she realized that being busy and taking care of Daniyyel and Jonah were the best avenues for coping with her heartache.

Rina had not always felt comfortable doing kitchen work. She did not like how Marcela worked only for the family by cooking, cleaning, sewing, and tending to the house. It was as if Marcela only served her husband and children. Although Rina would never say she disliked what her mother did, Rina did not want to repeat her mother's life. As a child, Rina had been to the weddings of many people in the community, but they had not meant anything to her until her friend Elena was matched with a man fifteen years older. Rina had known Elena since they were small children playing on the floor together. Now Elena's belly was bulging with her first child.

Some months ago, Elena confided how each time after her blood drippings completely stopped, her mother took her to the mikvah. Then, for the next seven days, she and her husband avoided contact. After the seven-day clean period, her husband would lie next to her, lift her sleeping garment, roll over onto her body, and say, "Open your legs."

"He separates my private part and puts himself inside me," she stated. "After some of his rough grunting and groaning, he takes himself out, leaving the bed linens and me with wetness that is not water or piss."

Rina did not understand what Elena had told her, but cooking and cleaning and having a man grunting on top of her were not what Rina wanted for herself.

Several times Rina had asked Marcela if it was required that all girls marry. The response was always vague and the same. "It is what is to be. It is what it is." That was all that Marcela said. That was all Rina knew. It was the only answer given.

Rina paused by the fire. She was angry that her life was predetermined. Marcela would say, "When you are a wife, you will do this for your husband" or "When you are a mother, you will take care of your children" or "You need to learn this so you can cook for your family." Cassela would tease Rina by saying, "Papa will never be able to find a husband for you. You do not like cooking or housekeeping." or she would say, "Your children will be ugly because you will only get an ugly husband." Rina did not want to do house chores all day and just wait until she had a girl child who could take over those duties.

So Rina asked her mother, "Do I have to marry?"

With loving sweetness, Marcela had said, "It is what is to be. It is what it is." With that answer, Rina felt like a cornered goose up against the barn wall, waiting to be taken by the executioner with ax in hand.

After Isaac died and Marcela became ill, Rina rallied her courage, and one evening after all her chores were done, when Benjamin was sitting by the fire with Jonah studying the Torah portion for the week, Rina said, "Papa, can I ask you a question?" There was no response. No head looked up. Nobody moved. "Papa," Rina repeated, a bit more strongly the second time. "I want to ask if I can begin to go with Tio Roffe Michah and learn healing. I want to help people be well." Benjamin looked up. His face was quizzical and annoyed at the same time. "I do not want to be confined to a life of cooking and cleaning. Cassela is suited to this life. I want to keep people from dying."

Benjamin said nothing. He looked up and then back down at

his book. He paused and then, with a crisp tone, said, "No. You will do as you should." His face was bland and neutral as he said, "You cannot disrupt what is."

Rina's eyes saddened. Her shoulders sagged, and her head dropped to her chest. She knew she could not broach her father with an argument, no matter how logical.

Now Rina walked with a fast pace around the kitchen. She checked the pan of sweet lamb heating on the fire. The smell of the berries and meat with spices of cumin and cinnamon left her with a smile on her face. She would be serving a lunch that was a favorite family meal.

Rina set the table with metal dishes that clanged as she put them out with the forks and knives. Adding a bottle of red wine and flowers made the table look inviting. Earlier in the day, Rina had cut the flowers from their garden in the courtyard, smelling each white aster to ensure the bouquet would be not only attractive but also aromatic. She combined the delicate daisies with some *eguzkilore* (large sunflowers). They had big, bright yellow centers surrounded by silver leaves with sharp serrated edges. Superstitious Basque women grew these flowers to keep evil spirits away from their homes. Rina did not believe in these Basque good luck charms. She had her Hebrew amulets for protection. For as long as she could remember, there had been a *hamsa* hanging on the kitchen wall and a *mezuza* nailed on each doorpost. However, Rina was not taking any chances with luck. She believed God watched over everything and everyone, but she did not understand why so much tragedy had visited her family. Rina did not want to hang eguzkilore on the door as Christians did. That would attract too much attention from the neighbors and certainly from Tia Agamit. But she could put them on the table mixed with other flowers and no one would notice. "I am not taking any more chances with luck. I want to use whatever power is available to keep evil spirits away from the Crevagos."

Daniyyel and Jonah walked into the kitchen and interrupted Rina's conversation with the dead. Another man was with them, but it was not Ezra. As was the custom, he went home to eat with Roffe Michah.

"Avram happened into the shop to see the new shoes we are making. He has been weaving cloth for our shoes for the last year or so. From the shop, we could smell lunch. So I invited Avram to join us. You have learned to cook well, little sister, but you always make too much," Daniyyel said. "Avram, sit here at the table, next to Rina."

Avram was surprised to be asked to sit next to a woman.

"Thank you. I am glad to do so," Avram said as he sat down. He tried hard to keep his eyes from looking too much at Rina as she set a place for him. "You look very nice today," he said in a shaky voice that did little to cover up his excitement at being close to her.

Avram had grown into a handsome man. His long black hair rested on his shoulders, framing his face and emphasizing his skin, which had become bronzed from being outdoors selling his cloth. His neatly trimmed moustache and beard accentuated his full lips. His rosy cheeks puffed up when he smiled. He towered over Daniyyel and Jonah by a whole head. Unlike most street vendors, his brown shirt and trousers were not worn looking; they had no tears or tatters. The pockets showed tailored detail. His clothes were a walking advertisement for the cloth he wove. Only his shoes showed the wear of a street vendor who walked the streets of Vitoria and nearby towns.

"I happened to be in front of your shop and thought I would stop in," Avram said. In truth, he had timed the route of his wagon so he would be at the Crevago shop for the midday meal. Since Cassela's death, he visited Daniyyel more often so he could see Rina.

As Rina uncovered the pot hanging over the fire and spooned the stew into a large bowl, the smell of the cooked lamb filled the room. She put roasted greens on each plate, using her mother's ladle to serve the men.

Rina climbed over the bench and sat across from Jonah and

Daniyyel and next to Avram. Her skin tingled as she seated herself on the same bench as the guest.

What was that I felt? Rina asked herself. *Is it that I am close to a man who is not my brother, or is it that I am close to Avram? I like how his face is expressive as he talks. His eyebrows are not too bushy, like those of some men, but they move as he makes his points. I liked his kindly face from the first time I saw it."*

Rina did not join the men in their conversation. They talked about shoes, cloths, and market values. But she saw how comfortable Avram was with her brothers and what an intelligent person he seemed to be.

"When will Vidal be back?" Avram asked.

"Within a few weeks," Jonah said with his customary frown. "I am anxious to hear the news he brings. I am sure it will not be good for the Jews."

"I have not heard anything about what has gone on in Aragón or south Castile. I think there is a war being waged against Moors in the south, so there is little concern by the monarchs about the Jews," Daniyyel said.

"The king and queen are always concerned about the Jews, as are the priests of the land," said Jonah.

The men continued to make small talk, but Rina did not say a word. It was not a woman's place to join in a conversation about the affairs of the state or its economics. She knew nothing about business, so she could not contribute anything to this talk.

"Very good food," Daniyyel said. "You are learning to keep a good house."

Jonah nodded his head in agreement. He smiled slightly.

When they had finished their meal, the men left their dishes for Rina to clear and wash. The roles in the household were always well defined. The men walked back into the shop feeling full and ready to continue their workday.

Rina did not know which thrilled her more—that her brother had given her compliments or that Avram sat at the same table as she did. The mood of the household had changed since Benjamin's death. His children were saddened by their loss but uplifted by the happier tone of conversations and the absence of criticism.

"Daniyyel, you are the oldest, so I will ask you," Avram said. "Did your father make a marriage match for Rina?"

"No," Daniyyel said as nonchalantly as possible.

Avram knew the tradition of boys being matched up with girls. He did not know what determined that one person should be with another. He certainly did not understand the protocols for marriage arrangements. No father had offered his daughter to him. He was an outcast to some extent, having come from Segovia after his parents were burned at the stake. Fathers did not want to chance their daughters to marry a person with this history. He also could not provide a father with any dowry. Adela had married a man twenty years her senior who had been married before and had a gaggle of children. Adela had moved to his farm, about thirty leagues from Vitoria, and had visited Avram only once since then. Gaila lived as a servant to the Levi family—the couple whom she, Jeremiyo, and Adela lived with after Vidal brought them to Vitoria. Joshua Levi had done well as an apothecary and had become a man of means who could afford a servant. Jeremiyo had been Joshua's apprentice but Joshua treated him as an undesirable. Jeremiyo became a practicing Catholic and moved to Portugal. He never visited Vitoria. Esau moved to Burgos to work for a drapero there. He never returned to Vitoria either.

"I have a good living with my cloths," Avram said to Daniyyel. "I weave at night and sell during the day. I am about to hire an apprentice. I have a cow that gives rich milk. I could match her up with a bull for calves. Would it be acceptable to you if ..." Avram began to stutter. "Do you think Rina could marry me?"

"Avram," Daniyyel said. "After Cassela died, each shiva night you said prayers with the minyan, and then stayed late to sit with Jonah and me. Although the conversation was with us, your eyes were on Rina. I saw you two today, and the air was thick with each of you trying not to stare at the other. I think Rina is young but ready to marry. She knows how to take care of a house and family. My mother taught her well. You can marry her at the next *Rosh Hodesh*—the next new moon. Tonight I will tell Rina of this decision."

"Thank you," Avram said, trying to control his exuberance. "I will be a good brother to you and good husband to Rina."

Avram left the workshop skipping steps as he walked out to the street. He picked up the handles of his wagon and walked down the Calle with a smile on his face. He smiled so hard his rosy cheeks hurt him. His thoughts were not on cloth but on the new life he would have with Rina. He would be part of a family again. This is what he had missed these past years since his parents had perished. Avram would finish his day, go home, and weave new cloth and think about his future life with Rina.

The rest of Daniyyel's day was typical. "Avram wants to marry Rina," he told Jonah and Ezra as they worked in the shop. "The ceremony will be at Rosh Hodesh. I am happy for them both."

"Did Papa not make a match for Rina before he died?" Jonah asked.

"He never told me anything," said Daniyyel. "Even if he did, without telling me, no agreement would be upheld by the rabbi."

"What does Rina want?" Ezra asked. He knew what it was like to have his life predetermined by his father.

Daniyyel said, "I think Rina will like it, but it does not matter. This is what she needs to do—be a wife to a husband and a mother to his children."

The men worked until light in the shop was dim and no longer available for close work. "Ezra, go home. Jonah, let us go to dinner. I smell the vegetables that Rina has on the fire."

Rina had started preparing dinner as soon as she had washed all the lunch pots, pans, and dishes. She was happy in this work, thinking about how she would marry and have her own family, although this had not always been the case. Rina's entire point-of-view changed after Cassela's attack, because this was when she met

Avram. She had seen him around Vitoria, and once at Tio Vidal's home. But she had not noticed his eyes before—his kind and sweet eyes.

"What do you have for us tonight?" Daniyyel asked.

"I cooked cherry soup with wine, and I mixed heated cheese with beans."

"Sounds good," Daniyyel said. "Mother never cooked cherry soup."

Jonah said, "You will make Avram a good wife."

"What did you say?" Rina asked.

"Avram asked Daniyyel if you were promised to someone, but we do not think that Papa promised you to anyone. Did he ever say this to you?"

A smile came across Rina's face. She was surprised that her brothers were talking about this so soon after Benjamin's passing, but she felt happy with the conversation.

"If Avram wants to marry me, I will do it," she said, trying to control her joy at this prospect. "This is what you, my brothers, want."

"I like Avram. We have had honest dealings with him. It is clear that he likes you. I told him you would marry at the new moon. He can live here, and you can use Papa and Mama's room for sleeping."

Rina got up from her place at the table and walked over to Daniyyel. "Thank you, my brother, for allowing me this marriage." She did something she had not done since she was a little girl; she kissed Daniyyel on the cheek. Then she turned to Jonah and kissed him too. "I will make a good wife, a good mother, and I will always be a good sister. Maybe you both ought to think about marriage too."

Daniyyel let out a big laugh. "I can only think about shoes. Nothing else matters now. We have to keep the business going."

"I will never marry," Jonah said. "I am too much like Papa, and it would be heartless to be this kind of person and put it on a wife and children. We know how cold he was to us."

"Do not say that about Papa," Rina said. "He was as kind and good as he could be. He always took care of us. He taught you his trade. He loved Mama. Those are the important things."

"No," said Jonah. "The important thing is to let your children know you care about them and love them. He did not do this with us. It was all about work and study. I am angry that I did not have a father who loved me. And now it is too late."

"Enough of this talk," Rina said. She loved her father with his flaws, defects, and faults. She loved him because he was the head of her family. "Please tell me more about Avram. What did he say? You know him better than I do. What is he really like?"

Daniyyel said, "You will find out for yourself. Avram will go to the rabbi tomorrow for the *ketuba.* The rabbi will write the marriage contract."

⇒—┤ ◆⟩— ◉ —⟨◆ ├—◅

Rina married Avram three weeks later, on a Saturday night after *Havdala,* when Shabbat ended.

The rabbi performed the marriage ceremony just like always, in accordance with the traditions of the Jewish people. Daniyyel, Jonah, Ezra, and Vidal had tied the corners of Avram's prayer shawl, his tālēt, to the ends of four oak poles cut from trees in Vitoria's forest.

The rabbi's wife made Avram a new tālēt to wear. By doing this, she fulfilled the biblical commandment instructing men to wear prayer shawls with specially spun strings of wool. The knotting was a complicated task. This ensured that the tālēt was made with effort and care. She knew how to do it carefully and methodically.

The ceremony was held in the synagogue's courtyard, which was located in the back of the building off Calle Abrevadero.

The courtyard was small, but it was big enough for the Jews to congregate. First, the Crevago men came from their homes, and other men followed, all holding candles to light the proceedings. The street seemed joyous from the candlelight. Avram, dressed in a white shirt, wore his new tālēt and walked with Joshua Levi. They stood on the left side of the *huppah* with the men standing behind them overflowing into the street. The candlelight made the street seem iridescent. The stones of the buildings reflected the light to add to the romance of the evening.

Then the women walked out of their homes and down Calle Abrevadero. They held flowers picked from their gardens. The scent of yellow and white asters filled the air.

Tia Agamit walked with Rina. Agamit had taken this young bride to the mikveh the day before.

Rina wore a modest long white jacket over her fresh brown tunic that almost touched the ground. Around her waist was a wide cinch belt that gathered the cloth and made soft pleats. This was not the jacket that Marcela had worn when she married Benjamin. That outfit had long ago been given to others in the community for their wedding days. Rina's jacket had been worn by Della and her daughters.

A heavily brocaded headscarf covered most of Rina's hair. A lacy veil across her face had small sparkles attached to it. These gemstones had been meant for shoes that Daniyyel was fashioning for a highborn customer, but instead Daniyyel affixed them to Rina's veil. Rina's fancy shoes were made with silk cloth and adorned with precious stones. After the wedding, Vidal would sell these shoes to a Christian agent who would take them to the court of a noble.

Agamit lifted Rina's tunic so she could walk up the steps of the synagogue and sit in the large brocaded chair that had been taken from the sanctuary and placed on the platform in front of the synagogue's doors.

Avram walked over to Rina, bent down, and lifted her veil so he could look closely at her face. This ancient tradition verified that no switch in brides had occurred and that it was actually Rina sitting in the chair. He performed this *bedeken* ritual slowly and with gentleness. He wanted to avoid what had happened to Jacob in the

Bible story. Jacob's future father-in-law, Laban, switched brides. Jacob had been betrothed to Laban's daughter Rachel, but on the night of the wedding, the bride wore a thick veil and Jacob did not realize he had married Rachel's older sister Leah. Jacob had worked seven years for Laban to earn the right to marry Rachel, and after the switch, he had to work another seven years to earn Rachel all over again.

Avram took a quick breath when he saw his bride. She looked like a beautiful child and woman at the same time. He looked at Rina's face, saying to her what Genesis says Isaac said to Rebecca: "*At hayi le alfei revavah*, be the mother of thousands, of ten thousands." Avram turned and faced the men and women watching this ancient ceremony and even though it was not typical, he said the *Shehehekianu* prayer, giving thanks to God for bringing him to this moment of happiness.

As Avram replaced the veil over Rina's face, he smiled at her. Tears filled Rina's eyes. She already felt loved by this man. It was a new feeling of joy.

Avram's fulfillment of this rite meant that the marriage ceremony could proceed. As he took his place under the huppah, he said to Daniyyel, "Your sister is as beautiful as the sky's Diana star." Daniyyel knew this was a high compliment. This is what men in the Judería said when they saw a woman of striking beauty.

Avram watched as the women escorted Rina to the huppah in the center of the courtyard. On one side of the bride was Agamit. On the other side was Joshua Levi's wife, Ester. *Rina's face is so serious,* Avram thought. *Is she sad that she is marrying me? Does she think I am too low—not good enough for her? Should she be serious on her wedding day? Maybe.*

Rina looked young and fresh in comparison to Ester and Agamit, who looked spent and haggard. "Caused by their years of working by the heat of the fire," Avram thought as he wondered what Rina would look like when they stood with their children under the huppah. *Will she look worn out and weathered from childbirth and work? Or will her facial qualities of today persevere?* Avram let these thoughts leave him as he looked at Rina in her purity. He was happy and grateful for his forwardness—that he had found the courage to speak with Daniyyel. Rina was a good choice.

As Avram stood under the huppah with the community watching, he wished his parents could have been present to share this day with him.

Rina made seven passes around Avram symbolizing the seven marriage blessings, the seven days of creation, and a sign that this husband would be the center of this wife's world. On the seventh pass, Rina took her place beside him, the tears from her dark eyes flowed down her cheeks. She was wishing her parents were there, and she was thinking of her future. Avram's eyes filled with tears. He was thinking of his future.

The rabbi read the ketuba, wherein Avram promised to be a dedicated husband. The scribe in the Judería had written it carefully, knowing the rabbi would read it during the wedding ceremony and that it would subsequently be displayed in Avram and Rina's home. The marriage contract listed Avram's responsibilities as a husband. It specified what contributions Rina's brothers had made to the new household, as well as what Avram would pay in the event that the marriage was terminated.

The rabbi's face looked somber as he said the marriage prayers, gave the bride and groom cups of wine to drink, bound the hands of the couple with a piece of white linen, wished the couple well, and placed a glass on the ground to commemorate the loss of the second temple. As Avram prepared to step on the glass, he thought, *Things happen for a reason. God had a plan for me. Maybe if my parents had not died at the stake, I would never have come to Vitoria and would not have met Rina.* Then he broke the glass into shards. A bellow of "*Maazāl Tōbh*" went up from the crowd as they began to sing songs of joy as Avram and Rina took their first walk through the crowd as husband and wife.

CHAPTER 10

Not Even the Devil Can Have the Upper Hand with the Jew

Fall 1491

King Ferdinand of Aragón had named the Dominican priest Father Tomás de Torquemada as inquisitor general of the Inquisition in the kingdoms of Castile and Aragón nine years before. This was the first time an Inquisition was managed by a designate of a monarch instead of the pope. Ferdinand did not like Rome to supersede his royal influence among his subjects. The king preferred to have Father Tomás reporting to the monarchy rather than the papacy. Father Tomás also liked this approach. More control.

As Ferdinand walked slowly and nervously down the long hallway of the castle, his long royal red robe flowed in his wake. Its embroidered gold threads glistened as he moved. His rounded multicornered black velvet hat was decorated with royal ribbons and honors. His thinning hair was clipped in a circle around his neck and fell over the collar of his white silk shirt. He frowned as he thought about the conversation he needed to have with his wife.

Father Tomás walked with intention next to the king at an equal pace. Typically advisors walked two paces behind the monarch, but Father Tomás believed himself, in the eyes of God, to be equal to Ferdinand, maybe even more elevated than the King. The priest looked impressive in his snow-white tunic. The white symbolized

Father Tomás's purity of life with Christ. His thick black belt, the Dominican cincture, had a simple metal buckle that represented his vow of chastity. The black symbolized his struggle against his bodily desires. Rosary beads hung from his waist and rattled as he walked. The white scapular, a knee-length overlay, covered his shoulders. A long floor-length black cape was gently draped over his *capuce*—a short shoulder cape with a white hood.

Father Tomás pushed the black cape to his back to show off the large crucifix that hung around his neck on a long heavy chain decorated with bronze and rubies. The ring of hair circling his bald head gave the appearance that he was wearing a crown of thorns, just as Christ did at his crucifixion. The bulbous nose, large puffy cheeks, and long jaw line offset the priest's small ears, which stuck out from under the tufts of hair.

Small rooms lined the extended hall. Each room had walls covered with woven silk fabrics. Colorful tapestries depicting the crucifixion and various saints hung in most of the rooms. Large area rugs covered floors of stone brought from quarries in the hills of Italy.

"How shall I present this problem to Isabella?" Ferdinand asked the priest.

"Be honest," Father Tomás said.

Ferdinand's shoes tapped on the stone floor, making a clicking noise that announced the king's arrival. As the pair entered the sunroom for the morning meal, doormen clad in red velvet suits bowed to honor them.

Mounds of food on glass platters covered a long table set with perfectly appointed candelabras, elegant eating utensils, and plates. The scent of cooked goose drowning in animal fat drifted throughout the room. Aromas of freshly baked breads and pork sausage wrapped in cinnamon sweet pastry covered with almonds filled the air.

Queen Isabella was seated on a large red satin throne chair at the breakfast table. She had not waited for Ferdinand. Her plate was already filled with breakfast foods. She had pulled her long sleeves of satin back to her elbows so she could eat freely. The royals enjoyed taking their meals together, but Isabella was not a patient person. Either her husband was on time for breakfast or she began without him.

The room lent itself for a morning meal. The outline of the gardens showed through the panes of thick glass that denoted the luxury of this palace. The sunlight shone on the food, which created a shimmer off the serving platters and jeweled serving pieces. Servers in starched and pressed uniforms of red and yellow linens stood behind each chair and at the sides of the long table.

"Isabellita, darling, did you sleep well?" the king asked, posing his typical morning question.

"Just fine," the queen said. "And you?"

"Equally fine, my love," the king said as he sat down to the left of his queen. "As we eat, may I share with you our progress with the Inquisition? Father Tomás brings reports of new developments."

Isabella did not look up from her breakfast meal as she continued chewing pieces of goose meat. She reached for a goblet of wine to wash it all down.

After a pause, the king continued. "Our Inquisition of conversos has moved forward but has not been as far-reaching as we had hoped."

Isabella looked up from her plate.

"Our goal is to unify Spain under our one true Catholic religion. Soon we will remove the Muslims from the south. The reconquest of all Spanish lands is about to be completed. We seek truth and true believers in our unification. However, can we be successful when some places continue to resist the Inquisition because of their good relationships with conversos and Jews? In some towns, they will not let the inquisitors put into practice the Instructions of the Office of the Sacred Inquisition that Father Tomás wrote. Magistrates do not allow the rules to be enforced. Jews are not required to wear the badge of Hebrews. They still wear their ritual garments. The penitent are not forced to wear the sambenito. In Aragón, subjects have refused to allow some inquisitors to pass through the city gates. However, resistance has been less since the incident in Teruel, when the murderers of inquisitor Pedro Arbués de Epila were beheaded and quartered, and their parts nailed to posts around the plaza."

Ferdinand continued almost without taking a breath. "In Castile, the sermons denouncing heretics have been stronger and longer. We have had more confessions of heresy by accused conversos. The new forty-day window of grace—our grace period that allows for confessions of Judaizing—has been successful in proving heresy. This extra time has proven to be a good invention. We have identified more false Christians, received more secret testimony and more confessions, and witnessed more reconciled heretics testifying at auto-da-fés of friends and relatives. The unrepentant have been condemned by state authority to be burned, and our processionals of heretics have grown in their pageantry. The fires have burned longer and with larger audiences."

"What is the problem," Isabella asked as she returned to eating her breakfast.

"Our Inquisition depends on the fines and penalties levied on those found guilty and the properties we confiscate after a trial. Father Tomás has identified an obstacle to our plan for religious unification."

As Torquemada sat with the monarchs, he held his head high, believing that, as their advisor on all religious matters, he was closer to God than they were—and certainly more knowledgeable as well as influential in the Christianizing of Spain. He wanted his plan to go well. His desire to be forever endeared to the monarchs and to the papal powers would be fulfilled. His desires for power and control would be secure.

"We know the Muslims of Granada will soon fall. We can easily complete our reconquest by ensuring the exit of Muslims who do not convert to Christianity. We will expand the Inquisition of Jewish conversos in the new territory. These wicked Judaizing Christians infect us. They are a problem—but not the only problem we face in purifying Spain. Ultimately we cannot be a pure country if there are Jews anywhere in our presence. They subvert our holy ways by keeping conversos from being true Christians. Having Jewish quarters and separating these heretics from Christians is not enough. We must remove the Jews from our midst so we can be a purely Catholic and righteous country. Catholicism is the universal way of life that we must purvey to all your subjects. It is the only path to heaven and redemption. The Supreme Council of the Inquisition is the only governmental institution that unites the kingdoms within Spain. We must use this to purify Spain."

Isabella thought for a moment. "The Jews bring revenue into our treasuries. All the Jews in my realms are under my protection. Mine is the obligation to defend, help, and maintain them in justice. Our Jewish financial advisors have guided us well. My personal financial advisor, Isaac Abrabanel, is a Jew. He has directed me on how to broaden my wealth. Rabbi Abraham Seneor has faithfully collected the taxes and rents due to the crown. He has managed all the tax collectors in my realm. Jews have successfully managed our financial matters with foreign nations for years. As much as I do not like the Hebrews, it does not make sense to remove them from Spain. Convert them, yes. Be sure they are true Christians, yes. Stop the Judaizing with their prayers, festivals, and rituals, yes. Expel them, no."

The priest respectfully said, "Christian unification can never be attained with this fragment in our culture. We will give their jobs to competent Christians. The Christian artisans will take over the Jewish shops. Our merchants will prosper without competition from Jews. Their assets will be ours because we can limit what they take out of the country. Most importantly, we must think about the purity we want for Spain. Baptize and remain. Infidels must leave."

Torquemada himself had great-grandparents who were Jewish. His grandfather Alvar Fernandez de Torquemada had married a converso. In efforts to separate from her past, his grandmother swung very far into Catholicism to avoid any appearance of loyalty to her original faith. Torquemada's indoctrination of hatred occurred at home as a child and during his training as a Dominican priest.

He learned prejudice just as he learned Christian dogma. He took to both. Torquemada's zeal grew along with his fear that the economic and social growth of Jews and conversos would disrupt his goal for a purely Catholic nation of Spain. His attitudes were fueled by his hatred of his own Jewish ancestry.

"Your Royal Majesty Isabella, I defer to you on matters of state. You are the supreme ruler and have all the respect that I can possibly give you. I have been your confessor and advisor. As the person closest to Inquisition activities, I ask you to trust me in this guidance that I give you now. The Jews are a threat to the religious and social fabric of Spain. To have pure unification of all our kingdoms and provinces, we must have purity of religion. Think about this as your army assaults the Emirate of Granada. If Islamic heretics will not be allowed, why should you allow Jewish heretics? I present to you the thinking that no heretics should be allowed to live in Spain."

The king agreed. "Sweet Isabellita, we cannot say we are a Catholic country when Jews live here." However, Ferdinand's thinking easily gave way to his cold ulterior motive. *Let me realize how our riches will grow. The Jews will be restricted from taking money and possessions out of the country leaving great wealth for the crown to seize, loans that Jewish financiers have made to the crown and nobles will be cancelled without payment, and new conversos in a desire to curry favor will be willing to pay more in taxes.*

"Here is my plan," the priest said, looking almost annoyed at the interruption by the monarch. The Father did not want to leave this important topic to Ferdinand for fear that the he would yield to his wife's concerns.

"As we complete our agreement with the Muslim leader Boabdil, let us consider the hundred or so Jewish families that live in Granada. We will give them one month to convert to Catholicism or they can settle their affairs, pack one wagon of goods, and remove themselves from Spain. If that goes well, as I think it will, we will know what is possible. The new archbishop of Granada will watch closely and report to me on the disposal of Jewish property."

Ferdinand, already tasting his new wealth, nodded.

The queen looked over at her husband. Isabella, with all her royal finery and jewels gleaming in the sunlight that streamed through the castle's windows, said, "I accept this plan out of deference to my husband and because of the respect I have for you, Father, my confessor."

Isabella felt comfortable with these two men. She also recognized that the handsome navigator Capitán Cristóbal Colón [Christopher Columbus], with his ideas and ventures to find a new route to the treasures of the Indies would be good for her kingdom. She thought: *Jews are lending me the money to finance his voyage and perhaps expulsion would eliminate the need for repayment of these loans. The wealth acquired from the Jews will grow my treasury,* although for piety, she did not want to connect the expulsion with her desire for riches. Isabella wanted to keep the motive for expulsion purely religious—an act that would ensure she would go to paradise.

CHAPTER 11

The Nobility Is Visible in His Face

Early Spring 1492

Vanna, a tortoise of a horse, kicked up dust with each step in her slow trot. The morning air was cold, and the winds were blowing, but not as abrasively as they had been. Winter had finished early, and the road was dry. Being dressed in his traveling clothes, Vidal looked plain—almost poverty-stricken. He had been traveling around Castile for more than a month, bringing the local well-born the exquisite shoes that Daniyyel had designed. Each pair was more beautiful than the next. Avram had woven their linen fabrics. Jonah had cut, polished, and artistically placed the gemstones. The boots were made from the finest sheep hides, tanned and dyed by Ezra. They had buckles that gleamed, and some sparkled with inset crystals. Vidal acknowledged to himself that his nephews had more talent than anticipated. Benjamin had taught them well. The boys excelled beyond him.

"I like the temperate days of the coming spring," Vidal said to Vanna. Her brown tail swished the flies away. Her matted mane hung on each side of her long neck.

Vidal was about to enter Guadalajara, a city established by the Moors in the eighth century. They had named it *Wadi-al-Hajara*, meaning "valley of stones," because of the large pebbles that could be found by the riverbank and in the fields. However, in 1212, the city was conquered by Christians. From that point forward, Christians populated the land. The Church took over Moorish buildings, destroyed Islamic symbols and traces of the previous culture were obliterated. The city was on the eastern border of Castile, not too far from the kingdom of Aragón.

Vidal crossed over the Henares River on the old stone bridge—one of the few remnants from the Moors. The *clip-clop* of Vanna's hoofs made a pleasant sound of arrival. The pair rode by the tall city walls and into Guadalajara's small streets, where the merchant shops were located.

"We are finished after this," Vidal said to Vanna. "We will stay for a day or so, refresh ourselves, and then start for home."

Vidal stopped Vanna in front of Lorisino's shop. Lorisino was the most reputable cobbler in Guadalajara—the one who served the nobles in the area. As Vidal walked through the doorway, he said, "Hello, my friend. I am here with beautiful shoes." Lorisino's was typical of cobbler shops throughout Spain. It held workbenches and cutting boards, with drab hides and strips of leather lying around on the floor. Scrap material lay everywhere. The smell of hides, rough-hewn leather, and smoothed suede filled the room.

"Why are you here?" Lorisino asked as his face turned pasty. Lorisino was burly with dark olive skin and shiny black hair. Generations ago, his people had migrated from the south of Italy. In addition to shoes, he made gloves, tunics, hats, table coverings, and whatever else he could make out of hides. His family also had groves of olive trees in the hills of Guadalajara. This agricultural occupation kept him in the sun during warm days, when his skin turned even darker.

Vidal returned a startled look. "I always come to Guadalajara as spring is coming upon us."

Lorisino dropped his metal awl and knife on the workbench with a clang that rang throughout the shop.

"You do not know yet? I heard from the priest who heard from the bishop who heard from an inquisitor who passed through Guadalajara some days ago. Jews are leaving Spain."

Vidal cocked his head to the right and straightened his body as he stepped closer to Lorisino. "What are you saying? What do you mean?" asked Vidal.

Lorisino repeated what he had heard. "Our priest said the monarchs had a great victory in Granada. King Ferdinand defeated the Moors—those learned people of the south Iberian Peninsula. They were good with science, art, and literature of the classics, but they were not warriors enough to repel the king. The old ruler of Granada and our monarchs signed an agreement, which included the expulsion of all Jews from Granada. The Jews there had thirty days to sell their property and belongings. They have left to live in Muslim lands. The Muslim ruler has left. The Muslims have converted or left. Ferdinand and Isabella now rule Granada, and it is the model of an entirely Catholic country."

Vidal stood in shock as Lorisino continued.

"The priest seemed very certain that all Jews now living under Ferdinand and Isabella would soon be converted to the cross or banished from the country."

"Who is this man, the inquisitor? asked Vidal.

"I do not know his name. He conducts Inquisition trials of converso heretics."

Vidal's body wilted. Lorisino put his arm around this man who had been bringing him shoes for decades.

"Sit here, Vidal. Calm yourself."

Vidal felt weak. He made a fist with one hand and clasped his other hand over it, trying to show some defiance.

Vidal said, "I cannot believe our monarchs would do this...force us to become Christian or leave what we have known all our lives. What a choice. We have lived in this land for hundreds of years. We make no trouble. We pay our taxes. For what reason do they want us out?"

"I do not know," Lorisino said. "I do not even know if it is true. I should not have said anything about this to you. I am sorry."

Lorisino brought Vidal a jug of wine and poured some into two cups. Normally Vidal, being kosher, would not use the *treif* dishes or cups from a Christian home. Today, he needed the wine to soothe himself. Vidal and Lorisino sat quietly for a few moments and drank together as two old friends might.

Finally Vidal said, "I must leave sooner than planned. I am dirty from the road, but let us do our business so I can go."

"Stay for a day and refresh yourself," Lorisino said.

"I cannot," Vidal said. "On my behalf, you will have to give my regards to your family."

Vidal delivered the beautiful Crevago shoes, collected his money, and left immediately for the return trip to Vitoria.

Vidal pushed Vanna's strength and rode the rest of the day in an effort to reach Vitoria as soon as possible. As he held the reins, Vidal thought about his family, his work, and his community. "I did not ever think this would happen, but we should have left long ago. Maybe Benjamin and Marcela would still be alive if we had. Can it be true? We must be gone. Why? Should we leave or convert to Christianity? If we converted, would we ultimately be burned at the stake? What should we do? Where could we go? What is best for the family?"

In between the questions, Vidal tried to pray. He thought of himself as a lapsed Jew, but praying seemed like the only alternative. "God of my fathers, help us survive whatever is coming our way. Help us be who we are. Keep us safe from tyrants, from the pharaohs of today, from the Jew-haters. We are your people. I pray for the safety of my wife, my children, my children's children, my family, and my friends."

Repeating prayers, asking questions with no answers, and remembering the strength of his ancestors kept Vidal focused on his goal of getting home. He did not even want to take time for detours to go to an inn or try to find some space with a Jewish family. He knew if Jews lived in a house by the mezuza on the doorpost.

Instead, Vidal camped off the road for a few hours. He knew this was dangerous given road bandits, but he had to rest Vanna even if it was only for a very short time. In doing so, Vidal took as many precautions as possible. Vidal drove the wagon into the high brush. He muzzled Vanna with a blanket to avoid her reacting to the noise of any nighttime creatures or noise from the road. He did not make a campfire. He ate the cold salted meat and hard bread that Lorisino had given him. He slept in the empty wagon on top of hard wooden boards. The night air was cold, but Vidal was too tired to notice. He fell asleep quickly, but his fears would not let him sleep deeply. Visions of Antonio and Maria in their sambenitos and then burning at the stake came to him and stuck in his mind.

He had had these recurring nightmares before. They reduced his interest in traveling. He was no longer jovial or the jokester he had been before. Vidal would sit in the kitchen with Della and watch her cook, or he would walk by himself for a long time in the countryside surrounding Vitoria. Sometimes he would spend hours in the cemetery visiting his parents and ancestors.

It took Vidal months to shake the fears from the scene he had witnessed in Segovia until he was able to sleep at night. Now the visions had returned.

Vidal mulled his thoughts and asked himself what the family should do. No answers came to him. "I need to talk with my brothers. With the rabbi. With the leaders of the synagogue. I must listen to what the aljama has to say."

When Vidal finally entered the Judería, the moon over Vitoria was high in the sky and slightly covered by clouds. He rode through the Jew's Gate, down Calle de Judios, and around the block to Calle Abrevadero as he had so many times before. The shadows of the houses cast ghostly outlines on the streets. The darkness was only slightly broken by the leftover firelight in the hearths of the houses that shone through the thick pane windows of these Jewish homes. The street was deserted.

Vidal reached the Crevago courtyard ready to collapse from exhaustion. He opened the gate to the courtyard and directed Vanna in, closing the gate behind the wagon, making as little noise as possible. As soon as Vidal unhitched Vanna from the wagon and took off her bridle, she immediately lay down in the courtyard. Her big brown eyes closed, and her tail barely moved.

Vidal stepped quietly into his house. Dust from the ashes of the fireplace flew onto the floor from the slight wind that had come in when Vidal opened the door. The smells from the family dinner lingered in the kitchen. The glow from the hearth was low.

The floorboards creaked as Vidal walked up the stairs. He looked in on his sleeping grandchildren but did not wake them. He looked at Della sleeping on the bed in the corner. He crept over to the empty bed next to hers, pulled the covers back and lay down. She briefly opened her eyes and looked at Vidal as if he were a dream.

"You are home, my husband," she said softly. "Good trip?"

"We will talk about it in the morning. I am too tired to say five more words."

"I am so glad you are home. Tomorrow is the *bedikat hametz*. We have to clean the house. The next night is the first Seder for Pesah."

"Let the boys scour the house and look for bread and grain by themselves. Tomorrow night I have to talk to my brothers."

"No, the man of the house has to read the blessing and direct the removal of leavened foods. We are not breaking three thousand years of tradition because you have to talk to your brothers. You will go from room to room and cupboard to cupboard to make sure that no crumbs remain in any corner. You will do this by candlelight to see each corner and use a feather and a wooden spoon to clean out all specks of hametz. Then you will burn whatever crumbs you might find. This is what we do before the Pesah Seder. You can talk to your brothers another time."

Vidal was too tired to argue with Della on these points.

When he had left Vitoria, he had expected his homecoming would be a happy family reunion. They would be celebrating Pesah, the retelling of the Exodus of the Jews from Egypt. Even Yosef would be home from Murcia. Conversion or leave? This would put a pall over the Seder.

Vidal decided to hold Lorisino's information until after the houses had been cleaned for Pesah. He did not want to create fights between his brothers and their wives. If Benjamin were still alive, Vidal would have talked to him immediately about the unsettling news. However, for now, Vidal decided to keep silent.

CHAPTER 12

It Has Become So Dark That the Sun Is Sure to Rise Again

Pesah 1492

Agamit worried why Vidal had been over so early in the morning to talk with Rahav. They huddled in the courtyard talking, talking, and talking, with such serious faces. There was none of Vidal's old-style joking. She would press Rahav to tell her what Vidal was saying.

It was the fourteenth of *Nisan*, 5252, in the Hebrew calendar—Erev Pesah, the first Passover Seder. Mid-April was an aromatic month on the Calle. The new growth on the trees gave the air a fresh scent. More and more wildflowers bloomed each day. Various reds, yellows, pinks, and purples created an array of color around the border of the Crevago courtyard. Scents melded, sending perfume to the surrounding houses. When combined with the smells of cooking from each household, the aroma suggested an aura of blissfulness.

Agamit had been cooking since before the sun came up. Her kitchen table already had stacks of matzo she had baked. *El pan de la aflicción* (the unleavened bread of affliction) was made from plain dough of flour and water, mixed without salt or yeast, rolled out flat, and baked for about fourteen minutes, but no longer than eighteen. She measured the time by a water clock that slowly dripped water into a pail marked with lines to tell how much time had elapsed. When the pail was full, the matzo came out of the fire. By dawn she had already made sixty round discs of matzo. She had made three for the Seder, including the *afikoman* that would be hidden for children to find after the meal, and eaten after the other desserts. The rest of the matzo would be eaten by the family at the Seder and during the week when they could not eat leavened bread.

Agamit's forehead was beaded with sweat. As she put a new batch of matzo into the metal box that hung over the fire, she felt the heat fly under her long dress and swirl all around her. She stepped away from hearth to cool herself and walked to the long wooden table in the kitchen.

Haroset is next, she thought. *I have to make it before the children wake. Otherwise it will be all gone before Seder.*

Agamit stood over the table with her back to the door to the courtyard. She was about ready to begin chopping dates when Rina opened the door and came into Agamit's kitchen.

"Can I help you, Tia Mitty?"

Rina was the only one who used Agamit's childhood nickname. Marcela had kept it for her sister-in-law to soften Agamit's authoritarian personality. Rina liked to go to market with Tia Mitty and listen to her bargain with a caravan trader. "These spices should be a lower price," Agamit would loudly whisper, and then secure a lower price from the trader. Rina was in awe of Agamit when she talked to her older brothers. "Get out of my kitchen!" she hollered when the men trampled in to taste whatever was cooking in her pots. The brothers knew that of all the Crevago women, Agamit was the best cook, and that after some cajoling and teasing of their little sister, she would give each man a spoonful to taste. She then kicked them into the courtyard.

Rina walked in, her belly rounded from the child she was carrying. "What can I do for you?"

"Sit here. Cut the pits out of the dates and then chop them and put them in the bowl. Then chop the almonds and add them to the dates. I bought them in the Arab market. Paid too much. The Arabs know what we need for our Seder and overprice it. I tried to talk them down, but they were strong about it. And people say the Hebrews are the stiff-necked people."

"The dates smell very sweet," Rina said.

"Take a little home, and when you are alone, rub some on your belly so you will have a sweet child."

"Does that work?" Rina asked.

"Who knows? God will give you the child he wants, but rubbing a few dates on your skin cannot hurt. Let me ask you something else. How is Avram? I have not seen him for a few days."

"He is wonderful but always busy with his cloths. He is also spending more time at the synagogue. When I ask why, he just says, 'We are talking.' When I ask about what, he says, 'Nothing of concern for you, my love.' I do not know what is going on, but it feels like something big."

"Sprinkle some cinnamon in the haroset," Agamit said. "Then add some honey and a little vinegar. Taste it as you go to get the mix right. Then put it on the high shelf over the window."

"Has Rahav said anything?"

"No, nothing. But Vidal was over and not to eat my food. I think Della is doing a better job of cooking. She was a terrible cook when she first came to the family. I taught her how to make a lamb stew and many other things." Agamit said this with some prideful tones in her voice. "Poor Della. Her mother did not teach her well."

As Rina chopped, she asked, "When is Tio Yosef coming home? It is almost Seder. I miss him. When I was a little girl, he started teaching me to read Hebrew, but when Papa found out, he forbade it."

"Rahav received a letter from Yosef some days ago and read it to me. Of course you know that Yosef is really writing to me, but since I cannot read, he sends his letters to Rahav. Yosef said he would be here for Seder but that he is very busy with his languages. He seems to be working hard. He has tired of teaching, but he likes his work with the governor of Murcia. He is well but has no woman. I think he should marry, and I will tell him this when he comes. He should have a family and be educating his children by now. He will never move from Murcia. My little brother has become an important person in the provincial court, but he could take a girl from Vitoria and live near the governor's palace and raise his children there. I have to start roasting the lamb now."

As the morning wore on, the women cooked and talked. Agamit's grandchildren came into the house chattering and wanting to hug their grandmother.

"Just sit down and eat," Agamit said briskly.

The boys obediently sat down at the end of the long kitchen table, which was now filled with stacks of matzo, raw vegetables, herbs, spices, pots, and pans. Agamit gave each boy a bowl of boiled vegetable stew and eggs from the pot she had sitting by the side of the fireplace. As she plopped the food into the bowl in front of each child, she kissed each boy on the top of his head and said in Hebrew, "May the Lord bless you and keep you safe."

After their meal, the young boys joined Rahav in his silversmith shop that faced Calle Abrevadero.

With the grandchildren gone, the kitchen became quiet again.

"Agamit said, 'I am worried about what the future holds for my grandchildren. I cannot help but think something is going on. I just do not know what.'"

"Do not think about it now, Tia Mitty. The future will be whatever God wants it to be. Our hamsas protect us from the evil eye. What else needs to be done for Seder?"

"You may be right to say that, but I feel a black cloud coming."

"Why? Because a few men were talking and whispering? We do not know what they were saying. Maybe it is good that we do not know. Papa told me that women do not need to know what men know. If Papa was right, I only need to be concerned with the child in my belly."

Agamit realized that conversation with Rina was not going anywhere. Instead of pursuing it, Agamit asked, "Rina, can you fetch me three eggs from the cabinet by the door?"

Rina walked to the cabinet, and as she was grabbing some eggs, the door to the courtyard flew open. Because the sunlight streamed in to cause a glare, the women could not see the face of the person standing in the doorway. However, from the form and figure, they knew he was the one they had been waiting for.

"Tio Yosef!" Rina said. Her face brightened and her belly popped out in front of her as she stood up straight.

Before Yosef crossed the threshold, he extended his arm and put his four fingers to the mezuza case that held the parchment paper with the inscription of the *Shema Yisrael*. Yosef brought his four fingers to his lips and kissed them to show reverence for God that he might grant health and happiness of the people living in this house. Although he had a mezuza on the doorpost of his house in Murcia, he usually ignored it, being occupied in scholarly thought. But being home was different.

"It is good to be here, even if it is just for this short holiday season," Yosef said as he hugged his niece and looked at her pregnant body. "How can you be old enough to be bearing a child?" Yosef said, faking disbelief.

He walked over to Agamit, and looked at her carefully. He gauged whether she had changed much from his visit during the last Pesah.

He gave his sister a loving hug and judged her to be as fit as she had been a year ago. He never came home for the High Holy Days anymore. Too much work in Murcia.

Tears came to Agamit's eyes at seeing her youngest and most sophisticated brother. His impressive dress emphasized his elevated station as he walked into the sparsely appointed room. The long cape showed the emblems of the province of Murcia—six large crowns embroidered with golden threads, arranged in the center of the rich red cloak. On the sides of the cape were ten large embroidered fortresses, each castle separated by an equally large bright white square patch that had a standing red dragon sewn on it. The royal dragons, with two paws firmly planted on the ground and two paws lifted, ready to give a one-two punch, looked as ominous as the castles, which looked strong in their protection.

"You never come home for Rosh Hashana and Yom Kippur anymore. It has been a year. We have missed you," Agamit said, feeling somewhat diminished in the presence of her important brother. However, Agamit quickly regained her dominance. "Are you close to marrying a Jewish girl in Murcia? It is time you started a family. Studies are fine, but family is everything."

Yosef let out a hearty laugh. "You have not changed, Sister dear. You always want to know everything."

"Then tell me what is going on that our men are having secret talks all the time. Is there danger in the air that no one is telling me about? What is happening? Rahav will not talk to me about it."

"If your husband will not talk to you about it, then neither will I."

"I give up," Agamit said. "But only for now."

"You should know things in the world are changing. New ideas are coming to us, and we, the scholars, have to judge them. But with everything good comes something bad. It is the balance that the alchemists talk about." Yosef hid from Agamit the worry he felt over rumors he had heard in Murcia.

"What is the bad? That is what I want to know," Agamit said.

"Whatever happens in history, it is never good for the Jews," Yosef said.

Rina interrupted. "We will have time to talk about what is bad for the Jews. Tonight is Pesah, and the family will be happy to see you. I want to talk about happy things. We will have enough sadness as we tell the story of slavery and how we left Egypt. Tell us about court in Murcia. I want to hear about what the women are wearing and what the new dances are."

"Leave him be for now. You must be tired after your travel. Rina, get Yosef a cup of hot water. Pick some mint leaves from the garden. Then put some honey in it to relax him. The tables are in the courtyard. Cover them with cloth and set the dishes out. Then prepare the Seder plates—one for each table."

Agamit wanted some time for herself with Yosef. She knew that as soon as her brothers saw him, they would consume him with questions about politics. Agamit worried about what the future might bring for the Crevagos. Her life in Vitoria was safe. She knew what had happened to Avram's parents in Segovia and had heard chatter about conversos and their fates in other parts of Castile and in Aragón, but conversos did not seem to be in danger in Vitoria. Besides, the Crevagos stayed Jewish, and the Christians of Vitoria respected the Jews who lived here.

Rina brought the leaves in. She poured the hot water, dipped a spoon into the honey pot, and then put it into Yosef's cup.

"Now that I am sitting down, I realize how tired I am. I rode the entire night to get here. My horse is in the courtyard. As soon as I finish the tea and eat something, I will brush him down and then sleep.

≻—⦁⟩—O—⟨⦁—≺

Just before sundown, the Crevago brothers and their families, dressed in clothes they did not wear every day, filed into the courtyard. Long tables had been set with a bright white cloth covering each table. Avram had made these for the family's Pesah dinner. Dishes, forks, knives, spoons, and cups that had not been used since the last Seder sat on the table. Bowls of yellow, pink, and green flowers gave color to the tables.

Baruh, his sons, and Vidal's son David carried in large jugs of wine and put them on the various tables so that each adult and child could drink at least four full cups.

As more Crevagos entered the courtyard, each said "*Hag Samech* [happy holiday]" to the others. Each wife carried a pot of food. Each husband trailed along with more food. When the pots of food were set down, hugs and kisses on each person's cheeks were the next protocol. There were children and grandchildren, aunts and uncles, nieces and nephews, and cousins who lived on Calle de Judios or on another Calle in Vitoria. As the family had grown, new housing had been built to accommodate the expansion, just as with the Christians, whose numbers in the city had also increased.

When Yosef made his entrance into the courtyard, a bellow of happy wishes welcomed him. The brothers surrounded him and chatted like excited boys with new toys.

Yosef enjoyed the attention. He liked being with his older brothers. They were accomplished artisans however Yosef was the most learned. He finally felt a certain superiority given his position and education. Yosef missed Benjamin, but he was happy to be with Vidal, Roffe Michah, Juhuda, Baruh, Rahav, and his new nephew Avram.

Unlike Shabbat meals, when the young children sat at their own tables or with the women, all the male children, regardless of age, sat with the men. The holiday of Pesah was all about the children and making sure, they learned the Exodus story.

Vidal, being the oldest living Crevago brother, led the Seder. He was the only one with a *Haggadah*. Poorer families did not even have one. They told the story of Pesah from memory, as the Crevagos used to. Having a written Haggadah showed the family's financial success.

"Tonight we retell the story of the Exodus of the Jews from Egypt, bonding the elders and the young ones, as each child must learn that this is our story and know that it is when we left Egypt that the Hebrews became a people of freedom—the nation of Israel, of our forefathers Abraham, Isaac, and Jacob. We tell this story linking the past and future as if we are all slaves in bondage and controlled by unwanted masters. We prepared for the Pesah by searching our homes for hametz. We burned anything and everything leavened. This cleansed us so we could be prepared for our new life of freedom."

Yosef leaned over and whispered to Rahav, "There will be no freedom for the Jews in Castile."

"What have you heard?" Rahav asked.

"That the monarchs removed the Jews of Granada and want to remove the Jews from Castile and Aragón."

"Remove how?"

"I do not know. Force conversion. Take ownership of homes, livestock, and shops. Enforce the anti-Jew laws. I do not know for sure.

Vidal continued. "The Book of Exodus says to 'remember the day on which you went forth from Egypt, from the house of bondage, and how God freed you with a mighty hand.' We are free in Castile, but we must ask ourselves if something might change for the worse. For the Jews, it can always be worse." Vidal's mind was filled with thoughts of what he had heard in Guadalajara.

The Seder continued with Vidal asking the children questions about the symbols on the Seder plate. "Why do we have a roasted shank bone of a lamb?"

A young boy jumped on the question. "It symbolizes past animal sacrifices in the temple."

"What about the leafy green vegetable?"

Another child quickly said, "It symbolizes hope for the future and for dipping into salt water, so we can remember the tears Jews shed in Egypt."

And so on.

"Bitter herbs?"

"For the pain of slavery."

"Haroset?"

"The mortar Jews used to build Egyptian pyramids."

"Roasted egg?"

"The old-time sacrifices for festivals and is a symbol of renewal of life."

Vidal congratulated the children on learning their lessons. He pointed to piles of matzo that were strategically placed so fathers could pass it out to their sons. Mothers did the same for their daughters.

Yosef said in an aside to Rahav, "The symbols have meaning for today. Jews are oppressed by the monarchs and their church."

Vidal continued to ask the children questions about various other symbols: Elijah's cup of wine, pitcher of water for hand washing, and so on.

Vidal took the middle of the three matzot that sat in front of him and broke off a piece. He placed it in a woven bag and put the bag on his left shoulder. He let it sit there for a moment and then transferred the bag to his right shoulder. "This symbolizes the burdens that we carried as Jews in Egypt. Today we carry our burdens in our thoughts and at some point must cast them off as we cast off our loads in Egypt."

Vidal followed the various steps of the Seder. "We eat the bread of affliction tonight as our ancestors did when they left Egypt and as our people have done for thousands of years. We suffer along with those who have suffered. If we suffer in our lives now, our descendants will remember how we suffered under oppressive monarchs.

The youngest child at the table asked the first of the four questions: "Why is this night different from all the other nights?"

Vidal answered, "Because on all other nights, we eat either leavened or unleavened bread, but on this night we eat only unleavened." He continued with the expanded answer as it was written in the Haggadah, but then added, "And on this night we think about the past, our life today, and our future."

The child asked the other questions. Vidal gave the answers and then added, "We must think about the past but also the future."

He went on. "We lived in Egypt and then we left for a better place—for the Promised Land. We live in Castile, but in years to come, we may have to leave, and it could be for a better place—a promised land.

"The laws that put the Jews in bondage in Egypt are like the laws that have come to the Jews on the Iberian Peninsula.

"Just as our ancestors were freed from Egypt, we must ask how we can free ourselves if our rulers choose to put us in bondage as conversos."

The Seder went on for hours. Telling the story of the Exodus, quizzing the children about Jewish history, and symbolically reliving the Exodus with prayers and stories. However, after each step in the Seder, Vidal always brought the story back to their lives in Spain.

Roffe Michah said, "You are scaring the women and children, Vidal. You are scaring me. Let us stay with the story of the Passover as it was written for us. Let us think about the Jews of Egypt more than the Jews of Castile and Aragon."

"Vidal is right Roffe. We must think of ourselves too. We must consider yesterday, today, and tomorrow," Yosef said. "It does no good to dwell on the past without learning its lessons. You frighten me, Roffe. I thought you would be more aware of the future and the Jews on the Iberia Peninsula."

"I know all I want to know. I tend to my patients and try to keep people alive with the medicine I know. I am not going to try to foretell the future. I leave that to the seers and astrologists. No matter what happens, I trust in God and in his Divine plan for the Jews."

At last Vidal came to the part in the Seder where the meal was to be served. At Vidal's order, the wives and daughters took the covers off their iron pots and began serving the men, boys and children.

The men talked only about politics. They asked Yosef many questions, but he declined to answer them. Although he was worried, given what he had heard in Murcia, he wanted to relax with his family on this first night at home. Nothing would happen to the family tonight.

All waited for the children to search for the afikoman. The family ate it after eating the desserts that the women had baked: the sweet cakes made with dough from matzo flour and filled with berries from the hillside groves. Many small treats had been made using the sugar that the Moors brought to Vitoria in their caravans, knowing that the Jews needed specialties for their holiday.

"This life is so nice," Roffe Michah said as he sat on the bench next to his brothers. "Good to have you home, Yosef."

Vidal said, "Dinner is over. The Seder is complete. We have fulfilled the commandment to tell the story of our Exodus from Egypt. We have spent our evening on the past. It is time to talk about the present and future."

He told the men what Lorisino had said.

Yosef told his brothers what he had heard in Murcia. "I do not know what is true, but it seems that no matter how many sweet cakes we eat, once more our future feels as uncertain and bitter as if we were still slaves in Egypt."

Juhuda wanted to know what they should do to prepare.

Baruh said, "I cannot imagine leaving Vitoria. It seems like an impossibility."

Roffe Michah said, "We have to wait and see what God has planned for us."

Vidal said, "It is the monarchs who have a plan for the Jews."

When Pesah was over, Yosef returned to Murcia, vowing to verify the rumors that he and Vidal had heard.

CHAPTER 13

Drop by Drop, the Barrel Fills Up

End of April 1492

Everyone was eating bread again. Families had packed away their Pesah dishes, pots, pans, and cooking and eating utensils. The spring air was clear. Wind was causing tree branches in the courtyard to bang against the houses. The men talked about the rumors they had heard, but their lives in Vitoria continued as usual.

Juhuda, Daniyyel, Jonah, and Ezra were in the shop, preparing shoes for Vidal's next trip through Castile. Vidal was working at a small wooden desk in a dark corner of the room. A thick candle gave him the light he needed to look over the accounts and check how much each customer still owed for the shoes that would be delivered.

Vidal lifted his head and asked, "What is all that noise in the street?"

"I do not know," Ezra said as he walked to the door. "Men of the Calle are walking down the street. Alongside the crowd, royal soldiers are walking too."

A booming voice from the street said, "Jews of Vitoria! Jews of Vitoria! You are ordered by our royal majesties, their highnesses King Ferdinand and Queen Isabella, to gather." The man was dressed in a royal soldier's uniform with a dirty braided gold trim on his shoulders. His dusty black four-cornered beret sat on his head like an empty nest.

"Stop your work. Jews of Vitoria! Jews of Vitoria! You are ordered by King Ferdinand and Queen Isabella to gather in front of your synagogue."

Daniyyel said, "It is strange that we should be disturbed like this. I think we have to obey."

Vidal agreed.

The men did not remove their stained work aprons or remove their tools from the pockets. They joined the others in the street and walked up Calle de Judios toward the synagogue. The noise of their shoes against the cobblestones and the chatter of asking each other for explanations could have been the sounds of sheep being herded into pens.

As they approached the building, they saw Jews from all parts of Vitoria congregating in the street, including men who lived and worked in the Christian parts of the city. It was odd to be standing in front of the synagogue when the rabbi was not going to perform a service. A man stood in front of the big wooden doors dressed in a red jacket with a blue sash across his chest and a pin denoting the official insignia of the monarchs. These confirmed his status as a messenger from the royal court.

The synagogue, located between two shops in the middle of Calle de Judios, looked like any other storefront. The men who built the synagogue generations ago believed that there was no benefit in calling attention to the synagogue's location—no need to invite vandalism.

Rahav and Baruh sighted Vidal, Juhuda and the boys and walked up the sloping street. They greeted their brothers and nephews with the usual kisses on both cheeks—the same as what others were doing as more and more men joined the group. Avram pushed his cart of cloths through the crowd so he could stand with his family. Roffe Michah walked over too. They stood together, waiting nervously with others in the community. A low hum buzzed as more people arrived.

Vidal said, "For generations, the synagogue has been central to our lives. Now, for the first time, a messenger of such importance is in front of the synagogue. This cannot be good."

The rabbi emerged from inside the synagogue. He was not smiling or showing any signs of joy that the monarchs' emissary was visiting his synagogue. He had not changed to special clothes, suggesting that this was a surprise visit. He wore his basic brown tunic and a knitted kippa with its frayed brown edges and off-white Star of David in the center.

Collectively, the men standing in front of the synagogue gave a slight bow to the rabbi in reverence to his position. Daniyyel whispered to Vidal, "The rabbi looks blank, which is so unlike him. Usually he wears one of his two faces: happy for celebrations or sad for funerals and mourning days. What do you think?"

Vidal looked at his nephew but said nothing as the rabbi began to speak.

"This man is from our monarchs. He has an important message for us. Let us listen with the respect due our king and queen."

A silence came over the crowd. The messenger cleared his throat. In a loud and emphatic voice, he read from a scroll entitled "Jewish Charter of Expulsion."

"I read to you from the Alhambra Decree: 'We who rule by God's grace, Ferdinand and Isabella, rulers of Castile and Aragón, rulers of Leon and Murcia, rulers of Majorca and Sardinia, rulers of Granada and Navarra, etc: The cries of the Marranos have come up to us, upon some of whom we have decreed burning and upon others to be imprisoned forever, for they have been found wayward in our religion, while some of those who have remained free of these punishments have done so because they have repented of their ways completely.

"'Yet the hands of the inquisitors are still stretched forth to investigate the evil of their deeds, and they cried out to us bitterly that it is the Jew who to this day has been the reason for their rebellion and their forsaking of the Christian religion, by teaching them their ways, their laws, and their beliefs, as well as the laws of their feasts and festivals, and as long as Jews are to be found among them in Spain, it will be impossible for them to be complete and true Christians. We have therefore seen fit to totally banish the Jews from all places in our kingdom, even though they deserve a greater punishment than this for what they have done.'"

"How can this be?" and a wailing "Oh no!" were uttered by various members of the community. "This cannot be true" and "I do not believe this" rang out. And then the community stood in shocked silence.

"'However, we have had mercy on them, and we are content to limit ourselves to this punishment. We therefore decree and command that every male and female, young and old, who is a Jew and who lives in our kingdom is to be banished and is to leave all those places where they live and to go outside the provinces of our kingdom to another land within the coming three months, starting with 1 May and ending on the last day of July. And whoever disobeys us and does not leave will be sentenced to death by hanging or to convert to Christianity. Whoever wishes to convert and become a Christian from this day on for the coming three months may remain in his home with all his possessions, his land, and his movables, as before, and in addition will be exempt from any tax or servitude. So too will he be exempt from investigation by the inquisition for a period of ten years.

"'We also decree that all judges, officers, advisors, and leaders of the country or any official of any kind in every province and city is to look after the Jews, and any person of any rank who harms any Jew, either bodily or in his possessions through theft or robbery, whether within the city or outside it, is to be hanged immediately on a tree by the official or judge or leader of the city. In order to ensure this, we hereby decree that every official or judge in each province and each city is to place the royal seal on the home of each Jew, wherever he lives. And we decree and order every official and judge in every province and each city to send a crier in the markets and streets to announce this decree of ours, as well as in every Jewish community in every province and each city on the coming first day of May. And every official or judge or any other government employee who disobeys this order will be rebuked and punished as is seen fit.'"

Vidal gasped, "So it is true."

The rabbi's face had turned ashen white. "Had I known this was the message from the royals, I would not have been as inviting. This is an abomination."

The messenger added, "You will now go to your homes and plan for your conversion, expulsion, or death. Do not speak of this as you walk to your homes. You must leave the square in silence. If you take to violence, the monarchs will in haste send soldiers to put down any disturbances."

The rabbi looked at the ghostly faces of the men in the crowd. He then opened the synagogue door and went inside alone.

Because Vitoria was a designated city of importance and the capital of the Basque country, the royal messenger nailed the last page of the edict, the page bearing the official seal of Isabella and Ferdinand, to the door of the synagogue. Then he and his fellow soldiers left.

Vidal looked at his brothers. Their eyes were wide in disbelief. Their mouths hung open in the shock of what they had just heard. It was as if they had experienced a cosmic event.

Vidal said, "I did not believe this could actually happen."

Rahav asked, "How could these rulers do this to us? We have added to the culture, knowledge, and thinking of their kingdoms. How could they abuse us so and then give us so little time?" These questions were rhetorical and pointless.

Avram said, "These rulers are evil beasts. They burned my parents at the stake for their beliefs. Now they expel us for our beliefs. They do the work of their satanic priests. We live our lives according to their stupid laws, and these monarchs betray us anyway. They are the infidels—not us."

Juhuda turned to his brothers and asked, "What shall we do? How shall we do it?"

"We shall go home and tell our wives," Vidal said. "Our lives in Castile are finished. The monarchs do not care about the Jews, and they do not care about our families. We have contributed to the realm, but it does not matter. We are Jews, and for an intelligent people, we have been very stupid to trust these rulers. The messenger said the monarchs signed the edict on the Christian date of 31 March 1492. Why did they wait a month to tell us, giving us even less time to act?"

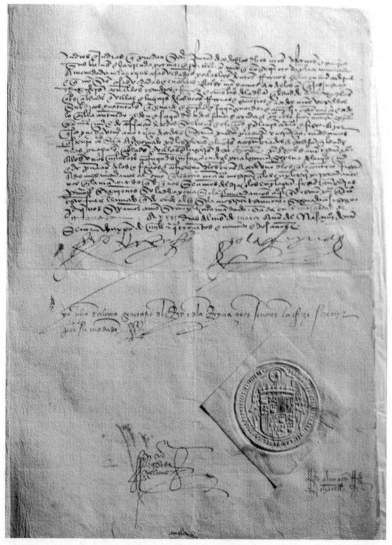

Alhambra Decree of Expulsion

"Because they are more evil than the most evil person alive," Avram said. "More immoral than the most immoral. More wicked than one could ever imagine."

"We have to move swiftly to put our work and dealings in order. We have to call a meeting of the community to plan our next steps," Vidal said. "This is what Benjamin would have done."

Roffe Michah, who had been silent to this point, said, "We have existed for more than five thousand years. We will survive this tragedy against us too, just as our ancestors survived theirs. If this is to be our exodus from Castile, then so be it. Let us fully understand what is happening and what our choices are."

Vidal turned to his brothers and said, "This move by the monarchs was inevitable. It is the logical next step after enacting the anti-Jew laws. Ten years ago, the queen banned Jews from Andalusia. Her magistrates dictated that Christian women and girls were not allowed to enter a Judería without a man. Christian women could not work for a Jew. Jews could not act as lawyers in lawsuits, and so on."

"No," said Roffe Michah. "The monarchs protected us with their *fueros*. They have placed Jews in high levels of government. This edict will be repealed. It is one more thing that will not be enforced."

Vidal responded, "I have been saying for years that we should leave Iberia, and now we are being ordered to do so not when we want but when the monarchs tell us to. I should have seen this coming and been more strong-minded. I should have convinced you to leave years ago."

Daniyyel walked over to his uncles. "Where will we go? Am I to be the next generation for Crevago shoes, or will there be no more Crevago shoes?"

Roffe Michah argued, "Vitoria has been our home for generations. The Christians of Vitoria have not disturbed us or made us abide by the anti-Jew laws. The edict will not stand."

Vidal interrupted. "Maybe I thought of myself as too much a part of Castile and not enough a Jew. Now we know. Jews are never a part of anywhere. It does not matter how accepting people may be. We must always take care of ourselves."

Vidal stepped away from his brothers and approached Duardo, a man he had known since childhood. As boys, they had studied the Torah with the rabbi; as adults, they visited with each other's families on holidays. Their wives and children were friends. Their mothers had been friends.

Duardo had fear in his face as he looked into Vidal's eyes and asked, "What is going to happen, my friend?"

Vidal looked back at Duardo and said, "No one knows what is to come."

Duardo said, "Faces that are normally calm now look distressed."

Confusion and bewilderment made the air that had been fresh and clear change to a heaviness that could be cut with a knife.

"I feel like I am in mourning," Vidal said to Duardo. "Mourning for my home, my city, and for my good life here. It is as though a loved one has suddenly died. What are the monarchs doing to our homeland?"

Duardo stood with his hands clasped in front of his belly, almost in a Christian prayer-like stance.

Without waiting for Duardo to speak, Vidal said, "This is what the king and queen want—no Jews anywhere. They are the royals, so all they had to do was write a decree on a piece of paper and we are to be gone. They did it with some strokes of a quill. They told all the ministers, nobles, and officials in the realm that the Jews are to be banished. Killing conversos was not enough. Now they say the problem is with unconverted Jews. That is all they had to do to ruin our lives forever."

Duardo said, "This is the destruction of our community and our people."

In Duardo's face, Vidal saw the reality of today's news had set in. He had a sadness that came from more than the uncertainty of his future.

"Duardo, do you feel betrayed by the monarchs to whom you have shown loyalty? What are you going to do?"

"In truth, I do not know. My wife has talked about conversion to Christianity for some time. She will probably want to stay in Vitoria, where she grew up and is the place that she knows. I want to leave, but I have no place to go and no relatives living outside of Castile. Anywhere we go, we will live the rest our lives being looked down on as people who are less than everyone else. If we convert to Christianity for safety and not for beliefs in the Christian doctrine, I will be a Marrano—a pig. I do not want that for my children. I have heard the news of what the Catholics have done to conversos. The fake so-called trials with the mocking and torture. The burnings. I do not know what my wife and I will do. I do not just feel betrayed; I feel forsaken, abandoned, and empty."

Duardo, forgetting that he was actually talking to Vidal, turned and walked away in a daze.

Vidal stood in place for a moment and then looked over to his brothers, who had begun the walk home. He walked down the street that he had walked many times before. This time, however, he felt as if this street no longer belonged to him. It never really had. Its familiarity had given him feelings of ownership. This was his community. Now he realized it was a place of false safety.

As Vidal walked slowly home, he saw Della standing in the doorway of the shop with Agamit. Della held some long greens, which she had been about to boil for the midday meal. Agamit's tunic was covered with flour, since she had stopped kneading her bread when the commotion began.

Vidal said, "We are leaving Vitoria. I do not know where we will go, but we are leaving. We should have done it a long time ago, but Benjamin was against it."

The women looked at each other.

"What are you saying?" Agamit said. "You have lost your mind and all of your thinking."

"No. There is an edict from the king and queen. It is nailed to the door of the synagogue. Take Jonah. He will read it to you."

"What are you saying, brother? That we are moving? Where? When? Just pack up? What about the business? The family? Our friends and their families? Why would we leave this place that we have lived in for generations?"

The women started crying. Their weeping evolved into sobbing and then into wailing. Crying also came from the houses of their neighbors as news of the expulsion spread.

Vidal's heart was beating fast.

"I have no answers for you. I have the same questions ... but no answers."

The happy people living on Calle de Judíos had, in a few short minutes, evolved into a panic-stricken, frightened, nervous, bewildered set of people.

Vidal went through the shop and entered the Crevago courtyard. The space was empty. No tables were set for a Shabbat or joyous festival. No children were playing. Even the flowers seemed bent over in sadness.

Vidal saw Roffe Michah and Rahav talking in a corner of the courtyard by the back gate.

"I spoke with some other members of our aljama," Roffe Michal said to Vidal. "We will meet later today and probably send riders to the aljamas in Segovia, Tudela, and Salamanca. They will speak with the leaders in these bigger cities. We will learn what Jews in other places will do. Once we know, we will make our own plans.

Vidal had no verbal response to give. The once jovial man had changed to a grim alternative self. Vidal nodded. However, he was really thinking that if Benjamin were alive, he would know what to do.

CHAPTER 14

Whoever Waits for Help from Another Person Can Keep Waiting

Mid-May 1492

In the large royal receiving room of Granada's grand Alhambra palace, Ferdinand and Isabella were holding court.

The Christian monarchs rejoiced in having this fortress as their new royal residence. It confirmed that they had obliterated the Arab presence on the Iberian Peninsula. Now they were doing the same to the Jews. The edict of expulsion had been circulated. The process of cleansing the realm was moving forward.

Ferdinand and Isabella sat on identical thrones. Richly woven red fabrics covered their large authoritarian chairs, improved with floral brocading of rose, gold, and deep green stitching. The legs of these thrones were seven-inch-tall wooden posts gilded with gold foil and decorated with various-colored gemstones that gleamed in the daylight. The back of each chair had two seven-inch-tall bronze posts with etchings of the royal seal attached at the top. The chairs stood on a three-foot-high platform made of large marble tiles. These matched the stone of the many magnificently sculpted columns that created a square entry to the space where the monarchs sat.

Previously on the site where the Alhambra was now located, there was a small Roman fortification. In 899 CE, the Arabs built a fortress over the ruins, and in 1333, Yusuf I, sultan of Granada, added hundreds of rooms and converted the fortress into a royal palace. Arab stonemasons had installed on the floors, walls, and ceilings large colorful handmade tiles with Islamic designs.

Ferdinand leaned over to Isabella and said, "We are the victors. We now enjoy these beautiful decorations and remember that the heretics who made them are either dead or Christians."

The monarchs' dress was everyday, yet it looked glorious to a person not familiar with the levels of grandeur that these royals thought commonplace. Isabella wore a circular crown of gold metalwork that included ornate filigree swirls topped with twelve prongs shaped into delicate arrows. Her crown sat atop her long, slightly curly light brown hair, which flowed like a cape over her shoulders and down to her elbows. Her yellow velveteen dress with royal insignia of satin woven into the fabric had a square-cut neckline trimmed in brown satin and fit snugly to emphasize her bosom and décolleté. The cuffs of her long sleeves were trimmed with tawny spotted fur from the Iberian lynx, a slant-eyed animal known for skillfully stalking and catching its prey.

Ferdinand's clothes paled in comparison to Isabella's. His black pants were simple except for the yellow braided edging on the cuffs that fell just below his knees. His black sateen jacket had no decoration at all. However, Ferdinand wore around his neck a heavy gold chain necklace that fell to the middle of his chest. A three-inch round medallion enameled with the crest of Aragón hung on the chain. His rough-shaven face gave the appearance of a man trying to grow a beard who had been unsuccessful in the task.

Standing in front of the monarchs were two important Jewish leaders of Spain: Don Isaac Abravanel and Rabbi Abraham Seneor. Also standing with these men were a dozen representatives from the most esteemed aljamas in Castile, Aragón, and León. They looked up at their monarchs and at the formidable minions hovering behind the royal thrones. Each advisor was dressed in his official garb of blue and black suiting, and each wore a colored sash denoting his appointment. There was the minister of the military. He wore his military honors with ribbons and medals hanging like ornaments around his neck. He stood in the most prominent place at the right of Ferdinand. The minister of farmlands stood to the left of Isabella. He wore a group of animal pins, which held his green sash in place. Others included the chief of the household as well as the attendants for culture, cities, and castles.

Isabella's ladies in waiting were off to one side, and Ferdinand's masters of the household guards stood on the other side.

Don Abravanel had served Ferdinand and Isabella as minister of finance, but his appointment had been terminated by the edict of expulsion. Rabbi Seneor was a personal friend of Isabella. He had arranged her betrothal to Ferdinand. She had appointed him chief rabbi of Castile and endowed him with a lifetime pension of one hundred thousand *maravedíes*.

"My royal monarchs," Don Abravanel began, "We thank you for giving us this opportunity. We have traveled to speak with you in an effort to preserve and give safe lives to the Jews in your realm. We believe that you, our king and queen of Castile and Aragón, have intentions for a legacy that can be perfected without exiling people who only seek to live in peace and tranquility within your kingdom."

"Our people are startled by your edict—your decree against the Jews. We, as your advisers, have been wrapped blithely in our security, believing in you and being your devoted servants. We have not felt the waves of hatred that others in our communities have felt. We have not been affected by the talk of pure Spanish blood. We did not live in the small houses of the Juderías. We have not felt the fury of the Inquisition. We have not lived with restrictions. We did not wear identifying clothes. Our loyalty to you, our monarchs, is solid and forever. The Jews in your kingdom are loyal to you. I ask that you save us. Do not exile your devoted advisors, counselors, and subjects."

Ferdinand sat in his throne, looking away from men who had served him with guidance and in dedicated deed and action. He was pretending to contemplate the pleas of these honorable men and the people they represented, but all the while he was determining whether allowing Jews to remain in the kingdom was a better financial decision than forcing them to leave.

Rabbi Seneor took over the plea. "We wish to again show you our loyalty. We ask that you stay the Alhambra Decree, this edict of expulsion, and in our extreme appreciation, we will increase your coffers by twenty thousand gold pieces, thirty thousand silver, and as many maravedíes as we can collect. We know that your treasury is low, and we, as your servants, want to help you."

Don Abravanel wanted to yell out his distress, his feelings of betrayal by these people whom he had served faithfully. Instead he just watched as the royals became increasingly bored with the talk of reversing the edict of expulsion. He had seen this look when going over obscure financial dealings.

"My royal king and queen, please consider our offer so that we can remain your loyal subjects."

Isabella stood up. She spoke softly. "God is guiding us. God is telling us to do this. I say to you in the words of Proverbs, 'The king's heart is in the hand of the Lord, as the rivers of water, he turneth it whithersoever he will.' We did not issue this order. It is God who has issued this order."

Ferdinand spoke. "You have offered us a large enticement to induce us to reconsider. Let us think on this. It is possible that we will change our minds and take your offer."

The Jews left the throne room with thoughts of a possible reversal or at least a postponement of the edict of expulsion. They were hopeful.

As soon as the Jews were out of earshot, Father Torquemada stepped out from behind the crowd of ministers and attendants. His face was red with anger.

"Here is our crucifix. Our savior is nailed to the cross." He pushed the symbol toward the monarchs and threw pieces of silver on the floor in front of their thrones. "Judas is again present in our midst. The enemies of Jesus Christ paid Judas thirty pieces of silver. Are we again to be paid by our enemies? I put this crucifix before you as protection against these purveyors of evil. It is God's will that we live in a Spain cleansed from heretics. We must be purified if we are to be ready for the Second Coming."

CHAPTER 15

There Is No Smoke without Fire

June 1492

The riders returned to Vitoria late Friday evening. The moon, which had appeared at sunset, was already high in the sky. Families had eaten their Shabbat meal, and most had gone to bed.

Normally, Ismael Moratan, Moises Yuda, and Lazar Matzor would never have ridden on Shabbat, but each wanted to arrive from his journey as soon as possible to deliver their news to the community. Ismael was coming from Salamanca, Moises from Segovia, and Lazar from Tudela. Vitoria's Jewish community had sent these men to learn how the other cities were dealing with the edict of expulsion.

The next day, Vidal and his brothers, sons, and nephews sat amid their family and friends in the synagogue for Shabbat services. Men saying ancient prayers of the Hebrew people filled the rows of benches. Vidal also said prayers for the future of the Crevago family, but with little enthusiasm. His faith in God had been shattered. He feared what news the riders might bring.

The sanctuary warmed up as the morning service wore on and as learned men read the Torah portion for the day.

Vidal thought about his final abbreviated trip through Castile. He had delivered the last sets of shoes and collected the money owed.

The men he had sold to for years were either warm and sympathetic, or cold and aloof.

In Palencia, José Perez would not let Vidal into his shop. Vidal had to do business from the street. "I am hurt by your rejection," Vidal told José. "I have known you for years, and we always were cordial with each other." José did not respond.

In Olmeda, Franco Felipo ushered Vidal into his shop and hugged him.

"This banishment is so unfair and unnatural. You are my friend for always." Vidal could only say, "Thank you," for Franco's heartfelt expression of camaraderie.

In Torrelavega, Berkio and his wife honored Vidal by inviting him into their home for a midday meal. "No one makes shoes like you Crevagos," Berkio said. "Maybe the monarchs will see that they should leave the Jews alone."

The rabbi finished the service and called Ismael, Moises, and Lazar to the *tevah*. The men rose from their seats. Ismael walked slightly bent over as he dragged his feet through the room. The others followed him as he stepped up to the square platform situated in the middle of the sanctuary. Each man kissed the rabbi's hand, and the rabbi muttered a blessing in return. This custom reflected respect for a learned man of Torah and for the Torah itself. By kissing the rabbi's hand these men showed the congregation that even in the worst of times, we should respect the Torah and its representative.

When Don Ismael turned toward the community, Vidal could see that Ismael's face had aged. He had more lines around his eyes and on his forehead. His beard looked unkempt and grayer than it did a few weeks ago. Moises and Lazar looked no better. They needed sleep and to be free from the pressure that comes with leading a community.

Ismael took a wide stance on the platform. He needed to steady himself as he gave his report to the congregation.

"I and aljama members Moises and Lazar returned last night

from each of our destinations. Here is what has occurred since the messenger read the edict of banishment.

"In the time since we left Vitoria, leaders of important congregations on the Iberian Peninsula had an audience with our monarchs. They sought a way for us to stay in our homes. The first of these was Don Isaac Abravanel, the esteemed advisor to King Ferdinand and Queen Isabella, who has been a member of the royal court almost from the beginning of his time in Castile, after his exile from Portugal. The second was the esteemed and famed rabbi of Segovia, Don Abraham Seneor. You may remember when Don Abraham came to speak to our congregation and did a special Torah teaching about the importance of being honest with yourself. Other Jewish community leaders also attended the meeting, including Don Abraham's son-in-law, the famous well-spoken rabbi Meir Melamed. He has served as King Ferdinand's secretary and has been very close to our monarch. Also included in the royal hearing were other Jews of wealth and learning. Offers of high payments to the royals were made, and for a time, there was hope that an agreement for a stay of the edict could be reached. However, after waiting for confirmation, word came from the queen. Her message was straightforward: 'The Jews will be expelled.'"

Vidal leaned forward and turned his head to look at his relatives. "Once more the Jews have been betrayed."

Roffe Michah put his hand up to his lips. "Stop talking. Let us hear the whole ugly thing."

Ismael continued. "With that, the delegation to the royal court knew all was lost. They returned to their home cities and in each location told the Jewish communities the same thing. We, the representatives from aljamas, must make ready for the exodus. I bring you this sad news and more. Rabbi Don Abraham Seneor; his son-in-law, Rabbi Meir; and all his family have converted to Christianity. They will serve the monarchs in various special positions designed to oversee the conversion of Jews who wish to remain in Spain."

Ismael gave a huge sigh. "I close by saying that it is time for the

Jews of Vitoria to decide what we will do and how we will do it. We will reconvene tomorrow to discuss our choices."

The riders left the podium.

The men of the congregation started talking to each other once again, creating a hum within the sanctuary.

Avram said, "I am relieved. At least we know for sure this is now an evil place for us. I do not want to live here with my new family."

"Where will you go?" Vidal asked.

"I do not know. First I must go home and tell Rina."

"Tio," Daniyyel said, "I was looking forward to expanding to more cities where we could sell our Crevago shoes. My plan was for Jonah to join you on your trips to the various cities and for you to teach others to go out and meet more people who could introduce Crevago shoes to more highborn in their cities. Our shoes are the most beautiful. Many people would love to wear our elegant footwear. I was about to take two more apprentices so we could increase the number of shoes we could make. I have new designs, and Avram is creating new fabric coverings for me. My plans are now worthless, just like our lives in Vitoria." His voice intoned his anger. "I hate Isabel and Ferdinand."

"My dear nephew," Roffe Michah said, "We cannot change what is to be. Let us go tell our wives and children. We will need to console them as we rip them from all that they have known for their entire lives."

The Crevago men walked on the Calle along with their neighbors, but there was only hushed talking. The soles from their leather shoes scuffed the cobblestones. Each man was stunned at the finality of the news.

The Crevagos walked into the cobbler shop so they could go to the courtyard where they typically ate Shabbat lunch. The shop was barren. No shoes were waiting to be worked on. No hides were waiting to be dyed and cut. The shop had been swept, so no scraps were askew on the floor.

Jonah said, "The cleanliness is odd. The shop has an unnatural feel to it. It seems to be dying a slow death."

Rina was sitting in the kitchen as the men walked through. The brothers greeted their sister with kisses.

Avram said, "Rina and I will talk now."

"Yes, I am going to see Della," Vidal said.

Avram prepared himself so he could comfort Rina. He tore a piece of bread from the loaf on the table and ate it. He walked a few steps to the hearth and looked into the pot that was sitting on the side of the fire. Then he drank a cup of wine.

Rina said. "Avram, stop pacing and talk to me."

"We must leave Vitoria. There is no hope to stay."

Rina said to Avram, "You have seen all the sadness that anyone should ever have to live through. Soon we will have our own child. Let us go where we can live happily in peace and without fear of persecution. You are a kindhearted soul, and you deserve a calm and tranquil life without upheaval. When do we go?"

Avram's eyes widened. "I thought you would be very upset and start crying."

"The women have talked. We did not know where we might go, but we knew we would be going. We will be together, and that is all that is important to us. We are prepared to go wherever it is safe for our children and for the family."

Each Crevago husband told his wife the news.

Upon learning that the edict of banishment would stand, each woman reacted in her own character and personality.

Agamit said, "Ferdinand and Isabella should end up in their own hell. And may they go there fast. If I could do it, I would kill them both. They do not deserve to live. I will pack up, and you will tell me where we are going. I will be ready."

Della said, "The monarchs want the wealth of the Jewish communities. These rulers are interested only in money and more money—not in the welfare of their subjects. I do not want to stay where I am not wanted. Just tell me what you are planning. I will be sure that our children and their children come with us."

These stoic women were like most others in the community. Once they heard the outcome, they were resigned to leaving. They had no alternative but to leave and go wherever their husbands wanted.

"Let us go immediately," Della told Vidal.

"No. We will wait to see what the aljama says, and then I will listen to what my brothers say. A few more days will not matter."

Vidal was correct to wait. Within a day, the aljama called for another community meeting.

The brothers walked up Calle de Judios to the synagogue in rank order of their ages: Vidal, Roffe Michah, Juhuda, and Baruh. Rahav and Avram walked behind them. Daniyyel, Jonah, and Ezra and other cousins followed.

As they walked, Roffe Michah said, "When I was tending to Argi Barker's wife, Argi suggested that we stay in the Basque country. He has a cousin who lives outside Baiona, which is in France on the other side of the Pirineos [Pyrenees]. This is something to consider. I know that some in the community are going to Holland, and this is a good choice too. Some are going south to where the Muslims live. These are the choices."

"Maybe we should go to Portugal," Baruh said.

"I like the idea of Holland," Vidal said. "I suggested Holland to Benjamin years ago, but he was not willing to leave Vitoria. What a mistake that was." Vidal's only comfort in this entire situation was that he had been right and Benjamin had been wrong. On this subject, the younger brother knew more than the older one.

Because it was late afternoon, the men created long shadows of themselves that were eerie and ghoulish like the circumstances they were facing.

The Crevagos approached the venerated building. It was a huge part of their lives and the lives of their families. So many occasions and events had occurred within its walls: services, celebrations, holidays, memorials, the education of their children, weddings, boys coming of age with their Bar Mitzvas, minyans, Torah readings, Talmud study, and talks with the rabbi. Their lives were integrated with this structure.

"I do not know what they will say, but whatever it is, I am ready to listen," Rahav said.

"What do you think they will say?" In his nervousness during the last days, Daniyyel had asked this question of his uncles many times. It was rhetorical. Daniyyel did not expect, nor did he receive, an answer.

The Crevagos walked in and saw about eighty men inside. Murmuring filled the sanctuary. People were asking the same question that Daniyyel had posed. Voices were not loud, but they were heated.

The leaders of Vitoria's aljama sat at a table in the front of the sanctuary: Ismael Moratan, Moises Balid, Samuel Benjamin Gaon, Abiatar and Jacob Tello, and Samuel de Mijaneas. Roffe Michah took his place in the last empty seat. Vitoria had the largest aljama in northern Castile. Each man had also served as head leader of the synagogue.

The rabbi stood on the platform in front of the ark, in virtually the same place where Father Ferrer had stood years ago when he spoke to the congregation and urged the Jews of Vitoria to convert to Christianity.

The rabbi said, "We stand here in the face of adversity, as our forefathers stood in Jerusalem before the destruction of the second temple. We pray to Adonay, the God of our fathers, for the strength that he has always shown the Children of Israel. We pray for ourselves and for any in our community who have chosen or will choose to leave us. A person may call himself a Christian, but in the heart of hearts, in the world of our God, the Lord will always recognize you as a Jew because you were forced to make this choice to survive the evils set before you."

The rabbi read a list of about twenty names. "These families have decided to convert to Christianity. Not willingly. Not with desire. But with fear and duress. For the safety of their wives and children. With the belief that their families and their economic and social lives will be sustained in the city they have known."

Murmuring became background music.

Duardo's name was on the list, along with other men Vidal and his brothers had grown up with, studied the Torah with, and socialized with. Vidal felt a loss. It was as if death had taken his childhood friends. The grief was obvious.

Vidal put his hand to his forehead to prevent his brothers from seeing the tears in his eyes. He said, "I am not stunned about Duardo and the others. It is much easier to be a Christian than a Jew. We have to work at it and really want it. People will escape to Christianity. It is the easy way out… as long as they are not burned at the stake."

However, Vidal had no time to grieve for these lost members of the Hebrew tribes.

Ismael Moratan began speaking. "I sadly reconfirm the edict of expulsion. The monarchs refused to rescind it. The edict is now the law of the land. We all must leave. The Jewish community of Vitoria, all two thousand and more persons, must move to locations outside the realm of Ferdinand and Isabella."

Another murmur rose from the group.

Ismael said, "I call on Physician Roffe Michah Crevago to speak. Roffe Michah stood up.

"We have been safe here. The Vitoria City Council has not caused disruption to our lives. For the past ten years, we have seen the various enactments by the provincial government that described rules of how we should live our lives. It was decreed that Christians and Jews must live with no commerce or social interaction. That did not happen in Vitoria. The Christian City Council never enforced this law. There might have been a few instances where a conversation between a Christian and a Jew was disrupted, but that was more for show. Maybe a court magistrate from Zaragosa or Madrid was visiting, or the archbishop from Toledo had come to visit one of the local churches."

Roffe Michah looked around the room as he spoke, gazing into the faces of his friends and neighbors. He had tended to the illnesses, the wounds, and the broken bones of many of those now sitting in the sanctuary. They looked at him with respect for his wisdom and kindness.

"Remember: it was decreed that no Christian could light a fire on Shabbat for a Jew, but Christians have come into our homes and lit fires for us and cooked for us on Shabbat and on the High Holy Days. No violence or penalties came to them or to us. Christians were not supposed to work or live with us, but some of the Christian families of our apprentices are poor, and we took these boys in as an act of *tzedakah* and kindness to our Christian neighbors. No repercussions occurred from these acts. Christians were prohibited from selling us fruits and vegetables on Calle de Judiós, so instead they sold us goods at the entrances to our street. No harm came to them or us. The Christians of Vitoria do not feel about us in an evil way—in the way of Christians in other towns and cities of Castile. We have been sheltered here because the Basque are good people and we have befriended them. Our ancestors chose well to live in Vitoria. We can choose well and go to France where Basque people live. We are a strong Jewish community because we act as one. We are not fragmented like the Jews in other towns. We are unified."

Vidal saw the men in the room nodding. He was proud of his brother and his ability to speak plainly and passionately.

Samuel spoke. "We know some families may go south to the lower continent to live peaceably among the Islamic peoples. Others will make their way to the holy city of Jerusalem. Still others will go to Holland, where we hear there is religious freedom. A few will go to live in the Anglo-English country. We believe these are reasonable choices. For those of you who have not yet decided, we have another choice. We are not like the Jews in the south who lived with Muslims. We do not know anything about them except for the occasional merchant who came to Vitoria to sell wares and spices to us. We do not know about England except that some of our families came from there many generations ago when the king expelled Jews from that country. We also thought about Portugal, but we have reports that Jews there are in danger. Holland may be a good choice, but who knows if the people be hospitable to us? Will we be a disruption to the Jews who already live there and are established? We do not know. Roffe Michah has suggested the Basque country of France."

Ismael uttered the final words of the meeting. "The aljama will take one day to consider recommendations and our next steps."

The congregation was anxious to disperse. Each man who had not yet determined his future had to go home to talk to his wife and family about the destination choices.

>-++>-O-<+-+-<

The next day the men of the community reconvened in the synagogue. Samuel stood up and said, "The aljama believes the best choice for our families is to stay in the Basque country. We are accustomed to living with the Basques: the sheepherders, the farmers who work the land, and the craftsmen. We understand them, and they understand us. The Basques are outsiders, as we are. They are Christian, but they are not zealots. They are willing to compromise about anything except their families and preserving their distinctive heritage and culture. We have lived well with the Basques. Now I ask Physician Roffe Michah Crevago to speak."

Roffe Michah stood up.

"Argi Bakar, a shoemaker from Calle Zapatería, told me he has relations beyond the Vascos Mountains and across the Pirineos, just inside France. This good man offers to give us letters to introduce us to his cousins in Baiona. We should consider this opportunity. We could not live inside the city of Baiona. Jews are not allowed.

However, Argi has visited his relations in Baiona, and there is land outside the city where the Nive and Adour rivers meet. Argi believes we could build our homes there and live unmolested. It may be a good idea for us to go east to live with the Basques of France."

A voice from the audience piped in. "The French hate us too. The Jews were banished from France."

"True," said Roffe Michah, "but we have to make haste in our leaving and the French in the east are accepting of us. We believe the French monarch Charles from the House of Valois has allowed Jews to live in France without too much resistance or harassment. For right now, this is a good choice, since we must leave Spain very soon. However, we will not go deep into France but just across the border. This is in the event that Ferdinand and Isabella come to their senses, see their error, abolish the edict, and allow us to return. Our people have provided Spain with learning, culture, education, and service. Once the Spanish monarchs feel the loss of our taxes, they will invite us to return. But for now, we have little time and must leave before the end of July."

"Our deadline is the ninth of Av," Ismael said. "The same date as when the second temple in Jerusalem was destroyed. We mourn that event that our ancestors lived through just as we mourn our banishment. Spain will regret its mistreatment of the Jews. Isabella, that cruel and merciless woman, will come to regret her stone-heartedness toward the Jews. She and Ferdinand will live in disgrace for this act; they have been so misguided, so narrow, so hateful. Their names will be cast off from Spain. They will become, in the history of the Jews, the embodiment of immoral monarchs to be loathed, like Pharaoh. Plagues will befall them. Sadness will be theirs. This country will suffer without the intelligence and wit of Jewish scholars—the learned men of science, literature, law, finance, and medicine. The country needs the Jews because we are a serious and thoughtful people. The towns and cities need us for our humble shoemakers, blacksmiths, carpenters, tailors, silversmiths, jewelers, barbers, leatherworkers, woodworkers, builders, and other artisans. We have been faithful residents to this kingdom. Our families added to the color of the country. The monarchs want sameness and uniformity. They will have it now, and they will suffer for it."

Roffe Michah stood back up and said, "We cannot live in our anger and resentment. We must keep our trust in God no matter what happens and believe God has a plan for us. We must think about the present that is upon us. We must appreciate the Christians of Vitoria who are concerned about our future well-being. We will respond in kind. Physician Tornay will stay in Vitoria for a short time to care for the ill until a Christian physician can be brought to the city. The city councilors have sought protection for him from the crown. He will be safe … for a time."

Ismael smiled. He embraced Roffe Michal. "This is a good thing to do. We shall leave Vitoria in good stead, with the same respect with which we lived here. We will clean our houses before we leave. We will clean our mierda pots. We will put our property in readiness for the next occupants. We will make our ancestors proud as we exit our homes of these many generations."

The crowd clapped.

"Here is the rest of our plan," Ismael said. "We will talk with the leaders of the city council. Aljama member will go to the Town Council and tell the councilors that we speak on behalf of the Jewish community of Vitoria. Because some of us were the tax collectors in Vitoria, we know these counselors well."

Vidal stood up and asked, "What is your purpose? What will you speak of?"

Moises said, "We can ask them to let us stay. They have protected us in the past."

A mix of positive and negative responses went up from the group.

Vidal said. "The crowns are telling us we must leave or convert, and the Christians must enforce this. As convivial as the Christians of Vitoria might be, they cannot override the edict. It is much more significant than any in the past. This is not enforcement of specific rules. This edict is not a censure of Jews who have not conformed to rules. This is a denunciation, a rejection, and an elimination of all Jews in Castile, León, Aragón, and Granada. This edict will be easy for soldiers to enforce. It does not rely on testimony that a Jew has infringed on a Christian or that a Jew has erred in behavior in some way. The soldiers will search every home, every cave in the hillside, and every shelter in the forest. They will find those who tried to circumvent the edict. By staying, we put our own lives in danger, as well as the lives of our Christian neighbors."

Baruh offered, "After a short time, the royals will see how the kingdom has failed without us. We can ask the Christians in Vitoria to preserve our homes until we return."

Again, the crowd uttered a mix of groans versus shouts of support. Others offered points of view.

"Once we leave and settle elsewhere, why would we return? Our homes will have been taken over by Christians. Even if the Christians promise to save our homes for us in the event of our return, how do we know what the Christians will do once they are comfortable in our homes? Can we trust them?"

"Our homes are precious to us, but once we leave, squatters will come to our vacant houses and claim them for their own. Someone will take possession of our land or will rent it out for their own profit."

"Can we sell our homes to Christians who want them?"

The response was quick in coming. "Jews do not have the right to sell land, and Christians are prohibited from buying land from Jews."

"What will happen to our ancestors who are buried here? Will Christians desecrate their graves?"

Moises said, "Not the Christians that live in Vitoria. They know that our cemetery is sacred to us."

Vidal said, "But what about their children and their children's children, who will not remember us and will not know the good that we did in Vitoria? They will not know that during the great illness, our physicians saved the lives of their parents, grandparents, and great-grandparents. They will not know that they owe their lives to the Jews who once lived in Vitoria."

"What is important to us?" Ismael asked.

Members of the community gave other suggestions: our synagogue, our street, our fields....

Roffe Michah stood and said, "Since we are banished from the kingdom and we are living with uncertainty of our future, the most important thing must be that we must ask for the preservation of the generations that came before us—those who lay in their eternal resting places."

Daniyyel jumped to his feet. His eyebrows rose, and his face reddened with anger. "Why would the Christians of Vitoria do this? What is their incentive to do this for the Jews?"

A short silence ensued. Then Moises Balid offered a simple solution. "We will pay them."

Collective sighs of "Ah" were released in unison.

Daniyyel said, "The Jews always pay, and we pay more. Everything has always been made more difficult and more expensive for us."

"What are our choices?" asked Vidal. Then he answered his own question. "We only can choose how to leave and where to go."

It was agreed. A delegation from Vitoria's aljama would go to the city councilors and ask for preservation of the cemetery.

Vidal looked at the men leading the discussion and said, "What will you say? How will you ask? Will it be with bent heads lowered in shame? How do you know they can or will do anything for the Jewish community of Vitoria? They will take our property after we leave and use it for their own purposes."

Daniyyel was also skeptical. "Do you really think the Christians will care for the Jewish cemetery? What do the Christians care about those who built the Jewish community in Vitoria?"

The community discussion continued until the men seated at the table made the final decision.

The Jews would ask that the cemetery be preserved. In payment, the Jews would give the city the synagogue building for their use. If *maravadies* were required by the Christians, the community would pay.

CHAPTER 16

A Good Neighbor Is Better Than Relatives

Late June 1492

On Wednesday, June 27, the representatives of the Jewish community of Vitoria Ismael Moratan, Moises Balid, Samuel Benjamin Chacon, Abiatar Tello, Yuda Farral, Joséph Farral, Samuel de Mijaneas, and Roffe Michah Crevago walked slowly through the streets of Vitoria. The morning air was full of fog and chill—unusual for late June.

Ismael had sent a messenger to City Councilor Juan Martinez de Olabe, leader of Vitoria's city councilors, requesting a meeting. Word came back swiftly: "We will meet with you."

The men of the aljama walked in silence toward the castle of Vitoria, the Church of Santa Maria, which also served as the city hall. Roffe thought about the life he had lived in Vitoria. This is where he was born, where he had had his Bar Mitzva and had entered the Jewish community as a man, and had married and seen his children born and grow up and have their own children. It was where his parents had died and where his ancestors were buried.

The Jews walked into the alcove of the cathedral. Roffe Michah looked up at the structure's awe-inspiring high ceiling and arches. "I think God is holding this structure up. Their God, not ours."

Because city meetings were held in the church, these men had rarely ventured into the city chamber. The Jews preferred to be invisible and left city operations to Christians. The exceptions were those who collected taxes for the royal government.

The group walked into the sanctuary. "Overwhelming," Ismael said as his words echoed against the stone walls. His fellow aljama members nodded in agreement. The architecture, combined with the statues of the Virgin Mary, Jesus, and the many crucifixes, mesmerized the men.

"How can anyone pray in here?" Ismael asked his friends. "The statues are so distracting." He was used to praying in a simple unadorned room in isolation, with a prayer shawl covering his head and with his eyes closed as he swayed from side to side while reciting the liturgy, establishing *kavvanah*, the feeling of oneness with God.

A boy met the men as they walked through the building. He ushered them down a long, winding brick hallway to a room on the right. Inside were the Catholics who sat on the City Council of Vitoria: Juan Martinez de Olabe, a landowner; Andres Martinez de Herendio, a shopkeeper; Pero Gonzales de Junguitu, a provisions dealer; Juan de San Juan, a tailor; and Basegilero Pedro Galarreta, a carpenter. The families of these Basque men had lived in Vitoria for more generations than Jewish families had.

"Come in," Andres Martinez de Herendio said. He gave a half bow as the Jewish group entered into the room. He was a diminutive man with long hair pulled back into a braid that fell down his back. Usually he had a booming voice, but he welcomed the Jews in somber tones. "I am sorry that we are meeting under these dire circumstances that have been presented by our monarchs. Tell us what you have to say at this difficult time for you and your families." He did not offer any niceties or casual conversation. Time was of the essence, and Andres knew it.

The Christians seated themselves on a long bench behind a rectangular table. The Jews stood in front of the table in an uneven line.

With his head purposely held high, Ismael began. "We, the

Jewish community of Vitoria, in advance of our departure from this city wish to thank the Christian leaders of Vitoria for the general regard they have shown the Jews of this city."

Ismael stretched his body tautly so it appeared as if he were becoming taller as he spoke. "Thank you for giving us a quick response to our request for a meeting. We appreciate the kindness and goodwill we have had from the Christians in our city. It is with the support and endorsement of our community, in recognition of the friendly treatment we have received from the people of Vitoria, that we wish two things. First, we wish to give our synagogue building with all its furnishings and possessions to the City of Vitoria. We hope you will use well this structure, which has been so central to our lives, for learning and for good purpose; that it will not fall into collapse or disrepair."

The Christians looked at each other with eyes widened, but none commented on the Jew's words.

"Second, since we do not know when we might return—and we think we might in some years when the edict of expulsion is rescinded—we present to you our cemetery just outside the walls of the city, with all its fields. This land holds the hallowed graves of our ancestors, which we have prayed over and tended to for all these generations. We ask that in exchange for these gifts that the city council will not let this hallowed ground be plowed or put to cultivation. We ask that you not do anything that would defile our ancestors or our history in Vitoria."

Roffe Michah added, "We recently celebrated the holiday commemorating the exodus of our people of Israel from Egypt. We have the requirement to tell this story to our children so they can remember it from generation to generation. We ask that this request to preserve our cemetery be told to your children and your children's children and so on."

The Christians of the city council, staying seated on their bench, huddled in discussion behind their official table.

After a few minutes, Juan Martinez de Olabe rose from his seat in the center of the table. He tottered a bit as he looked straight at Ismael, Roffe Michah, and the others. Speaking slowly and with intention, he said, "The councilors of the City Council of Vitoria, on this day in the year 1492, accept the gift of your synagogue building. And we accept the gift of your cemetery. We accept these from the aljama and the Jewish community of Vitoria. We thank you for the kindnesses and the service that your community has shown to the Christians of Vitoria."

The other Christians stood up. The one on the end walked to an ornately carved cabinet standing against the wall. He opened the cabinet and took out a large Bible the church had acquired from a traveler who had purchased it in France. It had been ornately written by the monks of a cathedral there.

Walking back to the table, he gave the book to Juan Martinez. All the Christians put their right hand on the Bible.

Don Martinez de Olabe said, "On behalf of the Vitoria City Council and all the Councils yet to come, we swear on our Holy Bible that the Jews' cemetery holding the people from whom you are descended, who lie on the *Judizmendi*, the Jews' Mount, will be cared for. We swear we will never wound this land. The land will never be tilled and will never be furrowed or defiled with cultivations. This is an oath that we swear and will keep in honor of the Jews who saved many lives when the great illnesses came to Vitoria, when our own Christian doctors fled to the forests in fear and your physicians and the people in your community worked to save so many from death. We are in your debt. Our children are in your debt. Their children and those who follow are owing to the Jews of Vitoria. It will be our privilege to tend to your cemetery and to tell this oath to our children, their children, and to all of the children's children who follow. We will write a document and meet with you tonight to sign it in your presence."

After exchanges of gratitude, the Jews left the church. They walked in silence and with swift steps to the synagogue, where the men of the community were waiting for a report on the outcome of the meeting.

"Here they are," Vidal said as soon as he saw Roffe Michah enter as the first man in the door.

Daniyyel asked Rahav, "What do you think the outcome will be? Do you think the Christians will agree to what was wanted by the aljama?"

"We will know soon enough," Rahav said.

The men in the synagogue waited for someone from the aljama to begin talking.

"It is done," Samuel said. "They willingly took an oath to preserve the cemetery."

Roffe Michah followed with, "They will sign an agreement tonight."

The room exploded with applause, but it lasted for only a few seconds. Vidal said, "You accomplished what you set out to do, but I do not have joy in this. It is part of the final acts that we must do before we leave our homes."

Rahav said, "I congratulate the group for this success. We should be happy that at least this part of our end here is done. We should be glad that our Christian neighbors are willing to watch over our ancestors."

Vidal uttered sadly under his breath, "We shall see."

>─┼─◀▶─◯─◀▶─┼─◅

On the evening of June 27, 1492, two copies of the agreement to preserve the Jewish cemetery were signed by the Christians and Jews. One copy belonged to the Christians. The other copy belonged to the Jews.

Juan Martinez de Olabe read the pledge.

"In consideration of the good and neighborly treatment we have received in Vitoria, the Jewish community of Vitoria presents an irrevocable gift of the field and cemetery of the said Jewry, called the Judizmendi, with all its appurtenances, entrances, and outgoings; that from now and forever hereafter, it may remain for a pasture and public common of the city of Vitoria. An oath has been taken by the city of Vitoria that this land will never be broken up or ploughed but will remain for the public benefit of Vitoria."

"Thank you," Ismael said.

Andres Martinez de Heredio, Pedro Gonsalez de Tungiter, Juan de San Juan, and Pedro Galaretta witnessed the signing.

"We are done," Ismael said, shaking the hand of each Christian man. Before this event, rarely, if ever, had he touched a Christian.

All that was left was the leaving.

CHAPTER 17

Going Down Is Easy; Coming Up Is Hard

Early July 1492

As the Jewish community of Vitoria slowly began to disperse, people went to the cemetery to say good-bye to their loved ones. Old trees shaded much of the area, which gave the cemetery a feeling of protection from the elements. Where the sun shone, wildflowers had grown, offering sprays of color on the otherwise gray ground. Many graves had piles of stones on them, showing that visitors had been there.

On the Tuesday before they left for France, the Crevago family visited the cemetery.

Vidal walked down the middle rows of graves with his brothers, sons and nephews.

"It is a solemn moment," Vidal said. "We are the descendants of Erini and Rebeca Crevago. They settled here in the early twelve hundreds, and we leave at the end of the fourteen hundreds. Almost three centuries."

"And all because we are Jews," Daniyyel said.

"Stop complaining," Roffe Michah said. "Being Jewish has kept us strong for more than five thousand years. Do you realize how long that is?

Daniyyel took a deep breath as if to inhale this information.

"We will stay with our beliefs and survive elsewhere. That is all. I am not happy about having to leave, but being Jewish gives me the strength to know that I can survive anywhere. My ancestors did, and we will too, and so will our children and our children's children."

"Easy to say," Daniyyel replied as he splintered off from the group to go to the graves of relatives buried at the edge of the cemetery.

Following the men, the women walked slowly, holding some of the small children in their arms and leading others by the hand. As the women walked, they whispered to the children the name of each person who lay in a grave. Rina, whose belly was huge with the baby, stopped at the graves of Benjamin and Marcela.

"I cannot bear to leave you," Rina said softly. She could not bend down to put a stone on each grave. Avram, who had been watching her as he stood with the men, walked over to her. Typically a man would keep his distance from women in public—even his wife. However, Avram was less interested in these customs and more interested in helping his wife during this sad time.

"I will put the stones for you. When I first came to Vitoria, your mother was kind to me. She would give me sweet cakes that I would take to my brothers and sisters. I know you miss her, as I miss my parents."

"Thank you, dearest. We have many relatives, but you and I are orphans. You have never been able to reap comfort from visiting the graves of your parents. And now I will be without graves to comfort me."

"We will take comfort from each other," Avram said.

"And from the strength of the family," Rina added as she wiped her tears away.

Agamit walked over to Rina. "Be strong," Agamit said. "Are you feeling near your time?"

"The baby is big and moving around, but nothing more yet."

Agamit grimaced. She looked at the graves of her brother Benjamin and sister-in-law Marcela. "Life goes on," she said. She put a stone on each and said,

"Oh God, full of compassion, who dwells on high, grant perfect rest beneath the sheltering wings of your divine presence among the holy and pure who shine with brightness, unto my brother and sister, Benjamin and Marcela, who have gone into their eternal home. God of mercy, bring them under the shelter of your wings and let their souls be bound up in the bond of eternal life. May you be their inheritance, and may their repose be in peace."

Rina looked at her aunt's bloodshot eyes. "A new baby," Rina said. "We have a new beginning. What can we do but pray for a good life for ourselves, our children, the family, and all the Jews who have been in the clutches of Isabella and Ferdinand."

"I know you are right. I am hoping Yosef will come with us to France."

Rina shook her head. "Yosef has his own mind. He will do whatever will give him more knowledge. He loves the family, but it is not enough for him."

In the background, Rina and Agamit heard men weeping as they said Kaddish over dead parents, grandparents, children, and relations. The mourners swayed from side to side, lost in their moments of prayer as if these dead had gone to Heaven yesterday.

Avram left Rina in the care of Agamit and walked along the rows, looking at the myriad of graves with no stones. He began to put a stone on each of these graves so that no grave would be without a sign that someone had visited.

Vidal and Roffe Michah were standing at the graves of their parents, Levi and Estrela.

"They have been gone a long time," Vidal said. "This having to leave Vitoria would have hurt Mama many times over,"

Roffe Michah said, "You are right, but she was strong. She would have accepted this fate and done what we are doing—saying good-bye as best we can."

The men stood silent for a moment until Roffe Michah started to say Kaddish.

"Magnified and sanctified be the great name of God throughout the world, which he hath created according to his will. May he establish his kingdom during the days of your life and during the life of all the house of Israel, speedily and soon. Amen. May his great name be blessed for ever and ever. Exalted and honored be the name of the Holy One, blessed be he, whose glory transcends beyond all blessings and hymns, praises, and consolations, which are uttered in the world. Amen. May there be abundant peace from heaven and life for us and for all Israel. Amen. May he who establishes peace in the heavens grant peace unto us and unto all Israel."

Together, with their arms around each other, the men said a final "Amen" over their parents.

The women wept while they cleaned the graves. Seeing their mothers and fathers weeping, the young children wept for a sadness they did not fully understand. The tears dripped down the cheeks from the eyes of the descendants onto the graves of the ancestors.

The family walked back to the Calle slowly and in silence.

Avram hoped his brothers and sisters were alive and going to safe places. He did not have the luxury of time to visit them in the various towns they had moved to. Also, with Rina nearing her time for delivering their child, he could not leave her. He did not want to leave her.

"I am so angry; I feel like my limbs are ready to fall off. The monarchs, in their Catholic zeal, have robbed me of my future," Daniyyel said. "They think Catholicism is the one true religion for all. They do not accept people who are not like them. And I think they do not like that Jews are prosperous and know how to build strength around them."

"No use to be angry. We cannot change what we have no control over," Roffe Michah said. "Nephew, you will have a different future. A French future. You do not know what it is. It may be better than the one you would have had in Vitoria. Maybe we will have a life without fear and narrow-mindedness—without intolerance and bigotry. We do not know. We hope it will be better. Maybe when one door closes, another can be opened."

Vidal agreed with both of them, the young and the old viewpoints. *Life will unfold as it might.* Vidal knew that all he could do was be a good husband to Della regardless of her hard-heartedness years ago, be a good father and grandfather, and be a good brother, uncle and cousin. He had no other choices. He was too old to worry about anything except his family. Daniyyel's concerns would work themselves out.

As the Crevagos entered the Jew's Gate of the city, they saw the row of wagons that lined Calle de Judios. Women carried household goods out to the street. Vidal heard voices giving instructions to the husbands and children..

"Be careful."

"Pack the parcels tightly."

"Tie those knots securely."

"Hitch the cow with a shorter lead."

"Make room for more."

Some food for the two-week walk to Baiona was packed, but they would glean most of their meals from the forests and the livestock they were taking.

Vidal and his nephews had arranged for the Christian cobbler, Gorka Iturri, to take up work in their shop. He had worked with the Crevagos to supply shoes to the nobles in Pamplona, San Sebastian, and other towns and cities in northern Castile. Vidal would have left the shop to Argi, but Argi was too old to move and did not have any living sons.

"So sorry to see you Crevagos leave," Gorka said. "Your shoes are brilliant."

"I appreciate your kind words," Vidal said with a cracking voice. "I cannot believe we are leaving. Very tough. Very tough."

Vidal, Daniyyel, Jonah and Ezra gave whatever furnishings and tools Gorka did not want to the Christians who stopped by to wish the family well on their journey. The Jews did not receive much in compensation. The short time did not allow for bargaining.

The Crevagos and only a few other families chose to go to

Baiona. Most others went to established Jewish communities in Portugal, Holland, England, the south of France, and the Muslim countries. Some chose Jerusalem. They did not want to be in range of Inquisition spies who might be sent to neighboring countries looking for conversos, who could be taken back to Castile and tried for Judaizing true Catholics.

The rabbi was going to Baiona with the Crevagos. The new Jewish community would need a rabbi.

Rahav helped the rabbi dismantle the ark and pack up their few prayer books. They took the bells off the silver *rimmonim* used as crowns to decorate the top ends of the Torah's scroll rollers. Rahav blackened the rimmonim and the Torah's silver breastplate with ash so they would not look like valuable pieces in the event soldiers checked their wagons before allowing the family to leave. Rahav wrapped each bell tightly in linen. Daniyyel and the rabbi hid these precious bells inside the swaddling bands of the infant children. Rahav hid other precious items in a false bottom of Baruh's wagon, underneath the grapevines he had uprooted from his vineyards. Rahav hid the Torah in Avram's cloth bolts.

Since 1480, a proclamation prohibited the removal of precious metals from Spain, and even in light of this cruel displacement of the Jews, the monarchs did not see fit to relax this law.

Della, Rina, and Agamit packed their Shabbat candlesticks and Seder plates, the dishes, and cooking and serving utensils that had been passed down through the generations or received as wedding presents. The women sewed their gold beads and earrings into the hems of their skirts and long coats and into the clothes of the children. Family members took what they could: limited amounts of money and one wagon of goods per family.

The women took down their hamsas and mezuzas. The rabbi had said that when a person moves out of a house, he or she should leave the mezuza for the next tenant, but in this case, the new tenants would not be Jewish, and therefore, if the Jew wanted to take the mezuza, this act would be permitted.

"If you respect the person who is moving into your house, leave your mezuza so they will be blessed. If someone evil is moving into your house, take your mezuza so it will not be defaced. If you do not know who will be moving in, remove it so you will leave no opportunity for the mezuza to be disrespectfully discarded." Then the rabbi uncharacteristically said, "I spit on the monarchs. They are worse than dogs." And then he spat on the ground.

After the women finished the packing, they did their cleaning and sweeping.

On the Thursday morning following their visit to the cemetery, the Crevagos left Vitoria. As the wagons and carts wound through the Jew's Gate and into the field next to the monastery outside the city walls, a weary traveler approached the first wagon. His clothes were dirty but had signs that they had once been rich looking. His pleated shirt and vest gave a square to his shoulders as his blue cape with its small geometric patterns swirled from side to side as he walked. His puffy sleeves were turned over to reveal a satin lining of yellow and black. His boots showed the dirt of days of travel.

"Yosef," Vidal said. "How wonderful. You have come to join us in France. An educated place for an educated man."

The brothers surrounded Yosef. They each embraced him and kissed his cheeks to celebrate his homecoming.

Yosef felt superior to his brother, having served at court in Murcia, having mixed with nobles, and having taught the children who would be the future governors and magistrates of the province. He liked the feeling of superiority, because as a child, his brothers had tormented him, as brothers do. They had constantly annoyed him while he was studying and bullied him into doing their chores. However, Yosef also liked being with his brothers and feeling their warmth and love for him.

"My darling boy," Agamit said with a loud grating voice. She pushed her older brothers aside so she could get closer to Yosef. She looked admiringly at him, and for the first time she saw him as the tall, handsome man he had aged into.

"My sweet brother, I am so happy to see you and know you are safe."

"Agamit, you have cared for me like a mother would care for her son. You have given me food and shelter. On my visits, you have listened to me talk for hours about my work and studies, although I know you had no interest in this other than that it was me talking."

"Most of the time I did not understand what you were saying and talking about, but I loved knowing that you did. Now we will be together in France. Maybe you will go to Paris, but hopefully it is not too far from whatever place we are going."

"I have come to say good-bye. I am not finished with my learning. To gain new knowledge is important to me. I am going to sign on with a captain who is set to leave from Sevilla."

Vidal said, "Yosef, they will not take you, a Jew. Come with us."

"Dear brothers and sister, some months ago a navigator from the crew of this visionary sea captain visited me in Murcia. Because of my expertise in Hebrew and other languages, literature, and culture, he invited me—in fact, he enticed me—to accompany them on a voyage to find a new route to the East Indies. I cannot go with you, because I have already agreed to this adventure. You know me. I would not be happy in a place with only a little learning. I am different. You are content in your limited world. My world is bigger. I have no wife or bindings. I will witness the finding of this new route and new knowledge. This is my destiny."

Crying and speaking in low tones, Agamit said, "Yosef, I cannot keep you from going, and my pleadings will be useless. I have lost my home. I have lost my brother. Will I lose you to Christianity?"

Yosef looked into his sister's eyes with tears of his own. "I will convert to Christianity. Not because I believe in the cross, but because being a Jew is the barrier to learning more and to using the knowledge I have. This is my fate. I want to be part of this great journey. I want to be there when the unknown becomes the known. Once I do this, I will be a valuable scholar to all the kings in all the kingdoms. A Jew will become part of the explorations of the seas."

In this moment, Agamit sensed the expanse of her loss. She put her arms around her youngest brother. After a minute or so, she pulled away and looked up into his eyes. She took his face in her hands and said, "Remember to love God and keep his commandments. Remember your family. Remember who you are. You are Yosef Ben Ha Levi Ha Ivri. Yosef, son of Levi the Hebrew."

Yosef said, "I promise I will be Christian in name only. I am a Jew in my heart and in my head, and I always will be."

As the troupe climbed back onto their wagons or began walking along the sides, the creaking of the wheels sounded like a cacophonic symphony. Slowly the group continued on.

Yosef watched the wagons get smaller in the distance. Agamit kept turning back to take one more look at Yosef as he stood at the Jew's Gate, waving good-bye.

He waited until the cows' mooing and the goats' bleating could no longer be heard as they were pulled by their tethers to the wagons or ushered alongside these carryalls. As they moved farther away, Yosef wondered if, had he married, would he have had a fulfilling life—with children and with a wife whom he could sleep and feel. He quickly displaced these thoughts into a small corner of his mind. He needed to focus on the challenges that he wanted to face on the seas with a captain who had great ideas.

Yosef walked inside the house where he was born. It was empty except for the long table in the cooking area. This is where his father, Levi, had been laid out as the men prepared him for burial. The same was true of his mother Estrela, as well as Benjamin, Marcela, Isaac and Cassela. People had eaten for sustenance at this table and were prepared for their graves on this table.

Then Yosef walked into the Crevago courtyard to Agamit's empty house. He walked inside and looked around. The rooms were spotless but cold and uninviting. No sweet cakes were on the table, no broom leaning by the hearth, no pots or pans, and no noise of children running through. Yosef felt as empty as the house but as excited as the butterfly he saw flitting on the flowers in the courtyard.

Yosef visited the cemetery and then left for Sevilla. Once there, he converted to Christianity, and as his disguise, he took the name of Luis de Torres. This new Christian signed on with Capitán Cristóbal Colón to serve as interpreter of languages and to set sail on the very day the expulsion order required that all Jews must be out of Spain.

>─┤─◆>─•─O─•<─┤─◄

After about two hours of travel, when they were far enough away from Vitoria, Vidal called the men together.

"We will travel quickly," Vidal said assuredly. Because he had traveled these roads for years, he was their wagon master and had planned the travel route. His brothers, nephews, and friends trusted him.

"We will reach Baiona in about two weeks. We will leave the kingdom of Ferdinand and Isabella by walking north through the Basque country. We will sleep the first night in the wooded hillsides of Alava Province. We will go to Salvatierra and through the tunnel made by nature through the Vascos mountain, to Tolosa and San Sebastian. We will sleep in the woods and then cross the Pirineos into France. We will take the old Roman Road—the same road that old Erini Crevago, when traveling west, walked before he ended up in Vitoria."

With their wagons, livestock, and treasured belongings, the Crevagos passed through small Basque villages and into the French city of Saint-Jean-de-Luz. They saw Jews with wagons—some intending to settle in various towns in Navarre, others in France, still others intending to go further north and east.

Finally, the Crevagos arrived in the area of Saint Esprit, across the Adour River from Baiona. Including the time for rest and eating, and for Shabbat when they did not travel, the trip took about two weeks, as Vidal had predicted.

Saint Esprit was forestland that would need to be cleared. The Crevagos were starting over. They would have to plan for homes, for a synagogue and a cemetery, and for Rina's baby, which was sure to come soon. It would be the first Crevago born in France.

When their temporary home site was decided on, the women cooked a lamb and seared green vegetables they had found in the forest. The men sat around a fire and reflected on the lives they had had in Vitoria and the work they had in front of them. They talked about the Jews who had decided to go to other places instead of Baiona. They talked about the Christians who had lived because of Roffe Michah and the other Jewish physicians. They talked about the Jews who had converted to Christianity.

"It is strange to think of our people from Vitoria whom we have known forever now being cast in so many different directions and having made so many different decisions," Daniyyel said. "I wonder who has made the best decision."

Baruh asked, "Did you know that Zentolla the tinker converted? He took the name of Tristan Bogado. What a disconnected name! It has no link to his past."

Vidal said, "That is what those who convert want—to forget their past. Now in each Judería throughout Spain, there will be Franciscos, Juans, Diegos, Jerónimos, Pedros, Alfonsos, and Rodrigos where before there were Yudas, Simeons, Naphtalis, Ashers, and Dans. Now in the Juderías, the names of de Perez, Fernandez, Nuñez, Gomez, Ortiz, Molino, Coronel, Santa Ana, Santa Maria, Santa Cruz, and Cortez will be as familiar as Ha Simuel, Ha Levi, or Ha Benjamin. After they are baptized, each converso will pick a name to show he is more Catholic than his neighbors."

Roffe Michah looked at his brothers and with all seriousness said, "It is a contest that I do not want to be part of."

CHAPTER 18

Everything In Its Time

January 1952

Bayonne, France, is a stone's throw from the Spanish border. In the early Middle Ages, it was often considered part of the Aragón kingdom.

The city started as a Basque village called Baiona, or *ibai*, meaning "river." The rivers Nive and Adour flow together as they run through the Pyrénées-Atlantiques region. The Adour connects Bayonne to the Bay of Biscay, which takes ships out to the Atlantic Ocean or north to the English Channel and North Sea. Romans occupied the land in the third century, the Vikings in the 800s, and the Germans in the 1940s. Each of these conquerors developed agricultural and munitions industries that kept Bayonne commercially alive. One factory invented a rifle with a sword attached, which became the bayonet.

Descendants of Vitoria's Jews focused on manufacturing, shipping, and service enterprises. They became physicians, dentists, teachers, attorneys, clothiers, retailers of all types, and public servants.

>⊶⊶◇⊷⊷◂

Zokal Esquile liked visiting Bayonne. It was an easy drive from Vitoria—just under two hours. The superhighway through the Vascos and Pyrenees was the old Roman road. This was Zokal's fourth trip to Bayonne since the end of World War II. In past years, he timed his visit for July so he would be in Bayonne during the Grand Basque Festival. This year, however, his manager directed him to go in January so he could attend meetings about the new disease control services that Bayonne had instituted. At least, he would be able to visit with his cousins who lived close to the old Basque Museum. *A good getaway for a few days*, Zokal thought. His cousins always served him the best Basque foods, varieties of *marmitako* and lamb stews, and *Tolosa* bean dishes with paprikas from Lekeitio.

Even in winter, decoration lined the streets. Wide ribbons of alternating red, green, and white were wrapped around lampposts, and colored streamers were blowing in the wind.

Zokal was a senior member of the Spanish public health service. Whenever in Bayonne, he made a point of meeting with Dr. Michael Crevago so they could compare notes on program advancements.

As Zokal drove the streets of Bayonne, he saw Michael's government building. It was on the edge of the river where the streets were lined with four-story office buildings, some still showing their damage from the war.

The city was trying to forget the Nazi horrors and the tragedy of Jewish neighbors sent to death camps—often with the help of French collaborators. Although most Basques had opposed the Nazis, some French citizens supported persecution of the Jews—mostly so their property and wealth could be confiscated.

As he pulled into the parking lot of Bayonne's government building Zokal shifted his thoughts to his upcoming meeting. Crevago was intelligent and welcoming. These were two traits that Zokal thought were often absent from Jews. They seemed so serious.

Zokal walked toward the elevator and saw the sign saying it was out of order. He approached the dingy stairwell for the climb to the third floor. The olive-green walls and gray floor tiles still had wartime dirt embedded in the cracks. He walked the dim hallway to Michael Crevago's office. Long fluorescent bulbs flickered in their ceiling fixtures. The building had no architectural flair, no artwork on the walls, and no plants along the corridor.

"Are you busy?" Zokal asked as he poked his head in the door.

"Come in," Michael said as he stood up and extended his hand. The two men greeted each other like old friends. After the handshakes and talk of changes in their public health systems—the problems, the new ideas—Zokal thought the time was right to share the happenings in Vitoria.

"Michael, I heard that Vitoria's city council sent a letter to Bayonne's Jewish community regarding the cemetery. The councilors want to build on the grounds of the Judizmendi. The city has grown, and it wants to continue to grow."

Michael wrinkled his forehead. "I'm surprised that this is common knowledge to folks in Vitoria. Yes, we received a letter. It was sent to the rabbi, and he shared it with the board of directors of the synagogue and the Vitoria descendants."

Zokol said matter-of-factly, "The cemetery is just a plot of land now. I remember my grandfather telling me that he had heard stories passed down through the generations that after the Jews left, the Judizmendi was protected. A few grave robbers every now and then. Later on there were more. I think about a hundred years ago the city tried to build on the land, but there was a big uproar about it, so nothing ever happened. But I think this time the city council is committed to do this."

Michael did not move. He stiffened as the hair on his neck tingled. Was another betrayal in the air? He had never visited the Judizmendi, but nonetheless, he felt it connected him to his ancestors.

"Until we received the letter from Vitoria, we had almost forgotten about the agreement between our ancestors and the city council. We've known of the oath taken but never talked about it much. For generations this lore has been passed from down in our families too, same as you, from parents to children. I don't think anyone here has ever taken any action to verify enforcement of the agreement. The Nazis ransacked our city hall and synagogue. I think we don't even have a copy of the document anymore."

"We have a copy in the Vitoria city archives. Our city council knows of its obligation, as do the old Basque families," Zokal said. "The councilors want you to release them from the oath."

"We know. Tonight the community votes on whether to do this or require that the oath be upheld."

"Maybe it's time to let the cemetery go," Zokal said sheepishly.

"I don't want to offend you, my friend, but I don't support this. A promise is a promise. The Judizmendi represents all our community lost when we were expelled."

"But you've done okay in Bayonne. The Jews are prosperous here. You have made lives for yourselves in France."

"This is not the issue. The issue is that we could have been prosperous in Spain too. And more protected from the Nazis if our families had been living in Spain all these years. The cemetery, regardless of its present condition, is still the connection to our history. I think we'll have to agree to disagree on this."

"You make a good point. Let's have a drink and enjoy the day."

<hr />

Benjamin and Michael arrived at the synagogue early and were alone in the sanctuary. Streaks from water damage were evident on the walls and floor. The rows of benches were aligned in unadorned order. The simplicity of the room belied the complexity of the decision they would make on this night.

The benches creaked as they sat down to wait for the others. Michael put his jacket down on the seat next to him to save space for his wife, Estir. She was a critical care nurse at Bayonne's Centre

Hospitalier de la Côte Basque. She would come to the meeting when she finished her shift.

Michael and Benjamin waited for others to show up.

"Are the Crevagos from Paris coming," Benjamin asked. The Crevago Shoe Company had moved to Paris in the 1920's when the city of Chanel, Lanvin and Patou became the center of fashion.

"Jonah called Bernardo Crevago to see if he was interested, but Bernardo was consumed by design problems or something like that and couldn't come for the vote. He's living off the Champs Elysee now, and making a good living."

"He'll never go back to live in Vitoria, just like the Jews of Bayonne won't," Benjamin said.

"We might never go back to Vitoria, but we have to always be on our guard. When 1942 came, so did the Germans. Once again, we were the object of destruction because we were Jewish," Michael said. "We went into hiding—not that it did much good, because Bayonne was part of the German *Zone Occupée*."

"Yes, Benjamin said. "Not a good time for the world.

Michael's face reddened. "Not a good time for the Jews. Just thinking about those years makes me piss-mad. The German army searched for Jews in Bayonne, just like in Paris, Lyon, and the small towns and villages throughout France. Some collaborators helped willingly. Some were coerced into collaboration. It was a repeat of the Spanish Inquisition. Before the war, we were successful merchants, factory owners, businessmen, professionals. The French government only took an interest in us because we contributed to French revenues. We kept Bayonne healthy as an important strategic location."

"You shouldn't be so angry about it. Those days are past," Benjamin said.

"I'm angry that you are so quick to let the cemetery go. You should think of it as a special place for our family—for all Sephardim. It is a symbol of what once was. We should not let it be swept away by politics and planning departments."

"Let it go, brother."

"I can't. From 1940, when *Who is a Jew* was published to assist with the various waves of roundups, we were tagged one more time as outsiders of society. The unwanted. The Germans hated us. The French tolerated us. But eventually all wanted to get rid of us. Just like the Spanish monarchs of our ancestors. We had more than three hundred Jewish families in Bayonne before the war. Now look at us. Fewer than forty. Rabbi Ginsburger, he did our Bar Mitzvas. He perished. Our friends. Our neighbors. Family. All murdered. Our property was taken. If our ark and Torah scrolls that were brought to Bayonne by our Spanish ancestors hadn't been hidden in the Basque Museum, they would have been seized and lost to us. It's time to stand up for what is ours. Why should we let these people out of their promise?"

It was a rhetorical question.

The brothers stopped talking and stood up when their cousins and their wives entered the sanctuary. All hugged and kissed each other on both cheeks.

"I wonder how it will go," Saul said.

David responded, "I don't have a clue on this. There are no Jews in Vitoria so why should there be a Jewish cemetery there? The Basque of Vitoria kept their oath, but what does it matter now? We've a good life in Bayonne."

Michael said, "That's why our ancestors made a good decision to stay in the Basque country. I think the Basque don't feel fully French. They admire us because we chose to leave Spain rather than give up the religion of our forefathers. That's why we have lived cooperatively for centuries."

Benjamin, Michael, and their cousins often relished the good decision that their ancestors made in choosing Bayonne.

Saul said, "Bayonne is removed from Paris life. No *faux aires*. Here we have our own culture and personality. We're almost more Basque than Jewish. We settled this land hundreds of years ago, and we're its people—Basque-Jewish."

Michael grimaced. "What are you saying? That Jews are from the Basque people? No, we're from Abraham, Isaac, and Jacob."

Jonah said, "We're our own people. Have you forgotten that just a few generations ago, a Jew visiting from a foreign province could not stay more than three days in any French town? A Jew could be imprisoned if he stayed in the province more than fourteen days. Our rites and rituals, our Torah and Talmud, set us apart. The state laws and rules have always been against us."

"We need to keep our identity, practice our way of life, and keep the cemetery as a remembrance," Michael said.

"We need to fit in. We need to integrate. We need to be conciliatory. That's why we need to release Vitoria from its oath," Benjamin said.

The men of Bayonne's Jewish community loved each other. They prayed together, talked together, celebrated together, and shared sadness together. Regardless of differences of opinions, they all got along. Until, that is, the issue of the cemetery arose.

Benjamin was angry because of Michael's stubbornness. Michael was fuming at Benjamin's shortsightedness.

The men stopped their conversation when other descendants started to flow into the sanctuary. The congregants filled up the rows of benches. These were original from the 1600s. Some very prominent men came in: Albert Alcalay, owner of the leather goods factory; Daniel Boli, owner of numerous honey farms; and the men who owned several of Bayonne's chocolate factories. They sat in the front row. Their wives accompanied them. More people entered the sanctuary. The room was a mix of descendants from the Spanish expulsion as well as from the Portuguese and Navarre expulsions that had followed. There were also some more recent immigrants who had settled in Bayonne after the war. People who had survived Hitler's death camps had come to watch the proceedings. Men and women sat together.

The group's cross talk sounded like ducks quacking in a pond.

Jonah, as the de facto head of the descendants group, called the meeting to order.

"We are the remnants," he said, "left over from a previous age." Jonah walked up the three stairs to a cabinet on the left side of the ark. He slowly opened the cabinet door and pointed to the contents.

"In 1492, this Torah was brought to Saint Esprit by our ancestors. This is our heritage that our old Crevagos—Vidal, Roffe Michah, Juhuda, and Baruh—and their relations Rahav and Avram, and all the others, brought from Vitoria."

The dark blue velvet cover over the antique Torah was original. The silver *rimmonim* and their bells gleamed in the light of the synagogue, even though they had not been polished for many years.

Jonah closed the cabinet and looked at the men and women sitting on the benches. "Tonight we must answer the question before us. Should Vitoria continue to uphold the oath to preserve the Judizmendi, or should we release the city from the oath?"

Members of the audience started their cross talk again. Jonah quieted them by putting up his arm and stomping his foot on the floor.

"Let's have some final discussion, and then we'll vote. I see hands. Benjamin, you first, then Michael, and so on. And make your comments short and to the point," Jonah said tersely.

Benjamin said, "We have to let go of our past."

Michael countered. "These are our ancestors. With Jewish Europe in disarray, we are among the few who have some stability because our cemetery is intact."

"It is time to let go," Saul said.

"No," Alberto said vigorously. He had been nodding in agreement with Michael. "What are we if not our past? It is everything for us."

David stood up and turned to face the group. "Back in 1850, when Vitoria wrote our community saying the city wanted to build on the Judizmendi, some Saint Esprit Jews rejected this request. They wanted the promise of our ancestors upheld. I say to you now, we should repeat this position. Let us honor our ancestors and let them be a symbol of remembrance for all families who were by force, edict, dictator, or discrimination removed from their homes."

Eli Levi said, "Knowledge of the oath has been passed down from generation to generation. L'Dor V'Dor. We should keep the oath so we can pass the history of good Christians on to future generations."

After each statement, depending on their points of view, men and women broke into applause and cheers of "Yes, yes," "Right," and "Not ever."

Miriam Saavaedra raised her hand, and Jonah pointed to her. She walked up to the front of the audience, where Jonah was standing, and looked at the group. The blue ribbon that held her dark hair was loose and coming untied, causing her hair to softly frame her face. Her blue-flowered dress was ill fitting, and its uneven hem gave her a disheveled look. Showing from the short sleeves of her dress on her left arm was a tattoo of numbers from Auschwitz. She wore a small *Magen David* on a gold chain around her neck.

"You know me. I work in the synagogue's office. I was president of the sisterhood. I deliver food to the poor. I organize shiva minyans for grieving families. My father was a Crevago. My husband who was killed in the war was a distant Crevago cousin. I am a Crevago. I believe our family and its story has, with each generation since 1492, given us the strength to build successful lives in Saint Esprit. This is very special. However, at Kol Nidrei, people can ask to be released from oaths taken at the time of persecution and torture. We should allow Vitoria to be released from a vow that was taken at a very emotional moment in history. The Kol Nidrei tells us that all vows, oaths, and consecrations that were sworn to can be repudiated. Why not liberate Vitoria from this oath that was taken more than four hundred years ago? We live in Bayonne now—not Vitoria."

The men and women of Saint Esprit continued to give their points of view. Comments begat new comments. Repetitious comments were uttered more loudly for emphasis.

Still the community had not arrived at a consensus.

Jonah finally called a halt to the discussion. "We have heard many reasons and rationales for each side of the vote. Will we require the oath to be upheld by Vitoria's city council, or will we allow the city to be released from the oath? To uphold or to release? I will pass out the ballots. Mark 'uphold' or 'release,' and we will do the tally together."

SEMI-CODA

When Making a Decision, Come Out Clean

February 1952

The city council of Vitoria-Gasteiz, as it was now officially known, convened. The mahogany horseshoe table with a seat for each councilor gave the room an air of authority. White plaster walls reflected the lighting from the ceiling chandeliers. The Mayor, a stocky man of Basque heritage, sat behind a desk in the front of the room on an elevated platform. His suit was not pristine, but it was not too wrinkled either. His small feet stuck out from under the desk.

"I am calling this meeting to order. There is only one item on the agenda. Yesterday I received a letter from the Israelite Consistory of Bayonne, France."

Slight aahs and ohs sounded in the room.

"I will read this short letter to you. It is dated February 1, 1952. 'Dear Honorable Mayor of Vitoria, on this day in 1952, we the descendants of the Jews of Vitoria who were subject to Spain's edict of expulsion in 1492 hereby release the City Council of Vitoria, Spain, from its oath to preserve the cemetery of the Jews now known as the Judizmendi. This new understanding frees the municipality of Vitoria from any obligation that its ancestors made to the expelled Jews of Vitoria. We thank you for preserving the cemetery to this date. Signed by: Israelite Consistory of Bayonne, France.'"

Quiet engulfed the room—but just for a moment.

"I thought for sure the Bayonne Jews would not allow the Judizmendi to be discarded—that the Jews would not release Vitoria from its oath," the mayor said. "I am grateful to the Jewish community of Bayonne for this allowance."

"For the record, this day will bring us to a new point of city growth," a vice mayor said with his characteristic emphasis on every key word in a sentence.

Another councilor said, "We have done our best for over four hundred years, and the Judizmendi has been conserved."

"The tradition of the contract that was agreed upon by our predecessors, our ancestors, has been upheld," added another.

"We, the councilors of Vitoria, should congratulate ourselves for preserving to this point the agreement between the city council of 1492 and the Jews who were expelled by Isabella and Ferdinand," said another.

"That we respected the oath for almost 500 years shows that we Christians are an honorable people," said a man gloating with pride.

"Wait one moment," the Mayor said humbly. "We are congratulating ourselves on the longevity of keeping the oath of our ancestors, and now we are going to terminate it?"

There was silence. No one moved or spoke as each man recalibrated his thinking.

The mayor stood up and said, "Do we want to be known as the magistrates who broke this centuries-old oath: an oath of our forefathers, our ancestors—people who valued the presence of these Jews in their community?" He looked around the room for concurrence, but none came.

After some hesitation, he said, "I, for one, do not."

"But what about the city's growth? Its need to expand? What of all the talk we had in favor of converting the Judizmendi into a cemetery for Christian use?"

Each man around the table looked down at his papers or looked up at the ceiling or to the walls; they did not look at each other.

"I am thinking back to 1492, when conversion or expulsion was decreed," Mayor Ibarra said. "I feel like I am a stand-in for the ancestors who served on this very same governing body."

A chorus of comments sang out:

"I cannot support rejection of the oath."

"Nor can I."

"I will not deny what my ancestors wanted us to do."

"We must continue to uphold our oath."

"We owe it to the Jewish community of Vitoria and to the doctors who saved our ancestors from the plague and illnesses of death. Some of us might not be here if it hadn't been for the Jewish doctors."

"It's our sacred duty as Catholics that we show respect for the Jews."

With rounds of passion for their ancestors, for the oath that had been taken, and for the Jews who had suffered expulsion from their homes, the City Council of Vitoria, Spain, in 1952, refused to be released from its obligation to preserve the Judizmendi.

"As mayor of Vitoria, I will write to the Israelite Consistory of Bayonne, France, of our decision to continue to preserve the Judizmendi. Together the two communities, as our ancestors did, will create a new agreement that will be fitting and proper for our times."

Over the next months, representatives from the two communities worked together and determined how to proceed.

The remains from the old cemetery were collected and reburied in a common grave according to the laws of the Hebrew burial society Hevra Kadisha. With care, with all the rituals and propriety required, the bones of the Jewish community of Vitoria were blessed and reinterred.

To memorialize the Jewish community of Vitoria, the city council authorized that a plaza be built and a park be developed to surround the area of the Jewish cemetery.

Epilogue

1992

The families descended from the Jews of Vitoria clustered together on the plaza and under the mature trees of the park. Concrete and stone walkways bordered the large rectangle of grass. The breezes brushed on the cheeks of the crowd.

Michael, Benjamin, David and Jonah Crevago had aged, but they were not old men. Longevity ran in the Crevago family. However, even with age these men stood erect alongside the younger members of the Crevago family. Standing with the Crevagos were several descendants of expelled Jews from Portugal and Navarre. Also included in Bayonne's delegation to Vitoria were European Jews who had settled in the city after surviving Hitler's extermination camps and some Jews who had migrated to Bayonne from Russia and other former Soviet countries. The Jewish community of Bayonne had been enhanced by Ashkenazi Jews of Eastern Europe. Children, grandchildren, great-grandchildren, cousins, sisters, and brothers stood together.

The group gathered on the area of the Judizmendi to be dedicated as the Plaza de Sephard—the Plaza of Spanish Jews. Surrounding the Jews were Christians of Vitoria. All stood solemn. Each man wore a kippa to cover his head, in reverence to God and the moment.

The city leader of Vitoria spoke. "We welcome the descendants back to their home in Spain. Many of us would not exist if your ancestors, the physicians of the Jewish community, had not saved our

Christian ancestors. I read from the dedication plaque of the Plaza de Sephard—the Plaza of the Spanish Jews: 'In this place was the Jewish cemetery that the aljama of Vitoria-Gasteiz ceded in perpetuity to the city on 27 June in 1492. The city and city council loyally respected the conditions of the ceding for 460 years, until on 27 June 1952 Vitoria was freed of the condition by the agreement signed on that date with the Consistorio Israelita of Bayonne (France).

"'In homage to the friendly coexistence of the Basque-Hebrew cultures, to the religious tolerance of this city, and in remembrance of the Jewish community of Vitoria-Gasteiz.'"

Jonah then spoke on behalf of the descendants. "It is amazing that the city council and the people of Vitoria faithfully stood by its pledge for hundreds of years. It's impressive. We are humbled by the goodness of the Christian people in Vitoria. It is fitting that this area should become a park. People of all ages and faiths, all races and creeds, will come here and remember the good relationship between the Jews and Christians of Vitoria. This plaque that cites the history of these people is inspiring. It serves to remind us of what is possible."

The Judizmendi in Vitoria-Gasteiz, Spain

Final Notes

On August 3, 1492, the Niña, Pinta, and Santa Maria set sail for a new route to the Indies.

On November 2, Columbus sighted an island, which today is known as the Bahamas, and sent a two-man expedition to explore. Luis de Torres, the former Yosef Ben Ha Levi Ha Ivri, was the first man ashore, the first Jew to set foot in the New World.

On December 16, 1968, the government of Spain officially rescinded the Alhambra Decree—the edict of expulsion of the Jews.

On June 11, 2015, Spain passed a law granting citizenship to descendants of Jews expelled in 1492.

Glossary

Afikoman: Hebrew for "dessert", the piece broken from the middle matzo at the Passover Seder, it is put in a bag and each person at the Seder puts it on his shoulder as a symbolic gesture of the burdens carried by Israelites in Egypt. After the meal, the bag is hidden so children can search for it, and once found, the afikoman is eaten by all after other desserts.

Alhambra Decree: A decree issued March 31, 1492, by the Catholic monarchs of Spain, Ferdinand II and Isabella I. It ordered the expulsion of Jews from the kingdoms of Castile and Aragón and all properties belonging to the monarchs. The decree required Jews to leave no later than July 31, 1492, and limited what and how many possessions they could take.

Aragón: A kingdom located in northeastern Spain in the late fifteenth century, ruled by Ferdinand II. When he married Isabella I, Aragón was united with the kingdom of Castile.

Ark: Where the Torah is kept. Jews of Sephardic descent call the ark Hekhál; Jews of Ashkenazi descent call it *Äron ha kodeš*.

Aljama: A self-governing Jewish community whose leadership group consists of three to five esteemed men. These few men, usually including the rabbi of the synagogue, govern the community and deal with its administrative issues, such as the assessment of government taxes to be paid by each Jewish family in the community.

Ashkenazi Jews: those of central or eastern European descent versus Sephardic Jews of Spanish (Babylonian) descent.

Bar Mitzva: Hebrew for "son of commandment," this term refers to a boy, usually at the age of thirteen, who is obligated to lay tefillin, read from the Torah, and serve the Jewish community.

Basque: A unique ethic group living in an area between north central Spain and southwestern France. It is termed *"Vasco"* in Spanish, *"Basque"* in French and English, and *"Euskaldunak"* in the Basque language.

Bedeken: A ceremony in a Jewish wedding in which the groom looks at the bride and then puts a veil over her face. This custom is derived from a mistake described in the Torah, in which Jacob married Leah because her face was veiled, when he intended to marry Rachel. The ceremony provides verification that the groom is marrying the intended woman.

Ben Zakhor: On the first Friday night after a boy is born, he is celebrated by the community during a gathering in the baby's home. People bring food and pray. This enhances the newborn's holiness and joyously welcomes him into the Jewish community.

Berit Milá: The covenant of circumcision. In Genesis 1:10–14, God commands Abraham to be circumcised and for all of his descendants to be circumcised. Leviticus 12:3 says, "And on the eighth day the flesh of his foreskin shall be circumcised." Jews of Ashkenazi descent call it a *Bris*.

Boca: Spanish for "mouth."

Book of Numbers: The fourth book of the Hebrew Bible. The book describes how the people of Israel consolidate into a community.

Botillo: meat-stuffed pork intestines.

Calle de Judios: Street of Jews.

Calle de Zapaterías: Street of Shoemakers.

Capitán Cristóbal Colón: Captain Christopher Columbus.

Cathar Movement: A movement that thrived during the medieval period in southern France and northern Italy. The movement refused to accept various Church rules and rituals, such as baptism or the Eucharist, because Cathars did not believe that a wafer could be the body of Christ. The Cather Movement was perceived as a threat to the Catholic Church of Rome, which created the first Inquisition to eliminate the Cathar Movement. This effort took over one hundred years, but the Church of Rome was finally successful in eliminating the Cathar Movement.

Castile: A large and powerful state on the Iberian Peninsula during the Middle Ages located in eastern Spain. In the late fifteenth century, Castile was ruled by Isabella I. When she married Ferdinand II, Castile was united with the kingdom of Aragón.

Converso: A man who has converted to Catholicism, particularly during the 1300s and 1400s in the Iberian Peninsula. The term also refers to the descendants of those who converted. A woman would be a *conversa*.

Covenant with Abraham: In Genesis, God promises to make Abraham the father of many nations and of many descendants and give "the whole land of Canaan" to his descendants, create a great nation, and bless all those who follow Abraham. Circumcision is the permanent sign of this everlasting covenant with Abraham and his male descendants. This covenant is with each Jewish male and is known as the Berit Milá or Brit Milah.

Covenant with Isaac: Because Abraham obeyed and followed God, God promised his son, Isaac, that his seed would be innumerable, his descendants would possess the Promised Land, and the nation descending from Abraham and Isaac would be blessed.

Deuteronomy: The fifth book of the Torah.

Disputation of Tortosa: A conference held in the city of Tortosa during 1413–1414. Church leaders required that Jewish scholars participate. No authentic debate occurred because the Christians would not allow it. The disputation was a method for forcing Jews to convert to Christianity.

Don (Name): Title of esteem, like Mr., but with more reverence and respect.

Edict of Expulsion: See "Alhambra Decree."

Estupido: Spanish for "stupid."

Exodus: The second book of the Torah.

Five Books of Moses: Genesis, Exodus, Leviticus, Numbers, and Deuteronomy, which comprise the Torah.

Fuero: During the medieval period, Castilian kings could give special privileges to specific groups of people. For example, Jews could not be harmed or their homes desecrated.

Genesis: First book in the Five Books of Moses.

Granada: A territory known in the 1400s as the Emirate of Granada. It was established in 1238 by Muslim generals who ultimately conquered most of the Iberian Peninsula. Over the centuries, Christian leaders fought to take back these conquered lands (known as the Reconquest) from the Muslims. The last Muslim emirate was Granada, which fell to Spain on January 2, 1492, after thirteen years of assaults by Ferdinand II and his Christian army. The last Muslim leader, Boabdil, ceded control of the remaining Muslim lands to Ferdinand and Isabella, whose objective was to have a pure Catholic country.

Haggadah: Hebrew word for "telling" and is a written guide for the Passover Seder so fathers (now mothers too) can fulfill the Torah's requirement to "tell your sons" (now daughters too) about the Hebrews' liberation from slavery in Egypt and the Exodus.

Hamsa: An amulet for magical protection from the envious or evil eye. In Hebrew, "Hamesh" means "five," referring to the number of digits on the hand. "Hamsa" is the Arabic word for "five."

Hametz: forbidden food, at Passover it is any crumbs or residual that has leavening or yeast in it, such as bread or cakes, any utensils or dishes that have been used for bread or cakes. Ashkenazi Jews call it "chametz".

Havdalah: A Jewish ritual ending Shabbat and Jewish holidays. The ceremony includes lighting a candle with seven wicks, saying a blessing over a full cup of wine, smelling sweet spices to symbolically represent a good week to be had, and dousing the candle in the cup of wine.

Hekhál: Sephardic name for the holy ark in which the Torah scrolls are housed. Jews of Ashkenazi descent call it the Ark Ăron ha kodeš.

Hevra Kadisha: A volunteer organization of Jews responsible for ensuring that the bodies of Jews are prepared for burial according to Jewish tradition and ensuring that a body is protected from desecration, willful or not, until burial.

Huppah: A canopy under which a Jewish couple stand during their Jewish wedding ceremony. During the Middle Ages, a tālēt was typically used for the canopy.

Iberian Peninsula: During the Middle Ages, this was the collective name for the kingdoms of Castile, Aragón, Navarre, León, and Portugal, as well as part of the Islamic Empire.

Inquisition: Method for combating heresy by the Catholic Church. In the Iberian Peninsula, it was designed to seek out conversos who secretly remained loyal to their Judaism. Ferdinand II and Isabella I empowered Tomás de Torquemada to institute state-sponsored torture, trials, and executions of anyone suspected of being a false Christian. No one knows how many people were burned at the stake, but estimates range from two thousand to one hundred twenty-five thousand. More people were tortured than were executed.

Jew's Gate: The entrance into the medieval walled city of Vitoria by Calle de Judios.

Judería: The Jewish quarter of a city or town.

Judizmendi: This Spanish term means "Jew's mount." In Vitoria, after 1492, the Jewish cemetery was called the Judizmendi.

Kaddish: A prayer said when mourning a death to show that Jews praise God even in sadness and despite a tragic loss.

Kavvanah: A sense of ecstasy felt while praying—a deep concentration precipitating a feeling of oneness with God.

Ketuba: A marriage contract describing the rights and responsibilities of the groom to the bride. Jews of Ashkenazi descent spell it *ketubah*.

Kiddush (or Kiddish): A blessing said over wine to sanctify Shabbat or Jewish holidays.

Kippa: The Hebrew word for a skullcap worn by Jewish men during prayer and religious study. Some Jews wear a kippa at all times to show respect for and reverence to God. Yarmulke is the Yiddish term for a skullcap.

Kol Nidre: A passage that annuls vows and pledges made under coercion or distress. This passage is recited in the synagogue before the evening service of Yom Kippur, the Day of Atonement.

Ladino: a mix of Hebrew, Arabic, and medieval Spanish spoken among Sephardic Jews up to this day and used in Sephardic texts.

L'Dor V'Dor: Hebrew for "from generation to generation."

León: Until the year 1230, this was an independent kingdom situated in the northwest region of the Iberian Peninsula. In 1230, by force, León joined with Castile, and the two kingdoms were ruled jointly by the same monarch.

Leviticus: The third book of the Five Books of Moses.

Magen David: Star of David or Shield of David, referring to King David, the second king of the United Kingdom of Israel (1040–970 BCE). The symbol consists of two equilateral triangles overlaid to create a six-pointed star that is a generally recognized symbol of Jewish identity and Judaism.

Manna: Food God provided to the Hebrews while they were roaming the desert.

Marrano: A pig or dirty person. This was used as a derogatory term for a converso, new Christian, false Christian, or any Jew who had converted to Christianity.

Mear: Spanish word for piss.

Medieval period: The era from the fifth century to the fifteenth century, also referred to as the Middle Ages.

Midrash: A book containing the study of Torah texts with guidance and moral teachings.

Mierda: Spanish for "shit."

Minyan: A quorum of ten men required for various religious obligations, such as saying Kaddish for the dead, reading from the Torah, or giving the seven benedictions at a wedding ceremony.

Mitzva: a good deed. Jews of Ashkenazi descent spell it "mitzvah".

Nachala: Hebrew for "legacy." This is the Sephardic name for the annual remembrance of a dead person. Jews of Ashkenazi descent call it by the Yiddish term *Yahrtzeit*, meaning "time of year."

Navarre: A kingdom in the northern portion of the Iberian Peninsula. It was an independent monarchy until 1515, when it was annexed by Ferdinand II and the kingdom of Castile.

Ner Tamid: Everlasting light—a light that burns in front of the ark, in which the Torah is kept.

Ninth of Av: An annual day of fasting to commemorate great sadness in the history of the Jews: the destruction of Jerusalem's first and second temples and the expulsion of the Jews from Israel.

Numbers: The fourth book of the Torah.

Orina: Spanish word for urine.

Parasha: A section of the Torah. A parasha is read and then discussed.

Pesah: Sephardic spelling of the Passover holiday. Ashkenazi Jews spell it Pesach.

Prepucio: Foreskin of the penis.

Psalms: An anthology of Biblical poetry and songs.

Quemadero: A place of execution during the Spanish Inquisition— usually an elevated platform where conversos were burned at the stake.

Rabbi: A spiritual leader of a Jewish community.

Recitative: Melodramatic conversation that is sung, usually in an opera, typically as a back-and-forth between people discussing or arguing about a subject.

Rimmon: An ornament, usually silver with bells, placed on top of the Torah scroll rollers.

Sambenito: Spanish spelling. A tunic of yellow cloth worn to show guilt of heresy during the Spanish Inquisition. Usually worn with a conical pointed hat. Conversos accused of heresy were paraded from the trial location to the quemadero, where they were typically burned at the stake.

Sandak: Man honored at a Berit Milá by holding on his lap the baby boy as he is circumcised.

Sephardic: Term for a Jew whose family lived in the Iberian Peninsula prior to 1492, or for one who is descended from a Jew who was expelled from Spain or Portugal so these countries could be uniformly Catholic.

Sifrei Torah: The Hebrew name for handwritten Holy Scrolls. Also known as Sefer Torah

Señora: A married woman; equivalent of "Mrs.".

Shabbat: The day of rest. Jews celebrate the Shabbat on the seventh day of the week, from Friday before sundown until Saturday night after three stars appear in the sky.

Shehehekianu: Sepharic spelling of a blessing to celebrate special occasions. It gives thanks for new and unusual events and experiences. Jews of Ashkenazi descent usually spell it *Shehecheyanu*.

Shasha: A ceremony at the first Shabbat after a boy is born (*ben zakhor*), where family and friends say the Shema, sing psalms, pray, and eat sweet foods.

Sheloshim: The secondary mourning period which starts immediately after shiva and is counted thirty days from burial. Mourners can work, but cannot attend celebrations, cut their hair or listen to music.

Shema: A foundational prayer of the Jewish religion that affirms belief in one God. "Hear O Israel, the Lord our God, the Lord in One."

Shiva: The primary mourning period that commences immediately after burial and lasts for seven days.

Strappado: An act of torture wherein a victim's hands are tied behind his back and the body is lifted by a rope attached to the wrists. It is extremely painful, as the arms become dislocated from the shoulders.

Synagogue: A Jewish house of worship and communal center.

Taharah: The Jewish ritual of cleansing a body to prepare it for burial. Prayers and readings from the Torah are sung during this ceremony.

Tālēt: Sephardic Hebrew and Ladino term for a prayer shawl. It is called a tallit in modern Hebrew and a *tallis* in Ashkenazi Hebrew and Yiddish.

Talmud: A writing that consists of two books of Torah study: the Mishna and the Gemora. These books analyze the Torah and describe laws for daily living and how to ethically deal with various situations and circumstances.

Tefillin: A set of small black leather boxes containing scrolls of parchment inscribed with verses from the Torah. These are worn during weekday morning prayers on the upper arm with the strap wrapped around the arm, hand, and fingers. The tefillin for the head is placed above the forehead, between the eyes. The Torah commands that these should be worn as a "sign" and "remembrance" that God brought the children of Israel out of Egypt.

Tevah: Hebrew for "box." This is the Sephardic term for the raised platform or pulpit from which sermons are delivered and the Torah is read. It is elevated to show its importance in the synagogue. Jews of Ashkenazi descent call it by the Hebrew word *"bimah,"* meaning "high place."

Tikkun Olam: This is a Hebrew phrase meaning "repair the world." Each Jew has a responsibility to do what he can to make life better for others.

Tio: Spanish for "uncle."

Tia: Spanish for "aunt."

Torah: Holy scrolls written by hand. The Torah is the narrative of the Jewish people describing the birth of their existence, their history, and their covenant with God. It consists of the Five Books of Moses: Genesis, Exodus, Leviticus, Numbers, and Deuteronomy, and is used by rabbis to teach moral and religious lessons.

Tribunal of the Holy Office of the Inquisition: An organization established in 1478 that administered the Spanish Inquisition to seek out false Christians. Tomás de Torquemada was appointed by the Roman papacy as the inquisitor general and supported by Ferdinand II and Isabella I. Trials in Spain were administered by the Dominican order of priests and monks.

Vasco: Spanish term for a person of Basque heritage.

About The Author

Marcia Riman Selz spent her business career as a marketing consultant to financial institutions and investment companies. Her company, Marketing Matrix International, conducted studies on communications, service, product development, and branding.

Dr. Selz earned her PhD in executive management from the Peter F. Drucker & Masatoshi Ito Graduate School of Management at Claremont Graduate University, her MBA from Loyola Marymount University, and her bachelor's degree from Indiana University. Dr. Selz also has a master's degree in psychology from the Chicago School of Professional Psychology. Dr. Selz grew up in South Chicago in a neighborhood of mixed ethnicities and religions.

Currently, Dr. Selz volunteers as a life coach at Beit T'Shuvah, a Los Angeles treatment center for people with drug, alcohol, or gambling addictions. She also participates in the Volunteers for Israel program, where she spends two weeks each year working on an IDF base in Israel. In 1994, she chaired the Los Angeles Media and Marketing Division of the United Jewish Fund. In 1981–82, Dr. Selz served as president of the Southern California Chapter of the American Marketing Association.

Dr. Selz currently lives in Los Angeles (Century City) with her husband, Dr. Eduardo Subelman.

Dr. Selz is donating 20 percent of the profits from *At Vitoria* to charities providing social or health-care services and to organizations that conduct pancreatic cancer research.

Acknowledgments

At last, my head is clear of this story. In 2006, my husband and I were traveling through Spain with our friends Enrique and Kathy Mannheim. The focus of our trip was Jewish history. Our travel agent from Heritage Tours suggested we take a side-trip to Vitoria-Gasteiz during our drive from Barcelona to Bilbao. We visited the Judizmendi, and that was the inspiration for this book.

When I returned home, I told the story of Vitoria to my father, Bernard Riman, who at the time was living with my husband and me. I sat by his bedside and told him of my interest in writing a book about Vitoria. My father was always my supportive rock for educational and career endeavors, and in his usual very calm style he said just a few words: "Do it, but expect criticism." Well, Daddy, I did it. I don't know what criticism will follow, but I thank my father, who died in 2008, for his everlasting encouragement.

Writing this book has been a wonderful experience. Three years of basic research served my love of history. One month of concentrated effort to write the story (it literally flew out of my fingers, onto the keyboard, and onto the pages), followed by years of editing the text, conducting additional research, inserting additional information, deleting where needed, modifying where necessary, learning the craft of writing a novel, rereading, rewriting and finalizing the details. This book would not have reached completion without the help of many people.

I am so very thankful to Harriet Rossetto of Beit T'Shuvah for her incredible insights into human behavior and for being a role model of how to live a giving life.

Thank you to Ian Wilson, my teacher at a UCLA writing class on behalf of the National Novel Writing Program. He kept me on track to ensure I was writing for a sufficient amount of time each day to complete the novel in a month.

I appreciate all the help given to me by Aitor Delgado of Aitor Delgado Tours. During a research trip, he served as my interpreter, guide, and bridge to the Basque communities in Spain and France.

Thanks to Clara Navas Romano of the office of tourism in Vitoria, who prior to my visit identified medieval records for review and arranged for my visit to the archives of the City of Vitoria. Also, Ana Larsarte Sarasola, manager of the office of tourism, offered additional suggestions for research.

I thank Ricardo Garay Osma of Kale Arte Turismo for his time in providing specific details about the Jews of Vitoria and their journey to Saint Esprit.

Thank you to Lynn Hightower, my mentor from UCLA who helped me craft my story into a novel.

Thanks to Aaron Greyson, who read my manuscript and offered salient comments that led to insightful edits.

I give thanks to Toti Martínez de Lezea, Basque writer extraordinaire, who invited me into her home, a medieval cottage in Larrabetzu in the province of Bizkaia, in the Basque country of northern Spain. Toti generously gave me her time, knowledge, and herbal tea.

Thank you to Maria José Marinas at the library of the archives of the City of Vitoria, who directed the retrieval of medieval documents for my review.

José Ramón Díaz de Durana, professor of medieval history at the University of the Basque Country, responded to lists of questions about the Jews of Vitoria, their Christian neighbors, medieval society in Vitoria, the edict of expulsion, and more. I thank Professor Díaz de Durana for sharing his insights and thinking on these subjects.

My thanks go out to Anne Oukhemanou, president of the Israelite Consistory of Bayonne, France, which represents the Jewish community in Bayonne. She provided additional information about the settling of Jews in Saint Esprit and today's Jewish community at the Synagogue of Bayonne.

With great appreciation, I thank Georges Dalmeyda, a descendant of Jews from the Iberian Peninsula, who has lived in Bayonne for many years and has been a leader at the synagogue in Bayonne, Nefoutsot Juhua, and is active in the Jewish community, at large. He provided valuable information about the attendance of descendants at the ceremonies in Vitoria in 1952 and 1992, as well as historical perspective on the synagogue, the Jewish community of Saint Esprit, and the city of Bayonne.

The librarians at La Fundación Sancho El Sabio researched documents from the medieval era and provided literature describing the events of 1492, 1952, and 1992.

I profoundly thank Leslie Fischer, my wonderful niece. Leslie is my hero. As I worked on *At Vitoria*, Leslie was battling stage IV pancreatic cancer. Her courage, perseverance, positive outlook, intelligence, and strong grasp of reality continue to inspire me. Beautiful Leslie died when she was forty-five years old, on August 11, 2016, but she will be in my heart and mind forever.

Last, but certainly not least, I must thank my husband, Dr. Eduardo Subelman—my advisor, research aide, translator, discussion partner, best friend, and fuel source for my inspiration to write the book that was swirling around in my head. It is because of his love and support that I was able to offer this story about the Jews and Christians of Vitoria.

From my first visit to Vitoria in 2006 to my final editing session, the people of Vitoria were part of my being. I could not stop thinking about their history. For generations during the medieval period, the Basques and the Jews lived a peaceful coexistence. Then the monarchs abruptly uprooted the Jews to satisfy religious objectives and prejudices. I hope this book serves to honor Vitoria's Christians and Jews of the medieval period and their descendants who so beautifully resolved to honor their ancestors. We can all take hope and guidance from their story.

Marcia Riman Selz, PhD
Century City in Los Angeles, CA
2017

Sources

Angel, Rabbi Marc D. *Exploring Sephardic Customs and Traditions.* New York: KTAV Publishing House, Inc. in association with the American Sephardi Federation, South Florida Chapter, Sephardic House, 2000.

Ausubel, Nathan. *Pictorial History of the Jewish People: From Bible Times to our Own Day Throughout the World.* New York: Crown Publishers, Inc., 1954.

Baer, Yitzhak Baer. *A History of Jews in Christian Spain: Volume from the Age of Reconquest to the Fourteenth Century.* Philadelphia: The Jewish Publication Society, 1992.

Bronstein, Herbert. *A Passover Haggadah.* New York: Central Conference of American Rabbis, 1982.

Cardini, Franco. *Europe 1492: Portrait of a Continent Five Hundred Years Ago.* New York: Facts On File, 2000.

Carroll, James. *Constantine's Sword: The Church and the Jews.* Boston: Houghton Mifflin Company, 2001.

Collins, Kenneth. "Jewish Medical Students and Graduates at the Universities of Padua and Leiden: 1617–1740." *Rambam Maimonides Medical Journal* 4, no.1 (January 30, 2013), .https://www.ncbi.nlm.nih.gov/pmc/articles/PMC3678911/

Constable, Olivia Remie. *Medieval Iberia: Readings from Christian, Muslim, and Jewish Sources.* Philadelphia: University of Pennsylvania Press, 2012.

Crow, John A. *Spain: The Root and the Flower: A History of the Civilization of Spain and the Spanish People.* New York: Harper & Row, 1963.

de St. Jorre, John. *The Insider's Guide to Spain.* West Palm Beach, Florida: Hunter Publishing. 1990.

DK Books. *Spain.* London: DK Books, 1996.

Dolander, Miguel Ángel Motis. *Los Judíos de Tarazona.* Zaragoza: Centro de Estudios Turiasonenses, 2004.

Dyson, John. *Columbus: For Gold, God and Glory.* London: Hodder & Stoughton/Madison Press, 1991.

Elliott, Lynne. *Medieval Medicine and the Plague.* New York: Crabtee Publishing Company, 1968.

Epstein, Perle. *Kabbalah: The Way of the Jewish Mystic.* Boston: Shambhala, 2001

Freedman, Harry. *The Talmud: A Biography.* London: Bloomsbury, 2014.

Gaon, Yehoram. *From Toledo to Jerusalem.* Ramat HaSharon, Israel: United King Films Ltd., 2007.

Gerber, Jane S. *The Jews of Spain: A History of the Sephardic Experience.* New York: The Free Press. 1992.

Gilad, Elon. *Columbus Day: Who Was the First Jew in the New World?* Haaretz (October 5, 2014) http://www.haaretz.com/jewish/features/.premium-1.619195

Gitlitz, David M., and Linda Kay Davidson. *A Drizzle of Honey: The Lives and Recipes of Spain's Secret Jews.* New York: St. Marin's Press, 1999.

Gómez, Carmen. *Los Judios.* Vitoria: Fundacion Sancho El Sabio, 1992.

Gorsky, Jeffrey. *Exiles in Sephard: The Jewish Millennium in Spain.* Philadelphia: The Jewish Publication Society, 2015.

Grew, Francis, and Margrethe de Neergaard. *Shoes and Pattens: Medieval Finds from Excavations in London.* London: Boydell Press, 2001.

Groves, Marsha. *Manners and Customs in the Middle Ages.* New York: Crabtree Publishing, 2006.

Hartley, Dorothy. *Medieval Costume and How to Recreate It.* New York: Dover Publications, Inc., 2003.

Ingpen, Robert, and Wilkinson, Philip. *Encyclopedia of Events that Changed the World: Eighty Turning Points in History.* New York: Viking, 1991.

Jewish Encyclopaedia.com. *America.* The Koppelman Foundation, 2002-2011 http://www.jewishencyclopedia.com/search? utf8=%E2%9C%93&keywords=Luis+de+Torres&commit=search.

Kohen, Elli and Kohen-Gordon, Dahlia. *Ladino-English/English-Ladino: Concise Encyclopedic Dictionary (Judeo-Spanish).* New York: Hippocrene Books, 2000.

Kurlansky, Mark. *The Basque History of the World.* New York: Penguin Books, 1999.

Lindo, Elias Hiam. *The History of the Jews of Spain and Portugal, From the Earliest Times to Their Final Expulsion From Those Kingdoms, and Their Subsequent Dispersion.* Translated. London: Longman, Brown, Green & Longmans. Reproduction of book published before 1923.

Litvinoff, Barnet. *Fourteen Ninety Two: The Decline of Medievalism and the Rise of the Modern Age.* New York: Charles Scribner's Sons, 1991.

Lowney, Chris. *A Vanished World: Muslims, Christians, and Jews in Medieval Spain.* New York: Oxford University Press, 2005.

Mann, Vivian B. *Uneasy Communion: Jews, Christians, and the Altarpieces of Medieval Spain.* New York: Museum of Biblical Art in association with D Giles Limited London, 2010.

Mann, Vivian B., Thomas F. Glick, and Jerrilyn D. Dodds, editors. *Convivencia: Jews, Muslims, and Christians in Medieval Spain.* New York: The Jewish Museum, 1992.

Markman, Sidney David. *Jewish Remnants in Spain: Wanderings in a Lost World.* Mesa, Arizona: Scribe Publishers, 2003.

Menocal, María Rosa. *Ornament of the World: How Muslims, Jews, and Christians Created a Culture of Tolerance in Medieval Spain.* New York: Little, Brown and Company, 2002

Morison, Samuel Eliot. *Admiral of the Ocean Sea: A Life of Christopher Columbus.* Boston: Little, Brown and Company,1970.

Reston, Jr., James. *Dogs of God: Columbus, the Inquisition, and the Defeat of the Moors.* New York: Anchor Books, 2005.

Rosal, Jesús Peláez del. *The Synagogue.* Córdoba: Ediciones El Almendro, 1988.

Roth, Cecil. *A History of the Marranos.* New York: Sepher-Hermon Press, Inc., 1992.

Rottenberg, Dan. *Finding Our Fathers: A Guidebook to Jewish Genealogy.* Baltimore: Genealogical Publishing Co., Inc., 1986.

Ruiz, Teofilo F. *Spanish Society 1400–1600.* Essex: Pearson Education Limited, 2001.

Singman, Jeffrey L. *The Middle Ages: Everyday Life in Medieval Europe.* New York: Sterling, 2013.

Siraisi, Nancy G. *Medieval & Early Renaissance Medicine: An Introduction to Knowledge and Practice.* Chicago: University of Chicago Press, 1990.

Stern, Chaim, editor. *On the Doorposts of Your House.* New York: Central Conference of American Rabbis, 1994.

Stillman, Norman A. *Sephardi Religious Responses.* London: Routledge- Taylor and Francis Group, 1995.

Trepp, Leo. The Complete Book of Jewish Observance. New York: Behrman House, Inc./Summit Books, 1980.

Tuchman, Barbara W. *A Distant Mirror: The Calamitous 14th Century.* New York: Alfred A. Knopf, 1978.

Wellcome Library. Image No. 43200i https://wellcomeimages.org/indexplus/image/V0041636.html. London. First published 1722.

Yoskowitz, Herbert A. The Kaddish Minyan: The Impact on Ten Lives. Austin: Eakin Press, 2001.

Zimmels, H. J. *Ashkenazim and Sephardim: Their Relations, Differences and Problems as Reflected in the Rabbinical Responsa.* Hoboken, New Jersey: KTAV Publishing House, Inc., 1976.

A Reader's Guide to *At Vitoria*: Questions for Book Club Discussion Groups

1. When Benjamin says to Michael, "It's time. We'll never move back to Vitoria," Michael becomes angry. (See the prologue.) Do you believe their perspectives on the cemetery are justified? If you were a Crevago and had to vote, whom would you most agree with—Michael or Benjamin? What would be your compelling points-of-view?

2. Vidal goes to see Benjamin before going to see Della. (See chapter 1.) What does this tell you about the relationship between the brothers? What does it tell you about the relationship between Vidal and Della? How do these relationships change over time? Do you think that Vidal should have moved away from Vitoria, even if Benjamin did not want to go?

3. When Vidal visited Antonio in Segovia and watched as his children declared their loyalty to Judaism (see chapter 3), what feelings did you get? How do you compare these feelings to your own relationship with religion?

4. How do you compare your feelings from chapter 3 to those you felt after reading about Antonio and Maria's in the court of the Inquisition? (See chapter 5.)

5. Should Vidal have insisted that Della take in Antonio and Maria's children? Why do you say this?

6. How would you describe the evolution of Father Joaquin's and Sister Angelica's attitudes toward Jews? (See chapter 7.) Have

you ever experienced attitude shifts like this? Describe and compare.

7. Why did the Crevago family stay in Vitoria after Vidal described pogroms and pillaging in other Spanish cities? How do the behaviors of the Crevagos compare to those of families who did not leave Germany after the rise of the Nazis?

8. Are Jews really different? Do they always need to take care of themselves? Can Jews be fully integrated into a society? Why/Why not?

9. How did Vidal change his views of religion? Would you have reacted the same way? Why/Why not?

10. Compare and contrast the procession of the Inquisition (Chapter 5) to the procession of Isaac's funeral (Chapter 7). What can you learn from each?

If you wish to participate in the *At Vitoria* Travel Program with a guided tour of the Basque country in northern Spain and France, which includes specific locations cited in this book, and discussions about the book's content, contact Marcia Riman Selz at marcia@marciarimanselz.com.

Printed in the United States
By Bookmasters